Dream:
If not for Katie...

by Anita Massic

Dedications:

First of all, I would like to dedicate this book to
Toni and Tim.
There are too many reasons to list here,
but if not for them, this book would never be.

To My Children, Samantha and Justin, I love you.
My Family and Friends...
A special thank you to my sister Debbie
for her loving encouragement
and eternal inspiration

Acknowledgments:

Ellen Martin: for her help in editing.
Anne Beatty: for her help in editing.
Kay Ellis and her mother Dorothy: for their help in proofing.
Suzanne Langley: for her belief.
Brenda Smith, Celena Russell, and Travis Patterson: for putting up with me.

Dream: if not for Katie
by Anita Massic

Katherine Hampton has a unique and mysterious ability.

Through a kindred Indian spirit, Katherine Hampton witnesses her great, great, great grandmothers life. As each detail is revealed to her in her dreams, Katherine realizes that a higher Indian power has cursed her lineage. The only way to stop the dreams will be to solve the mystery, and break the curse.

Mary Kate Martin is Katherine's great, great great grandmother. A beautiful, vibrant, young girl forced to leave her homeland to travel along the Oregon Trail. Her journey is an epic one, filled with tragedy, love, sorrow and finally happiness.

An action-packed and riveting story, you will not soon forget.

Chapter One
The New Dress and The Candy Stick

Katherine Hampton stood alone in front of her mother's grave, watching the men lower the beautiful, white casket into the ground. She was the only one attending the funeral. In fact, she was her mother's only living relative.

Katherine's mother was the late Margaret Hampton, a widow of a rich and influential man. When Margaret's husband died, she hid away in an estate on the shore of Maine. She was never the same. Becoming a recluse, she had no friends.

Katherine was never particularly close to her mother. In fact, she felt like she hardly knew her. A nanny raised Katherine, and when she was old enough, she went to boarding school. During her summer vacations, she was shuffled from finishing schools, to dance schools, and on to modeling schools. Margaret was involved in entertaining, charities and all sorts of social events. She did not have time for Katherine.

Her father, Greg Hampton, was no better. When he was home, he spent most of his time in the study.

Katherine's parents were especially unpleasant and antagonized each other when they were together for long. She rarely saw him when he was home. She suspected that he had a long-standing involvement with another woman. Mr. Hampton died during Katherine's first year at Harvard. Being a wealthy and well-known Financial Adviser, his office was located in one of the Twin Towers that stood vigilant over New York City. The Towers crumbled in flames in 2001 when terrorists crashed into it in commercial jets. Mr. Greg Hampton went down with it.

Katherine knelt and placed her hand on the casket, putting a single red rose on it. She said, "Good-bye, Mother." Shedding no tears, she stood and walked toward the limo that she had rented for the funeral. On her way home, she gazed out of the window at her reflection on the buildings. She realized, for the first time, that she was all alone. Her mother was an only child and so was her Grandmother. She had no cousins. Her father was an orphan. Since her mother never spoke of it, she knew nothing about her heritage.

Last year, Katherine graduated from Harvard with honors, receiving her degree in medicine. Though she had several offers, she could not decide where she would establish her practice. Because her mother had left the estate and the family fortune to her, she did not have to work, but she wanted to make a difference in this world.

The limo pulled through the gate and down the long drive to her mother's house. Katherine stepped out, tipped the driver, and went through the entry. Walking up the spiral staircase toward her room, she took the pins out of her hair and lifted the black-veiled hat from her head, shaking her long, brown, curly hair out of the bun that she had fashioned on her head. Before going back down the stairs, she changed from the calf-length, black dress for an ankle-length sundress. She changed from her black pumps into a pair of flip-flops.

The study was at the bottom of the stairs, and after flipping on the power switch to the lap top, she went to the kitchen to make some coffee. With coffee in hand, she took the laptop from the desk in the study and stepped out to the patio. Looking at her seating choices, she decided to make herself comfortable on a lounge chair. She sipped her coffee next to the pool and typed, "ancestory.com."

Katherine spent the afternoon, evening and late into the night researching her family tree. She discovered some fascinating and puzzling information. First, in 1833 her great, great, great grandmother, Mary Kate Martin, was born. Mary Kate and every woman since her only bore one child. Second, each child was female, and each was born during her mother's thirtieth year. After refilling her coffee, she went back into the study and took a legal pad and pen off the desk. She listed each woman's name and date of birth on the pad. "How odd," she said. She double checked the dates and figures and became extremely curious about the phenomena. "Strange, could there be a medical reason for this?"

It was late, and Katherine decided to retire. Though anxious to explore further, she was exhausted and could not concentrate. She changed into her night gown and crawled into bed. Almost immediately after closing her eyes, she slipped into a deep sleep. An amazing dream, which proved to be the most significant event in Katherine's life, began to form vividly in her mind.

XXXX

In her dream, her vision was obstructed by a mist, and the screech of a hawk loudly screamed in the air. The fog lifted, and the sun shone so intensely that it blinded her. A loud rattling noise and the scent of sage triggered her senses. She could hear a woman's voice chanting "Itsike, Itsike, Itsike." First in the distance, and then closer and closer, the chanting and the rattling became louder and louder. She thought that her ears would burst when suddenly, the noise stopped, and the mist cleared so that she could finally see. She was in another place. Although she had never been there or seen the young woman that was in front of her, the girl was familiar to her. She knew that her name was Mary Kate Martin, and she felt entirely at home with her. She watched, but she could not be seen. She could hear, but she could not be heard.

It was a stormy morning in the mid eighteen hundreds. The thunder cracked wickedly, making the young woman flinch and the hair stand up on her arms. The young Jersey cow who she called Maggie was her best friend and only confidant. Because she had been milking her for three years now, she knew that if she did not stroke her flanks and speak to her softly from time to time that she might strike out and tip the bucket of milk over before she could finish. She told the Jersey her deepest secrets at every milking.

Lightening illuminated the dark, eerie, early-morning sky. The wind blew rain, dirt and grit up against the outside walls of the old, wooden, two-story barn, making the young cow especially nervous. Mary Kate had to keep a constant conversation going with her.

"Now, now, Maggie. I am here, sweet Maggie. Did I tell you that we are going to go to town today?"

Maggie turned her head to Mary Kate and looked at her with foamy, slobbery corn dripping from her mouth. Her eyes were open wide, showing the white that surrounded her dark brown pupils. Mary Kate could tell that she was frightened. She stroked her gently and told her, "It's

4

going to be my birthday you know. Mother is making a new dress for me. I am going to be sixteen, and I am going to look so grown up!"

Mary Kate giggled as she answered for Maggie, using a low voice, "Happy Birthday, Mary Kate!"

Lightening struck, and at the same moment, the thunder boomed so loudly that it shook the ground. Maggie jumped and planted all four feet firmly on the ground. She stood as still as a statue, not even chewing her mouthful of corn.

Mary Kate rubbed her belly and said softly, "Maggie, Maggie, it's alright, dear friend. I won't let anything happen to you." She rested her head on Maggie's flank and felt her heart beating wildly. She said, "Maggie, someday you will be a momma. You will be such a good momma."

Letting out a loud snort, Maggie relaxed and started chewing her corn again.

"Oh," Mary Kate sighed, "I will be very happy for you, Maggie. I want to have children someday but not for a long time. There are so many things to do first, and of course, unlike you, there has to be a wedding. I don't like boys. They are too much trouble."

"Oh, that reminds me! I have another secret for you, Maggie. June has a crush on Johnny! I don't know what she sees in him."

Mary Kate turned the subject back to her dress, "My dress will be tight around the waist, and it will drape down to my ankles."

Like all children, Mary Kate was in a hurry to grow up. She could not wait for the day that she would be on her own. She was independent and strong willed and did not like any of the boys at her school. She was not in any hurry to marry, and with her mothers encouragement, she wanted to teach for a while before settling down with a man.

She stroked Maggie gently and spoke softly to her as she pulled and squeezed the last drops from her teats. "I will wear my dress out here and show it to you when it is finished. You will love it, Maggie!" Mary Kate moved the bucket away from Maggie's feet and hugged her neck. She untied her and put her into her stall.

Mary Kate threw her a pitch fork full of hay, not wanting to take a chance by letting her out in the storm. She took the milk bucket and the basket of fresh eggs and headed toward the house, running as fast as possible to avoid the rain, lightening and the wind.

On a small farm three miles from Masontown, Pennsylvania, the Martins lived in a small, stone and stucco house. One half of the main floor had a wood cook stove, a homemade cupboard, and a wooden table and chairs. The other half had a stone fireplace and a large chair each for Mr. and Mrs. Martin. When time permitted, they would rest in them before going to bed. Their bed was located at the back corner, separated by a curtain for privacy. On the back wall, there was a wooden ladder that led to the loft where Mary Kate and her brother, Matthew, slept. Each half of the loft was separated by a curtain that Mrs. Martin had fashioned. Mr. Martin hung it when Mary Kate began to "blossom," so she would have her privacy.

Mary Kate opened the latch on the door. The wind caught it, making it fly open and slam against the wall behind her. The lightening struck and sent a loud snap through the house. The wind made the lantern flicker and sway on the hook that it hung from above the table. Mary Kate's mother, Margaret Martin, scurried quickly behind her, closing the door as the thunder rumbled outside. "My goodness, Katie, were you born in a barn?"

Mary Kate set the bucket and basket on the old, rustic, wooden table. She started to remove the scarf from her head to hang it and her coat on the nail by the door. "As a matter of fact, yes I was, Momma!"

Mrs. Martin smiled and took two of the eggs and cracked them on the edge of the cast iron skillet. "Don't take those off yet, Katie! Go out and ring the bell for breakfast." Mary Kate's mother called her "Katie."

Margaret was a beautiful woman, but living her entire life on the farm, her skin was hardened from a lifetime of hard work. She was an only child, and unfortunately, her childhood was cut short at age twelve when her father became ill with pneumonia and died.

Margaret and her mother were left to the endless toil on the farm. They plowed, planted and harvested the crops in the fields to make the land payment at the bank. To keep them warm in the winter, they cut and split wood for the fire. They tended the garden and butchered the animals that provided their food. They survived through droughts and floods and toiled until the blisters on their hands burst and bled through the torn strips of cloth that were wrapped around them. By hard work and a great deal of luck, they managed to scrape enough profit from the farm to make it through the hard times. Margaret knew what it took to survive and did not have time for anything else. She did not waste a minute. To her, "Idle hands were the Devil's workshop." She knew that her destiny was only to be shaped by hard work as this is all she knew. Toward the end of her mother's life, Margaret endured the added burden of caring for her and finally had to bury her next to her father in the family cemetery plot. Her life of hard work gave her the determination that was necessary to make it through any obstacle that came into her path. She was bound and determined to pass those traits on to her children.

Everything flowed together perfectly, most of the time, at the Martin House. Mrs. Martin saw to it. Like a

Drill Sergeant, she had everything timed to a perfect routine. She was stern and demanded respect from her children, making and enforcing the rules without mercy. Keeping order and organization, she was the glue that held the family in place.

Katie put her scarf back on and went out to the porch to ring the dinner bell. Matthew was out feeding the rest of the animals while her father, Fred Martin, hitched the team to the buckboard for their trip to town.

Mrs. Martin took the biscuits out of the old, wood-fired oven and fried the rest of the eggs.

As Katie came back into the house, she struggled with the door, forcing it shut as the wind relentlessly pressed against it. She hung her coat and scarf on the hook and told her mother, "I left Maggie in the stall, so she doesn't have to be out in the storm."

Mrs. Martin replied, "That was good thinking, Katie. Did you feed her?"

"Yes, Momma, I did. She was very frightened with the thunder." Katie set the table and scooped the cream off of the milk, putting it in the wooden churn for butter making. She poured the milk into the tin cups that she had set by the plates on the table.

Mr. Martin took his muddy boots off and left them under the porch, fighting the wind as he came through the doorway. "Whew! It's a strong northern wind blowing this morning!"

Matthew attempted to step across the threshold when he noticed the infamously raised eyebrow of his mother and stepped back out to remove his boots. The wind blew into the house again, swaying the lantern on the hook. Mrs. Martin ran to the door to close it, leaving Matthew out on the porch, "Now take those boots off, or you will be scrubbing these floors."

Matthew replied, "Yes, Ma'am!" He removed his boots and came in and hung his coat next to his father's on the hook by the door.

As he and Mr. Martin started to take their places at the table, Mrs. Martin raised her voice, "Uh...wash those hands!"

Matthew and his father looked at each other and smiled. They rolled up their sleeves and washed their hands in the pot of warm water that Mrs. Martin kept on the back of the wood stove.

Mr. Martin was a tall, skinny man with thinning gray hair, a protruding Adam's apple, and warm, loving eyes. He wore common overalls at the farm and had only a couple sets of dress trousers that he wore to church on Sundays. He was a quiet, even tempered man and never reprimanded his children. He was a hard worker, a devoted husband and an honest man.

Breakfast was Katie's favorite time of the day. It was a new beginning, and there was usually lively conversation and wholesome food. Today's topic was the trip to town which was always an exciting time for the entire family.

Katie asked her father as he sat at the table, "Are we still going to be able to go to town today, Pa?" She was worried that the weather was going to put an end their shopping trip. If so, they would not be able to purchase the fabric needed to start her dress.

Mr. Martin looked at his wife and smiled as he took a biscuit and passed the plate. He said, "No, Kit, it's far too rainy to go." He called her "Kit" because he said she was as sly as a Kit fox.

Katie had a look of devastation on her face and tears were welling in her eyes when Mrs. Martin finally said, "We have been through much worse than a rain storm, and we do have umbrellas to keep us dry on the way."

9

Katie sighed with relief and passed the ham.

Matthew shouted, "We aren't gonna' let a little ole' rain storm ruin our day!"

Mr. Martin was buttering his biscuit. "Mrs. Martin, do we have a list?"

Still chewing her food, Mrs. Martin nodded her head, and put one finger up in the air in front of her as she stood. She wiped her hands on her apron and pulled out a paper list from the drawer of the cupboard. She swallowed and began reading the list. "Coffee, sugar, flour, salt...."

Katie interrupted with a mouth full of ham, "My dress, Momma! My dress!"

Mrs. Martin gave her a scornful look for talking with her mouth full and said, "Yes, Katie!"

Matthew spoke up, "A stick of candy for me!"

"Yes, Matthew." She continued with the list. "Dress fabric, lace, thread and a candy stick from the general store and axle grease from the livery stable."

Mr. Martin looked out the window and said, "We are in luck! The storm is passing!"

Matthew yelled, "Yahoo! Ha-rah!"

"Now, if the sun would come out," Katie sighed. "It would be perfect!"

"We can always use the rain, but hopefully, it will be dry enough to pull the plow through the ground within the next two weeks. I need to plant the corn seeds that we saved back from last year's crop." Mr. Martin always worried about planting season. It was the most critical time of the year, and if they did not get a decent crop, it was financially devastating.

When everyone finished breakfast, Mrs. Martin did the dishes, while Katie churned the butter. Matthew brought in some dry wood from under the porch to stoked the fire, and Mr. Martin went down to the barn and drove the buckboard to the house. He came in the house and got an old quilt to pad the bench for Mrs. Martin. "Are you ready, Mrs. Martin," he shouted. She came out from behind the curtain, and he said, "You look beautiful, Mrs. Martin!" He kissed her on the cheek and then opened the front door for her.

"Thank you, Mr. Martin," She stepped out to the porch and opened her umbrella.

"Wait one moment." He ran out to the buckboard and spread the blanket out on the bench. He boosted his wife up, giving her a light slap on her rump while the children were not watching.

Mrs. Martin turned around and looked at him with a shocked expression and a smile. She snapped, "Mr. Martin! I swear!"

Katie and Matthew climbed up on the back and dangled their feet from it.

"Hup," Mr. Martin shouted, and they started for town.

A buckboard was the most practical vehicle of the day. Shocks supported the bench seat in the front, and a large wagon bed stowed supplies, harvests, hay and children. The Martins could not afford the luxury of a buggy.

It was an easy three mile pull to town for Mary and Moe, Mr. Martins draft team. He loved his horses for a good reason. They were extremely valuable members of the family, and he would have a terribly hard life without them. Moe was a Percheron stallion and worked on the left side. He was pitch black and exceedingly strong with long, lean muscles. His mane was long, and his tail flowed to the ground. He lifted his enormous hoofs high with a proud stride. He was Mr. Martin's pride and joy, and he also pulled the plow in the fields.

Mary was a Belgian mare who was the same color as dried straw. She worked on the right. They were used to working this way, and switching them confused them immensely. Mr. Martin tried it once. Moe acted up so much that he had to switch them back where he could keep a closer rein on him. They worked from Mr. Martin's voice commands, and Katie swore that they understood him. Mary contributed a foal each year that was sold to supplement the farm income. Katie's father was easy on Mary this time of year when she was so close to birthing.

Matthew asked, "Katie, are you going to the general store with Momma?"

"Yes, I can't wait to pick out the fabric for my dress!"

"I want to go with Pa, but I don't want Momma to forget my candy stick. Will you remind her, Katie, please?" he asked.

Katie looked at him, noticing the innocent, puppy-eyed look on his face and said, "Yes, I guess I will."

Matthew loved his sister and respected her, almost as much as he respected his mother. Even though he pulled pranks on her every chance he could get, he would never intentionally do anything to upset her.

The main corridor of town ran from east to west, and on the north side was a general store, a boarding house with a small cafe and a barber. Situated on the south side of the street was a sheriff's office and a saloon. In the town's center, all the buildings were butted up against one another and were joined by covered boardwalks, watering troughs and hitching posts. The school house, a small church and a livery stable were situated on the outskirts of town. The community was small and simple, and its citizens, for the most part, were small-farm owners.

When they arrived in town, Mr. Martin and Matthew dropped Mrs. Martin and Katie at the general store. Mr. Martin stood and stretched and then got down from the buckboard. He walked around to help his wife down.

She smiled and said, "Watch your hands, Mr. Martin."
He smiled back at her playfully.

Matthew crawled across the bed of the wagon and sat next to his father. "Don't forget my candy stick, Momma!"

Mr. Martin stepped up on to the buckboard and sat back down. He raised his voice so that he could be heard over the street noise, "I will pick you up out here in just a little while." They started off for Wrigley's Livery Stable.

XXXX

Katherine woke and sat up in bed realizing she had just had the strangest dream that she had ever had. It was so much more vivid than any of the dreams that she had ever had. She was not in the dream, but it seemed as if she were watching it happen. It was so real that she could smell and feel things. She did not want it to end, so she fell back to sleep.

XXXX

When Matthew and Mr. Martin arrived, Gabe Wrigley, the local blacksmith, stopped pounding on his anvil and came to greet them. Mr. Wrigley was a big, strong, bulky man with enormous arms.

Mr. Martin had always said, "He could pound a set of shoes out in five minutes."

"Now, Mr. Martin, if you ever want to sell that stallion, you will let me know won't you?" Mr. Wrigley knew a magnificent horse when he saw one.

Mr. Martin shook his head and told him, "I will have that horse till the day he dies, or I do!" He and Matthew got down from the buckboard and followed Mr. Wrigley into the barn.

"Well, we might be able to arrange that, Mr. Martin," he tease. They laughed, and Matthew ran over to the anvil.

It was always a treat for any boy to go to the livery stable because Mr. Wrigley would allow him to forge iron on the anvil. He gave Matthew a piece of metal, a pair of tongs and a hammer. Matthew picked up the iron with his tongs and put it in the fire. He left it there for several moments while he listened to the men talk.

Mr. Martin knew it would take Mrs. Martin at least a half hour at the general store, so he took his time and enjoyed the visit.

Mr. Wrigley looked at Matthew and asked, "That iron red yet?"

Matthew looked at it and replied, "I reckon." He picked it up with the tongs and hammered it against the anvil.

"I could use a new nail punch if you think you can make one," Mr. Wrigley said.

"Right away, Mr. Wrigley!" Matthew said, pounding on the metal, "Comin' right up!"

The two men stepped into the barn and returned with a barrel of axle grease, putting it into the back of the buckboard. They talked about the weather, the planting season and their horses, while Matthew finished the nail punch for Mr. Wrigley.

"How's that look, Mr. Wrigley?" Matthew bragged as he held the punch up with the tongs. It was still bright red.

"Pretty good, Matthew! Pretty good! Now square off the end a little and harden it in that bucket of water, and we'll see if it holds up!" Mr. Wrigley placed the horseshoe that he was working on back into the coals. When Matthew finished, he took the shoe out and held it against the flat side of the anvil, holding Matthew's punch against the side of the shoe. He lightly tapped the punch with the hammer a couple of times and lifted it, leaving a perfect nail hole in the shoe.

"Good job, Matthew! You'll make a great blacksmith one day!" Mr. Wrigley took off his gloves and shook Matthews hand.

Matthew was glowing with pride and smiled. "Thank you, Mr. Wrigley. Thank you very much!"

Mr. Martin put his hand on Matthews shoulder. "Well, we better head back to the general store and get your momma and your sister."

Chapter Two
The Muddy Christian and The House Guest

Katherine's alarm sounded at 7:00am and woke her from her dream. She thought that she must have had the dream because of the research she had done the day before. Her great, great, great grandmother's name was Mary Kate Martin, but the dream was like no other dream that she had ever had. It was as if she were there. She was so anxious to do more research that she skipped breakfast and went straight to work.

She decided to start with Mary Kate. She typed her name into her laptop and found birth records. Mary Kate Martin was born in 1833 in Masontown, Pennsylvania. Katherine spoke out load, "Oh, my god! How could this be? Masontown, Pennsylvania, was in my dream last night!"

Katherine stood. She paced the floor, deep in thought. She opened a new document in her laptop and typed in everything that she could remember from her dream. She saved it as "Dream."

She went up to her room and showered. After putting on a sundress and twisting her long, brown hair up on her head, she put on a pair of sandals. She took a suit case from her closet and packed it. Tossing the suit case in her shiny, white, cobra mustang convertible, she drove to the nearest book store and bought a copy of a Rand McNally Road Atlas and a large Starbucks Latte. When she got back in the car, she searched her new atlas for Masontown. She found it in the southwest corner of Pennsylvania. Katherine filled her car with gas and headed south.

Driving nonstop, she wanted to visit Masontown and see what it looked like. Her mind was filled with excitement. Knowing that there probably would not be anything left from 1849, she still hoped to find some history there.

It was after 10:00pm when she stopped in Pittsburgh and decided to spend the night. She would wake up early and go to Masontown. She checked into a hotel and got a bite to eat at the restaurant before going up to her room. It was past eleven when she got into her bed, and she could hardly fall asleep, thinking about the dream that she had the night before. Thoughts of Margaret Martin's childhood kept running through her mind. Compared to Katherine's childhood, there were so many similarities. Her father died when she was a young girl, and her mother passed away when she was a young woman, leaving her all alone with no one to turn to. She finally drifted into a deep slumber.

XXXX

The general store was a wooden, plank building with a large, flat store-front boasting, "Sweeney General Store." There were two large windows on either side of the tall entry door. When opened, the door triggered an old cow bell which would let Mr. Sweeney know when someone entered. The interior floor was lined with barrels of bulk dry goods that, when combined, made a strong aroma that confused the senses. The shelves were filled with glass jars containing a variety of canned foods and other household items.

Mrs. Martin gave the list of supplies to Ricky who was Mr. Sweeney's assistant. He was a school mate of Katie's and had a crush on her as did most boys her age. Nervously Ricky said, "I will get these for you right away, Mrs. Martin" and smiled at Katie who thought he was an imbecile and glared at him.

He turned and busily gathered their order while Katie and Mrs. Martin went to the fabric section of the store where several bolts of fabric were stacked. Katie could hardly contain her excitement. She asked her mother, "What do you think about this one, Momma?"

Mrs. Martin reminded her, "Not too much white, Katie. It won't last as long."

She kept flipping through the bolts of fabric. She found a perfect pattern with small, pink flowers that matched her tiny frame and were the same tint as her beautiful, full, pink lips. The pink flowers were surrounded with baby's breath, and the combination of the colors complemented her ivory skin tone perfectly. She asked her mother, "Momma, I love this one. May I have it? Please, Momma!"

Mrs. Martin said, "It is a little lighter than I would like, but yes, Katie, you may have it. I found some ivory colored lace to trim it with and some thread."

Mr. Sweeney charged the purchase to Mr. Martin's account and wrapped them all for the trip home. "Thank you, Mrs. Martin. I will see you Sunday!"

Ricky clumsily carried their packages out to the loading dock, tripping and stumbling as he tried to stay close to Katie's side. She rolled her eyes at him as he set them on the wooden platform where she and Mrs. Martin waited for

Mr. Martin and Matthew. Mrs. Martin noticed Ricky's efforts and felt a little sorry for him. She said, "Thank you, Ricky. That's very nice of you."

Ricky replied, "Oh, it's all my pleasure, Mrs. Martin."

Mr. Martin was just clearing the corner and coming toward the general store. Mrs. Martin was preparing to open her umbrella, when a scruffy-looking, young boy grabbed Mrs. Martin's string tie purse from her hand and ran down the street with it.

Mrs. Martin ran behind him crying out, "Stop! Stop this instant!" She reached out and grabbed a hold of the tail of his tattered jacket. With all of the determination that everyone knew her so well for, she tried to pull him to a stop, but he kept running, pulling her behind him.

A crowd gathered fast, and everyone was yelling, "Get 'em, Mrs. Martin! Get 'em!"

She began to hit the top of his head with her umbrella. "Stop, boy, or I will knock you senseless."

After Mr. Martin had stopped the buckboard in the middle of the road, he and Matthew stood up on the bench to watch her. Mr. Martin had a grin on his face, but his eyes were filled with concern. He was not sure whether to join the crowed with cheers or to worry about her.

More people were gathered. They lined the streets cheering her on, "Stop 'em! Stop 'em!" Laughter filled the streets because she looked so comically relentless.

Katie heard Mr. Sweeney comment, "I would hate to be that boy when she gets hold of him!"

The boy ducked into a side street, pulling Mrs. Martin behind him. The crowd became instantly silent, waiting to see what was going to happen next. Katie looked at her father who now had a worried look on his face. There was dead silence, and it was perfectly still as the suspense built. The crowd stood on their tip toes and watched with excitement. All that could be heard was the faint rustling noise coming from the alley way. It seemed to go on forever when finally Mrs. Martin appeared. Her dress was covered in mud, and her hair was pulled half way down out of her chignon bun. Her bonnet laid crooked and somewhat smashed on the side of her head. She was pulling the boy by his ear with one hand and had her purse and umbrella dangling from the other. The boy was scurrying on his tip toes, struggling to keep up with her. The crowd roared with cheers and laughter. "Yay, Mrs. Martin! Yay!"

She picked up the skirt of her muddy dress and marched him across the street to the sheriff's office with the crowd following.

Mr. Martin pulled the buckboard up to the platform at the general store and told Matthew, "Help your sister load the supplies and wait for us here."

Mrs. Martin slammed the door shut behind them when she entered the sheriff's office. The sheriff, Jed Jenkins, had obviously been napping with his hat down over his eyes, his arms crossed and his boots up on the desk. He jumped up out of his chair and stood behind the wooden, makeshift desk that sat facing the door.

The sheriff's office was small with just one jail cell. It smelled dusty and musty, showing that it had not had a thorough cleaning since it was built. There were cobwebs hanging from the corners and dirt and dust on the wood plank floor. Mrs. Martin cringed when she saw the grimy, brass spittoon that was on the floor next to the desk.

She sternly pushed the boy down on the bench in front of the sheriff. The boy's face and clothes were filthy, and his hair was matted. Her face was beet red with anger and embarrassment. While looking at the sheriff, she pointed at the boy and shouted, "This boy stole my purse and ran down the street, trying to escape with it!"

The sheriff looked at the boy and with a little pity in his eyes, began to question him in a deep, authoritative voice, "Where you from, boy?" he asked.

The boy said nothing.

The sheriff continued, "You will have to tell me, or I will have to lock you up, boy. What's your name?"

The boy was staring at the floor when he finally spoke in an extremely low and quite voice, "My name is Billy".

The sheriff repeated, "Where are you from, boy?"

The boy looked at the sheriff straight in the eye and said, "My ma and pa are camped outside of town. We are just passing through town, Sir. We don't have any food to eat, and I was hungry."

Mrs. Martin's angry and rigid appearance suddenly melted. Her facial expressions changed, and pity and regret could be seen in her eyes. She asked, "Sheriff Jenkins, can I speak to you outside?"

He acknowledged and opened the front door, allowing her to pass in front of him. "Stay right here, boy. I'll be right back."

Mr. Martin was just walking up the steps that led to the sheriff's office and joined Mrs. Martin. As usual, he remained silent and let Mrs. Martin handle the situation.

The Sheriff said, "I'll feed the boy and take him back to his kin folk. I'll see how bad their predicament is."

Mrs. Martin suggested, "I would be glad to take them a home-cooked meal."

He shook his head and said, "Let me see what their disposition is first. Don't ya just be wandering out there when ya don't even know the folks, Mrs. Martin. Ya hear me now?"

Mr. Martin nodded his head knowing very well what the sheriff was trying to tell his stubborn wife.

Mrs. Martin reluctantly agreed, "You let me know

what I can do, Jed."

They returned to Sweeney's. Gathering their goods and their children, they set off toward home. The journey home was a silent one. Mr. Martin and the children knew not to speak until Mrs. Martin had gotten over her anger, and her humor lightened a bit.

After returning home, Mrs. Martin pulled the tub down off the nail on the outside wall of the back porch. Mr. Martin went out and drug it in the house, and put it behind the curtain where they slept. She warmed some water and cleaned up, while Katie fixed the midday meal.

Mr. Martin and Matthew unloaded the wagon, unhitched the team and let the horses out to graze. Matthew could not wait a moment longer, so, with his face aglow, he looked at his father and said, "Boy, Momma sure caught that boy in the act, didn't she, Pa?"

Mr. Martin somberly replied, "The poor boy was just doing what he thought he had to in order to survive." Mr. Martin told him, "You youngin's always need to remember to count your blessings every morning when you wake up, and be very thankful that you don't need to steal to get a meal."

On the front porch, they took their muddy boots off and went into the house to washed up. Katie had the table set and was putting beans and biscuits down on it. They all stopped what they were doing and looked at Mrs. Martin as she entered the room. The feeling of anticipation was thick as they all sat at the table, waiting for her to break the silence. She took her seat at the table, and they all sat awkwardly waiting.

The silence went on too long for comfort, so Mr. Martin spoke, "Would you like some bread and butter, Mrs. Martin?" He was testing her mood. He could tell that she was still disturbed by the near loss of her purse.

"Yes, please," she spooned some beans into her bowl. A sad look appeared on her face as she spoke, "The poor boy was probably half starved to death and desperate." As soon as the words came out of her mouth, her facial expression turned serious, her left brow rose, and she sternly said, "If one of my children did that, they would have switch marks on their backsides for it!"

The children glanced at each other before looking down at their plates and eating their lunch. It was a quiet meal.

Katie helped her mother clean up after lunch as the family slowly settled back into their normal routine. She was excited about cutting the pattern for her new dress and told her mother, "I can't wait until my dress is finished, Momma."

Mrs. Martin told her, "Patience is a wonderful virtue, Katie. You are young, but this is a hard world, and you will have to learn to be patient." Katie was drying the last dish when she heard a knock on the door.

Mrs. Martin answered it, and standing in front of her was the boy who stole her purse and his mother. The woman stood in the doorway, looking sheepishly at the ground. Her voice was low and shaky as she introduced herself and her son, "My name is Abby Sternwall, and my son's name is Billy." It was apparent that she was extremely shy, timid, and ashamed of her son's actions. She nudged him, pushing him in front of her and urging him to apologize to Mrs. Martin.

Billy apologized, "I am very sorry, Mrs. Martin."

Mrs. Martin nodded while noticing his pitiful appearance. She was regretting that she did not realize the poor boy's poverty when she was beating him over the head with her umbrella. "It's alright, Billy Sternwall."

He was tall and thin and appeared to be about

Matthew's age. His hair was long and matted with dirt and debris, showing that he had not bathed in a long, long time.

"Please, come in, Mrs. Sternwall." Mrs. Martin called Matthew down from the loft. "Matthew, this is Billy Sternwall. Go and get some sweet cakes, and take Billy outside to play."

Matthew looked at his mother with confusion but knew better than to argue. He replied, "Yes, Ma'am." He got some sweet cakes from the cupboard and took Billy outside.

She picked the hot pot up from the cook stove with her apron and poured Mrs. Sternwall and herself some coffee. "Please sit down, Mrs. Sternwall. Would you like some cream?"

Abby sat at the table where Mrs. Martin had motioned for her to sit. "Yes, please, Mrs. Martin. Thank you."

Mrs. Martin poured some cream into the tin cups that she had filled with coffee and put them down on the table. She sat down next to Mrs. Sternwall. "Are you new in town? Where have you traveled from?"

Mrs. Sternwall replied, "Please, call me Abby." She paused before suddenly breaking into tears and sobbing, "My husband and I have lost our farm. We are out of money, and our three year old daughter, Audrey, took ill. We are on our way to Pittsburgh to find a doctor to tend to her." Stopping for a moment, she composed herself, "My husband is hoping to find work there." Abby looked up at Mrs. Martin with concern in her eyes, "My husband is a good man, but he is a proud man, and he wouldn't take kindly to me tellin' our hardships to strangers."

Mrs. Martin took Abby's hand in hers to console her. She thought for a while. "Please, let us keep Billy for you until you have settled. He will be fine with us, and when Mr. Sternwall has found a job, you can fetch him. He can finish school here with my children."

Abby still had fear in her eyes. "You don't understand, Mrs. Martin. My husband would never agree. He would be angry with me for tellin' our problem to y'all."

Mrs. Martin squeezed her hand, "My husband will talk to your husband." She called Katie, "Fetch Mr. Martin for me." She continued speaking to Abby, "I would not be a very good Christian if I didn't do everything that I could to help."

Mr. Martin came into the house and introduced himself to Abby. Mrs. Martin poured him a cup of coffee, and he sat with them, listening to Mrs. Martin tell Abby's story.

He asked Mrs. Sternwall, "Can you take me and the boys to where you are camped, and I can speak to your husband, while the boy's play."

Abby reluctantly agreed.

Mrs. Martin packaged up some left over beans and bread and put them in a basket covered with a cloth. She handed the basket to Abby, "Please take this with you, Abby. Your husband must be hungry."

"I can't thank you enough, Mrs. Martin." Abby leaned over and hugged her.

When Mr. Martin arrived with Abby and the boys, Mr. Sternwall was cutting wood for the fire, and their small daughter was asleep in the wagon.

Abby introduced Mr. Martin to her husband, "Mr. Martin, this is my husband, Dirk Sternwall."

Mr. Sternwall was a tall, lean, strong, young man with curly, strawberry-blonde hair and light skin that had been reddened by the sun.

Mr. Martin asked, "Please, Mr. Sternwall, take a walk with me."

The two men walked toward the creek. "Nice day we are having today. Don't you agree?" Mr. Martin tried to break the ice.

"Yes, Sir. I am glad to see the cold weather pass." Mr. Sternwall engaged in the small talk.

When they reached the creek, Mr. Martin sat down on a log. He motioned for Mr. Sternwall to join him. "Your wife tells me that you are just passing through?"

"Yes we are, Mr. Martin." He paused for a moment, "Look, Mr. Martin, I am sorry about what my son did to your wife..."

"No, Mr. Sternwall, that is not why I am here. Your son has done the right thing and has apologized to my wife. She has forgiven him and has forgotten the whole thing. You can be proud of him."

"He is just a young boy, Mr. Martin, but I want you to know that he will be punished. I brought him up better, and he knows better," Mr. Sternwall explained.

"There is no need for that, Mr. Sternwall." Mr. Martin had been beating around the bush but finally asked, "I understand, Mr. Sternwall, that you are between a rock and a hard spot."

Mr. Sternwall exhaled loudly and said, "Mr. Martin, I don't know what my wife has told you, but we don't need any handouts." His voice became irritated, and he continued, "I've come on bad luck, but I am fixin' to get a job and can take care of my own kin."

Mr. Martin said, "Mr. Sternwall, I know how you feel about that, but you must think of the well being of your children right now. Please let Billy stay with us until you get settled in Pittsburgh. When you can afford it, you can fetch him. It will make it easier on y'all, gettin' settled and all. He is getting along fine with my son, and the visit will do them both nothin' but good."

Mr. Sternwall was silent as a tear rolled down his cheek. He quickly wiped it, cleared his throat and said, "I appreciate your help Mr. Martin. Let me speak with the boy." Mr. Sternwall threw a rock into the river as he stood.

Mr. Martin felt sorry for the man. It must be the most difficult thing to leave a child behind, even for a short time.

They walked back to the wagon, and Mr. Sternwall called his son. He walked him to the creek and sat him down on the log. He said, "Son, Mr. and Mrs. Martin wanna keep you for a while until I can come fetch ya. Can you do that for me, son?"

Billy smiled widely and said, "Really! Really Pa, can I stay!"

Mr. Sternwall realized that his son did not know how hard this was for him. He saw the separation as an adventure. His voice cracked as he told him, "I will be back to fetch ya as soon as I get a job."

"Alright Pa!" Billy said as he hugged his father.

Mr. Sternwall continued, "Ya promise to mind yourself, son. No stealin', ya hear?"

Billy said, "No, Pa! No stealin', I promise!" He ran back to the wagon calling, "Matthew! Guess what, Matthew!"

Mr. Sternwall walked back to the wagon holding the tears back that were trying to force their way out.

Abby kissed her son good-bye and hugged him. "Ya make me proud, son. I will miss you."

Billy was too young and too excited to realize the pain his parents felt, "I will be good, Momma. I promise." He pulled himself from her arms and ran to Matthew.

His parents stood with their arms around each other. Tears flowed from Abby's face as her heart ached over the parting. Mr. Sternwall was fighting his tears. His pride took a blow as he watched his son wave excitedly from the back of the wagon.

Katie and her mother were cutting the fabric to make her dress. The door flew open, startling them as Matthew and Billy ran into the house. The boys jumped up and down with excitement. Matthew yelled, "Come on! I'll show you where you will be sleepin'!"

Mr. Martin entered the house smiling from ear to ear just like a boy with a new puppy. He told his wife, "Mr. Sternwall was reluctant, but after a long conversation about Billy's well being, he agreed to your plan." He was proud of his wife and excited about having the company for Matthew.

He called Matthew and Billy from the loft and told Matthew, "Take the tub down and set it on the back porch. We'll fill it up out there for Billy." He joked, "If you're gonna stay in the same house as Mrs. Martin, ya gotta be clean shaven!"

"Can I? I ain't never shaved before!" Billy's eyes were wide.

Mr. Martin laughed, "No, Billy. I was just pullin' your leg, son."

When they came back into the house, Billy was clean, and his hair was cut. He wore a clean shirt and a pair of britches that he had gotten from Matthew. Being just a year younger than Matthew, they were inseparable already.

Mrs. Martin had pinned Katie's dress on her, and Billy blushed when his eyes met hers. She did not realize it, but he thought that she was the most beautiful girl that he had ever seen.

Mrs. Martin said, "Matthew, take Billy out to the barn and catch a good pullet for your Pa. We'll be havin' a picnic after church tomorrow. Then do your evening chorin'. If Mr. Martin will fetch me some wood for the stove, I'll start supper," she said, smiling at her husband.

Katie changed, and she went out to milk Maggie.

Mr. Martin kissed his wife, "Mrs. Martin, I am so proud of you," and he went out to bring in the wood and slaughter the chicken.

As Katie approached the barn, she heard a loud commotion. She looked around the corner, and feathers were flying as Matthew and Billy were chasing chickens around the barn. She laughed as she watched.

Matthew was yelling, "That one, Billy! That one! Get it!"

Billy was running from side to side, and the chicken was flying and jumping, trying to escape from its terrible fate. Billy grabbed it, and it flapped its wings and escaped, leaving Billy standing there with a hand full of feathers. All of the chickens were running back and forth and clucking loudly.

Matthew laughed as Billy stood for a moment empty handed and then took off again.

Finally, he cornered the pullet and grabbed its feet. It screamed loudly, trying to escape.

"Yay, Billy! Ya got it! Ya finally got it!" Matthew yelled.

Katie shook her head and went back out to call Maggie, passing Mr. Martin who stood at the barn door with an ax in his hand, "Good job, Billy! Good job! He took the pullet and walked toward the tree stump that he used to split wood.

Matthew dared Billy, "Come on! Let's go and watch!"

"Yuck!" Billy cringed. "Not a chance!"

Katie called Maggie, and she came trotting into the barn. She tied her up and set the milking stool down beside her. "What a day, Maggie! You sure miss out on a lot, settin' around this barnyard all the time! You wouldn't believe what happened to us today!" She told Maggie about

Billy and what happened in town. "Then we made friends with 'em, and Billy will be stayin' on with us for a spell." Like her father, she was proud of her mother and said, "I hope, when I grow up, I can be just like my Momma."

At supper, the Martin family watched as Billy gorged himself. It had been a long time since he had a decent meal and could not stuff the food into his mouth fast enough. The whole family watched speechlessly as the food was shoveled in plate after plate. Billy was so busy eating that he did not seem to notice the audience.

Mrs. Martin glanced at each member of her family and smiled with satisfaction. She was, indeed, blessed by God to have the luxury of enough food to feed her family.

Chapter Three
Hick-Ups and Pollywogs

The sun was just peaking in the window when Katherine woke. It was way before her alarm was to ring, and from the moment that she opened her eyes, she was puzzled by her dreams. There was a message, or a meaning; something she could not explain. Something or someone was taking her back in time, so she could witness Katie's life first hand. She shook her head from side to side and whispered, "It can't be. It's impossible."

She showered and packed her suitcase. After eating breakfast, she used the gps device on her cell phone to find the nearest Starbucks for some coffee. She opened her road atlas and headed south. It was noon when she passed the sign that said, "Masontown pop. 3511." She drove into the heart of the town, searching for anything that might hold a clue to Katie Martin's past. Masontown was a prime example of "small-town America." A quiet community filled with older, simple buildings and slow paced citizens slowly walking down the streets. It looked relaxed, unlike the cities where she grew up.

She found the small, public library and stopped. It was an old, brick, two-story building with a simple, but stately, federal look. There was a brick archway above the door with a half-moon window above the tall, double-glass doors. She went inside and immediately noticed the historical pictures of the town on the walls. Some were extremely old photographs dating back to the 1900's. There was one of the settlement in 1869. The details were almost identical to her dream. It was shocking. She looked at it and wondered, "Was Katie Martin in one of those buildings when they took this photo?"

A woman walked up behind her, "Can I help you find anything, Miss?"

Startling her from her deep thoughts, Katherine jumped, "Oh, thank you, yes. I am searching for any historical information about Masontown in 1849. Would you know of any?"

The woman looked at the picture on the wall and thought for a moment, " I know that City Hall has some land ownership records from that time period. You might check there."

"Can you tell me where I might find City Hall?" she asked.

"Of course! It's in the Court House just north of here." The woman gave her directions. The town was small, and it was not far, so Katherine walked. It was a beautiful day. She walked down the street and crossed it, finding the building. It was a large, brick building, and she was sure it held a lot of history, but it would not have been present in the mid 1800's. Walking up the steps and through the front door, it smelled like a court house. She could not explain it, but every court house that she had ever been in smelled the same. An old, tall, wooden door had a metal plaque that said "County Clerk", and she opened it and walked up to the clerk's window. The woman stood in front of a tall, index-card cabinet, filing cards in the drawers. Katherine cleared her throat.

The woman looked over at Katherine, a bit startled. "Can I help you, Miss?"

"Yes, thank you. I am looking for any land records that you might have for Fred Martin. He lived here in 1849."

"We do have some records that go back that far. Give me a few minutes, and I will look." The woman left the room for several minutes and returned with a piece of paper. "I have nothing for Fred Martin, but I have a record for Margaret Martin for that date. She sold her property to the Land Office." She handed the paper to Katherine. "Would you like a photocopy?"

"Yes, please!" She touched it gently and looked it over. "Can you tell me where I might find this property?"

"Let me see." She took the paper from Katherine and looked on the map, holding the paper up next to it. "Oh yeah, this is the Wilson place. It is about two miles west of town. Just go out main street, up over a couple of hills and across a river. Just past that, you will see their mailbox. The clerk made a photocopy of the record and gave it to Katherine.

While driving to the Wilson place, she thought about what it would have been like in 1849. Katie was young and beautiful and carefree. When she came to the bridge, she pulled over and stood on the bridge. She closed her eyes and remembered her dream and how they crossed the old bridge in the buckboard. It was not the same bridge, but it was the same location. It was just the same bend in the river, and looking behind her, she realized that the hills she had just driven over were the same ones that Mary and Moe climbed in her dream. It was the strangest feeling.

She got back into the car and drove down the little dirt road until she found the mailbox. She looked at the driveway and across the meadow at where the little, stone house had been. Then she followed the landscape with her eyes to the left where the big, old barn had been. It was no longer there, but the meadow was almost the same. The land was now planted in crops and well groomed.

After seeing the farm, she could almost feel the Katie's presence. She smiled and drove back into town. She felt at peace. It was a beautiful place, and she wondered why they sold it. What happened to them? It was at that moment that she decided to stay a few days. She needed to know more.

There was a small cafe where she stopped to eat, and she asked the waitress, "I am researching some family history and was hoping you might know of anyone that I could speak to? Someone with extended family history in Masontown."

The waitress put her fingers to her lips and thought a moment. "There is an old gentleman. His last name is Wrigley, and his family has been in the area since the 1700's."

"Wrigley, I know that name." She remembered Gabe Wrigley, the blacksmith. "Yes! Can you tell me where I could find him?"

The woman gave her directions to Mr. Wrigley house and told Katherine about a small Bed and Breakfast.

Katherine purchased a room there and decided to go for a visit in the morning after breakfast. She went to bed with a smile on her face. She had a fabulous day.

XXXX

The next morning, the Martin family woke up before

34

the rooster crowed. It was Sunday morning, and the house was busy with their Sunday morning routine. By working a little faster, they were able to fit in enough spare time to gussy up for church. The chores still need to be done and the animals fed, but other than that, it was a day of rest. Mrs. Martin always fried up some chicken the night before to ease her workload on Sunday. Sometimes, if weather permitted, they took the meal outdoors for a picnic.

Matthew was feeding the animals, while Billy was watching Katie milk Maggie. He could not keep his eyes off her.

"What are you doing starin' at me. Billy?" Katie was annoyed with him. She was at the age where she liked her privacy. She usually told Maggie things that she did not want anyone else to hear.

Billy could not help but watch her because he thought she was beautiful. When she was around, he could not help himself, but he did not want her to know that. "I was just watchin'. I ain't never milked a cow before."

"There ain't no such word as 'ain't', Billy." Katie looked at him and rolled her eyes. "You want a try at it?"

Billy looked at Matthew. He was scared, but did not want Matthew or Katie to know it. "I reckon, I could give it a whirl."

"Well, come on then!" Katie stood and pointed to the stool.

Billy hesitated and looked back at Matthew. If he had not already committed, he would gladly back out of the deal.

Matthew laughed, "Go on, Billy! Ain't nothin' to it!"

"How'd you know, Matthew, you have never done it!" Katie stepped over to Billy and took his arm. "Just sit down right there. I'll show you."

Billy sat down, and Katie knelt beside him. "Just hold her teats, one in each hand. That's right."

Billy wrinkled his nose, "Uck! They feel funny!"

"You'll get used to it, Billy. Now just squeeze with your thumb and then the rest of your fingers. One at a time, like you are pushing the milk out. All the way down and out."

Billy squeezed, and nothing came out.

"Keep trying! We Martins aren't quitters!" Katie grabbed another one of Maggie's teats and showed him.

He tried again, and some milk trickled from the teat. Again and again, a little more each time, and soon the milk was squirting out forcefully, hitting the side of the tin pail and spraying out onto his legs.

"You have to aim for the bottom of the bucket, silly. You are wasting it!" Katie laughed.

Maggie turned and looked at him. Her eyes got wide, and she stomped her foot.

"It's alright, Maggie. He won't hurt you." Katie rubbed her hip. "You have to talk to her and rub her, so she will get to know you and feel comfortable with you."

Billy smiled at Katie, "I think, I got it! I got the hang of it!" He gave Maggie a pat on the neck and said excitedly, "Good girl, Maggie!"

"You are full of surprises, Billy Sternwall," Katie said as she smiled and watched him finish. "Now you have to move the bucket, so the milk doesn't get any dirt in it." She picked up the bucket and set it aside while she put Maggie in a small paddock outside the barn.

Katie finished her chores and took the eggs and milk into the house as usual. "I showed Billy how to milk Maggie, Momma! He was excited to learn!"

"Now wonder it took so long, Katie. I have been waiting!" her mother snapped.

"I am sorry, Momma. I'll set the table," she said as she washed her hands.

"It's alright, Katie. I am glad Billy is having so much fun here. I just don't want things to get out of order, or we will be late for church!"

"Yes, Ma'am," Katie hurried as she set the dishes and utensils on the table. "Are you ready for me to ring the bell, Momma?"

Mrs. Martin put the biscuits and porridge on the table, "Yes, Katie, it is time."

Katie went out and rang the bell. After coming back in, she took the cream off of the milk. She poured some of the milk into the metal cups that she had put on the table as the boys and her father came in the door and washed their hands.

"Mmmm, this looks good, Mrs. Martin," Mr. Martin said as he dried his hands on her apron and smiled at her.

She slapped at his hands playfully. "There is a linen cloth over there, Mr. Martin."

Mrs. Martin looked at Billy, "I heard, you learned how to milk a cow."

"Yes, Ma'am! I sure did! Got real good at it too!" He started to take a bite of his biscuit.

"Not yet, Billy. It hasn't been blessed!" Mrs. Martin sat and nodded her head at her husband.

"Dear Lord," he said as he blessed the food and each child, one by one.

It would be Billy's first time in a church, and on the way to town, Matthew coached him on his expected behavior while they sat on the back of the buckboard. He told him, "Whatever ya do, don't speak a word, or Momma will slap the back of yer head."

Billy sighed, "How long do we have to sit?"

Matthew maneuvered a long stem of grass that was hanging from his mouth into one cheek and said, "Ain't no tellin', Pastor Robinson can be awful long winded."

Billy laid back on the wagon and looked up to the sky. "Do you reckon there is really a God up there, Matthew?"

Matthew did the same and laid back just as Billy had. He looked up and said, "There's no doubt in my mind, Billy."

Billy turned his head and looked at Matthew. "Why's he gotta make it so hard on us then?"

"I don't reckon I know the answer to that one, Billy," Matthew said.

As they entered the corridor of town, they passed the most beautiful carriage that Katie had ever seen. "Matthew, Billy look! Look at that carriage! It's beautiful!" Several covered wagons followed the carriage, full to the brim and covered with tarps. "Someone must be moving into the old Smith place."

Matthew and Billy sat up quickly. "Golly, Pa, those people must be rich!" Matthew shouted. "Did ya see that, Pa?"

Mr. Martin smiled and looked back, watching the wagons, "Yes, Matthew, I seen it."

The Smith family sold their estate to the Land Office and left last spring with the wagon train to California. Many families were going west for the Gold Rush. There were wagon trains leaving monthly. Conversations about the promise of fortunes and the adventure of traveling out west were the main topic among the men. Assured that he could provide a better living for his family, Mr. Martin wanted to go. "Sure wish we could of went out west with the Smith family, Mrs. Martin. We might be driving a carriage like that right now!"

"It is far too dangerous, Mr. Martin. There are too many Indians and bandits. We might not have been so fortunate. We could be dead and buried right now!" she teased.

Following the convoy of wagons, was a young man on a beautiful, sorrel horse. Katie leaned forward and squinted to see him better. He looked remarkably handsome. Goose bumps covered her arms, and she blushed and looked the other way. She felt a chill run down her back, and her face felt flush. She could not help but look again and noticed he was looking at her too.

Matthew ribbed her, "Katie's in love! Katie's in love!"

Katie looked at him with that same raised eye brow that her mother had, "Hush Matthew! You don't know anything!"

Billy felt jealousy surge through him and sat silently, watching the road move under his feet.

The church was a beautiful, little, whitewashed structure with a steeple that housed an iron bell. The church was the anchor for the community, and it brought them together every Sunday and any other time there was a need.

Several small boys tugged on the rope that rang the bell as the community arrived in horse drawn buckboards and carriages. They lined up and filed through the threshold, greeting the Pastor. Mr. Martin shook his hand, "Morning, Pastor Robinson. It's a beautiful day, don't you think?"

Pastor Robinson replied, "The Lord is on our side today, indeed!"

They filled the long, wooden pews and opened their Bibles. Almost every family in the community attended church every Sunday without fail. If someone was absent, then something was wrong. Katie's parents knew everyone and greeted their friends, hugging and shaking hands until the Pastor finally stood in front at the pulpit and cleared his throat. This was the signal for everyone to take their seats.

Mr. Martin sat on Katie's left, and on her right, Billy, then Matthew and Mrs. Martin. Aside from Billy, they had sat in that order ever since Katie could remember, probably to keep her and her brother still when they were younger.

Katie's father was in the habit of falling asleep in church. He would jerk his head back into an upright position, after it had fallen back and woke him up. Her mother used to poke him in the back with her finger and wake him, but she had long since given up and let him alone.

Mrs. Martin sang the hymns with zest. She had a beautiful voice, and it could be heard over Katie's and her brother's.

As soon as the Pastor started to speak, Billy broke out into a loud outburst of hick-ups. He looked at Mrs. Martin with his eyes wide open. She looked at him and drew a deep breath and held it. She was trying to show Billy how to stop them. He gasped a deep breath and held it until his face was red. His mouth was forced open when a hick-up burst from deep down in his chest.

Pastor Robinson glanced at Billy, trying to hold back a smile. He seemed to lose his train of thought and started to flip the pages of his Bible. It was terribly difficult for Katie and Matthew to keep from laughing. The more he tried to stop them, the louder they got. "Hick-up!" "Hick-up!"

The Pastor kept preaching as he walked towards Billy.

Billy's face became beet red with embarrassment.

Pastor Robinson scooted himself between the pews, "Excuse me. Excuse me." He placed his hand on Billy's head and said, "God bless this poor boy. Jesus, please let this poor boy's relentless problem ease." A hum of whispers and giggles move through the body of followers in the tiny church. Just then, like a miracle, Billy's hick-ups stopped immediately. The look on his face was priceless, and the crowd made sounds of disbelief.

It made a believer out of Billy instantly, and he shouted, "Praise the Lord!"

The Pastor smiled from ear to ear and said, "Yes, boy, praise the Lord," and continued with his sermon as he walked back to his pulpit.

After the sermon was over, everyone filed out just as they had entered. The Pastor stopped Billy and shook his hand, "Now you be good, son."

"Yes, Sir!" Billy replied.

Out in the church yard, the entire crowd shook hands, gave hugs and said good-byes. The carriages, wagons and buckboards formed a single line down the road as they all headed home.

Mr. Martin stopped the buckboard at the bridge, "Whoa, Moe! Whoa, Mary!" He set the brake and wrapped his reins around the handle. Jumping down off of the buckboard, he walked around to help his wife.

Mrs. Martin pulled out the blanket that was neatly folded under the bench. "Lunch time! Katie, help me set up the picnic."

"Yes, Momma." Katie laid the blanket out in the grass.

Mrs. Martin unwrapped the basket and laid out the food carefully, covering it so that the insects would not get to any of it.

The boys ran to the river, took off their shoes and rolled up their trousers to wade in the river. Matthew told Billy, "I can't wait until the water gets warm enough to swim!" Billy was watching Katie as she walked along the shore, picking up abandoned muscle shells. Matthew was searching for pollywogs in the weeds that lined the banks of the creek. "You like my sister, don't ya, Billy," he teased while he was bent over searching.

Billy turned toward Matthew and splashed him with some water. "Ha, got ya!"

"Don't be getting all wet, boys," Mrs. Martin ordered.

"Would you like some bread and butter, Mr. Martin?" Mr. and Mrs. Martin were laying on the blanket, propped up by their elbows. It seemed as though Sunday was the only day they could take time to relax together.

"Yes please, Mrs. Martin," he said, smiling as he placed his hand on her knee. "It's a beautiful day Mrs. Martin. Maybe we could take a little walk in the woods," he teased.

She slapped his hand playfully, "Don't get any ideas, Mr. Martin, last time we took a walk in the woods, we got Matthew!"

"Awe," he sighed, "It feels good just to lay here and do nothin'." He paused and was in deep thought. "Are you happy, Mrs. Martin?"

She looked at him curiously, "Sure I am, Mr. Martin! Why do you ask?"

"I just wanted to make sure, because I sure am." He laid his head down on the ground and looked up at the sky. "I would like to give you much more, but it is the simple things that seem to make us the happiest. Don't you agree?"

Mrs. Martin took a deep breath, laid down next to him and looked up at the sky. "I am as happy as I could ever hope to be, Mr. Martin." She sighed.

That evening, Katie walked to the barn and called Maggie. The Jersey cow came trotting around the corner ready for her corn and milking. She hurried through the barn door with her sides scraping the side of the doorway. She put her head straight into the manger, scooping up a mouth full of corn.

"Goodness, Maggie, someone might think you were starving to death." Katie was happy to see her and had a lot to discuss with her.   She tied her to the post on the barn wall and placed her stool down on the ground beside her. "I sure wish you could have been in church today! We saw a miracle! I know now, if you ever get the hick-ups, how to stop 'em."

Katie wiped the cows teats down and rubbed her belly. She placed the bucket under her teats and started to squeeze and pull. "Do you remember Matthew's new friend, Billy? You met him this morning?" Maggie looked at her as if she knew what Katie was talking about. "Well, he got the hick-ups in church today, and the Pastor got God to make them stop. It was amazing!"

"Momma and I are going to work on my dress again tonight." I can't wait to show you. We have it cut out and pinned together. Now, we just have to sew it and put the lace on it. It's going to be real pretty."

Maggie switched her tail and just missed stinging Katie's face with it. "Oh Maggie, the flies are coming out. I hate that!"

Katie sat quietly with Maggie, resting her head on her flank and milking her, when she remembered, "Oh Mag, I almost forgot to tell you!" She looked around and listened to make sure that no one could hear her, then she whispered, "I saw a boy, well, a man. He was very handsome, and he saw me too. I don't know for sure, but I think I like him, Maggie." Maggie looked at her, chewing and drooling wet corn from her mouth as if she were hanging on every word.

Mrs. Martin and Katie were sitting next to each other, each sewing a different section of her dress. Katie searched for the courage to asked, "Momma, how did you know when you were in love with Pa?"

Mrs. Martin looked at her curiously, "Why do you ask Katie? Do you like a boy? I hope not. I wouldn't want a boy to get in the way of your plans."

"No Momma, I was just wondering." Mrs. Martin was not sentimental, and it was apparent that she had no interest in discussing the subject, so Katie did not continue.

43

"We have done quite enough tonight, Katie. You best finish up your chorin'." Mrs. Martin picked up her sewing basket.

"Yes, Momma." Katie was disappointed that she was unable to confide in her mother.

Katie finished her evening chores and grabbed a lantern to check on Maggie before bed. She entered the barn and noticed that Mary was finally in labor, "Oh! Good girl, Mary!" She ran back to the house, "Pa! Pa! Mary is going to have her baby!"

Mr. Martin was sitting in his chair reading an old book that he had read several times before. He jumped up, "Coming, Katie!" They scrambled through the door and back out to the barn. The rest of the family followed close behind.

"I am coming too," yelled Matthew. He and Billy came running.

It was an exciting time on the farm, to see the foal being born. They all watched as Mary labored and delivered a sweet, healthy, little stallion.

Katie smiled and looked at her father, "He is beautiful, Pa! Are we gonna keep 'em?" Even though she was brought up knowing that farm animals are raised to be sold or eaten, she would be glad to keep each and every one of them.

"No, Katie, he will be sold," he replied. Young horses brought a fair price and now, could be sold as excellent cavalry mounts.

The family admired the young stallion as her mother cleaned him and he stood to nurse. When Mr. Martin was assured that all was well, they all returned to the house. Katie went to bed happy with her day. She looked forward to school tomorrow.

Chapter Four
The Fist Fight and The Pig Race

It was 4:00am, and Katherine could not take her mind off the little, white church. She wanted to see if any of the old buildings were still standing. Maybe Mr. Wrigley would know something about it. She wished that all of the old buildings were still there.

Not able to sleep, Katherine showered and went downstairs to the Lobby area. She lounged on the antique sofa that was situated by the fireplace and waited for the coffee to be made. She truly missed Starbucks.

After her coffee and breakfast, Katherine walked out to the sidewalk and looked at the downtown area. She tried to remember what the town looked like in her dreams. "Sweeney's might have been located there and the sheriff's office across the street, over there."

From her purse, Katherine took the napkin on which the waitress had drawn the map and drove to Mr. Wrigley's house. When she knocked on the old, wooden screen door, she heard a voice say, "Just a minute!" She could see a terribly old man slowly get up from a recliner chair. Taking several minutes for him to get to the door, he used a walker and crossed the floor so slowly that she wanted to open the door and help him. Since he did not know her, she decided against it. He must have been nearly deaf because he raised his voice loudly, "Look, Sweetie, I am on a pension, and I don't have any extra money to buy anything!"

Katherine began to explain, "No, Sir. I am not selling today..."

He interrupted loudly, "Your gonna have to speak up, Sweetie!"

"...My name is Katherine Hampton, and I am looking into my family history. I was wondering if you might be able to tell me about some of the people that lived here!"

"Now that, I can do!" He started to turn his walker around. "Come on in, Sweetie."

Katherine opened the screen door and walked into the house. The house was old and filled with old, musty furniture. The room smelled like dust and mildew, the way old people's houses often do.

Sitting down in his recliner, he said, "Take those photo albums down from that shelf up there and bring them to me."

The table next to his chair was filled with pill bottles, a gallon jug of water, a glass, a single electric burner and anything else that he might use during the day.

Katherine took the albums down, and dust fell from them like powder. She started to blow them off, but it caused her to cough. Setting them down close to him on the coffee table, she sat next to him on an old sofa.

"How far back ya wanna go, Sweetie?" he asked.

"My great, great, great grandmother lived here in 1849. I was hoping you might have some information from that period." She looked at him hopeful.

He reached out, "Give me that old, brown album."

Katie sat next to him as he opened the cover. The first picture that she saw was of several people in front of the old, white church. "Oh my," she said. "That is the church! Is it still standing?"

"I believe so. It is not being used, except for tours, but it is still there," he said.

"What was your great, great, great grandmother's name?" he asked.

"Mary Kate Martin," she said.

He pulled the page covers back, "Some of these pictures are labeled if you would like to look at them."

"Oh, thank you!" she said. She turned the pages slowly to see if any of them resembled the people in her dreams. There were pictures of Gabe Wrigley and some of Mr. Sweeney. She could see the general store and the livery stable.

She asked, "Are any of these other buildings still standing?"

"No." He shook his head, making the loose skin on his neck jiggle like jello. "None that I know of, Sweetie. They knock 'em down and build over the top of 'em." Mr. Wrigley gave her directions to the church, and after thanking him, she left.

As she drove, Katherine thought about the dreams that she had been having. Someone was trying to tell her something, and she was determined to find out what it was.

Katherine found the old church, and it was beautiful. There was a box fastened to a post outside the door, and she inserted $20.00 into it. Standing there, she paused and remembered the Pastor, shaking Billy's hand. Opening the door, she marveled at the resemblance. They had done a breathtaking job restoring the church. It was exactly as she had dreamed. She sat in the same pew that the Martins had. Katie's presence could be felt that afternoon while she sat thinking about her dreams.

It was after dark when she got back to her room. She crawled in bed exhausted, but she had hopes of learning more about Katie in her dreams.

XXXX

Katie woke up early and ran out to see how Mary was managing with her new foal. It was important that the foal was sucking because of the colostrum. It was a special milk that gave the foal what it needed to build it's immune system. "Good morning, sweet Mary. How's the baby doing?"

Mary turned and looked at Katie and then walked to her manger. She knew that her breakfast was coming, and she was hungry.

Katie grabbed the pitch fork and scooped up some hay. "I'll give you a little extra this morning. You will need your strength." She dropped the hay in her manger and gave her an extra scoop of corn.

The small foal was laying in the corner and stood up on it's wobbly legs. It teetered over to Mary like a drunk sailor in rough water. Katie laughed. "You are so sweet, little boy! I don't suppose that I'll give ya a name because you will have to be sold." This thought made Katie sad, but a young stallion is as good as gold bullion.

Matthew and Billy entered the barn to feed the other animals. They ran to Mary's pen, anxious to see the new baby.

Matthew stood on the wood rail and looked at him, "He is so cute. I wish we could keep him."

Billy said, "I would like to have the money that he will bring!"

"You two better get to your morning chorin' before

you are late for breakfast!" Katie gave Mary a pat on her neck and reached over to touch the foal who was nudging his mother's udder. The skin on the foal's hide flinched when Katie touched it. "It's alright, little one. I won't hurt you." She milked Maggie, gathered the eggs and went into the house. Mrs. Martin was preparing breakfast, as usual, and Katie set the table. Aside from the butter making, Katie's chores were done, and the morning went smoothly.

The Martins sat down for breakfast. Mr. Martin scooped the porridge into bowls and passed them down the table, "You excited to start school today, Billy?"

"Yes, Sir!" Billy was still a bit uneasy around Mrs. Martin and did not speak much when she was present.

Katie spoke up to break the silence, "Can I drive the buckboard to school today, Pa?"

Mr. Martin chuckled, "No, Kit. Mary is not ready to pull yet, and I need Moe today to plow the south field."

"Oh, Pa! We will hurry home to help you plant!" Matthew was excited to show off his masculine abilities to Billy.

He told them, "No, we can't plant today. The ground isn't warm enough. We will just plow."

Matthew said, "Just the same, Pa, can I help plow?"

Mr. Martin smiled, a bit amazed about his son's enthusiasm, "I don't see why not!"

Mrs. Martin and Katie cleaned up the dishes after breakfast. Mrs. Martin passed out their lunches and looked Billy straight in the eye, "I expect that you'll all be on your best behavior today."

"Yes, Ma'am," they all replied.

Mr. Martin walked them to school because he needed to pick up some things from the general store.

They arrived at the small, one-room school house on the outskirts of town, and Mr. Martin waved to them as they

49

ran toward the schoolyard.

"Bye, Pa," Matthew said.

Billy ran to catch up with Matthew, "Good bye, Mr. Martin."

"Good bye, Pa," Katie said and walked over to meet her friends. They immediately asked about Billy. "Isn't that boy the one who stole your Momma's purse?"

Katie defended him, "He is a good boy, just down on his luck is all."

They were early and were allowed to play outside with the other children until Miss Roberts rang the bell, signaling them to go in and begin the morning work. There were only two weeks left of school, and then it was time for spring planting in the community. The children would be needed at home to help on the farms.

Tom Johnson and some other boys were kicking the ball around the school yard when Matthew and Billy arrived and asked to join the game. Tom snapped at Billy, "You are a pick pocket, and no pick pocket is playin' ball with me!"

Matthew butted in, "Billy is okay, Tom!"

Tom began chanting, "Pick pocket...pick pocket".

"Stop it now, or you'll be sorry," Billy said in self defense.

"Pick pocket! Pick pocket!" Tom egged him on, circling him with his fists in the air, while the crowd gathered to watch.

Billy drew back so quickly that Tom did not know what hit him. He punched him right in the eye and knocked him down, "I told you to stop, now didn't I?"

Tom rolled back and forth on the ground holding his eye, "I'm gonna get you for this!"

The children quickly surrounded the boys to watch and were yelling, "Yay! You got 'em! You got 'em good!"

Billy jumped on Tom, pinning him to the ground and

was hitting him again and again as Tom held his arms up to protect his head.

Miss Roberts ran outside, pushing her way through the crowd, "Let me through! Move aside and let me through!" She pulled Billy off Tom by his shirt. Billy was swinging wildly before he realized that he was swinging at his new teacher. Miss Roberts pulled him into the school house by the scruff of his collar, "I don't know where you came from, but you cannot act like that in this school." She slammed the door behind them.

Miss Roberts was twenty-two years old and had finished school five years ago in the same school house. When Miss Taylor married, she took over for her. She was a homely, young woman with mousy, brown hair. Because she was a bit heavy, her face was chubby. Freckles covered her cheeks, and she had a wide gap in between her two front teeth. All of the children respected her because she was stern, but at the same time, she was nice. Because the single life made her happy, she did not mind living with her mother and father.

Katie overheard her mother speaking to some women once, and they said Miss Roberts seemed to have settled with teaching for the rest of her life. She did not seem interested in any of the local, single men, and none of them seemed to be interested in her. Katie felt sorry for her, not because she was a teacher, but because she would probably never do anything else.

A few moments later, Miss Roberts came out and rang the school bell. The rest of the children walked in single file. Knowing that Miss Roberts might still be cross, they were all dead quiet. She gave Tom a wet cloth for his eye and sat him on the opposite side of the room from Billy. "You too are in hot water, Mr. Johnson."

The school was a small, one-room school house with

desks forming rows on the wooden, plank floor. The youngest children sat in front and the oldest in the back of the room. There were four windows, letting the natural light shine in and a wood burning parlor stove in one corner. Gathering and stacking wood was a common form of punishment for boys. Even though wood heat was not needed this time of the year, this job became Billy's and Tom's for the next two weeks.

Miss Roberts' desk was in the front, left corner of the room, and a chalk board was on the front wall. There were twelve students from the age of six to sixteen. Billy was seated next to Matthew on one side of the room, and Tom was at the end of that row on the other side. Tom's sister, Jenny, was seated in front of Billy. She turned and whispered, "pick pocket" as Miss Roberts told the children to be seated and prepare for their reading lesson. Jenny glared a sinister smirk at Billy and turned to face the teacher.

Tom and Jenny had been raised by their father who lived in the hills to the north of town. Katie thought Mr. Johnson was big, scary and rude. He was a brazen man. He drank too much and had bad manners. His wife had passed away when Jenny was born. The children were raised with a hard hand and had not been taught any manners. Tom was a bully and Jenny was almost as bad.

Jenny had long, dirty, blonde braids and Katie watched Billy smile as he picked up one of them and dipped it into the ink well on his desk. Jenny must have felt a slight tug on her hair because she pulled her head forward quickly, splattering black ink onto the back of her dress. She sat unaware of Billy's actions all morning. Katie chuckled under her breath. She would have liked to have done the same thing to Jenny more than once.

Miss Roberts wanted to teach Billy a lesson, so when it was time for math, she wrote a problem on the board. She turned to Billy and said. "Alright, Mr. Sternwall, if a room is 10 feet long and 15 feet wide, what is it's perimeter?"

Billy was not at all embarrassed and answered instantly, "Fifty feet, Miss Roberts."

She looked at him surprised and smiled. She decided to see how much he actually knew. "Very good, Billy, would you like to answer another?"

He answered, "Yes, I can do more!"

"Alright," she said. "What would be the square footage of the same building?"

In an instant, he answered, "One hundred fifty feet, Miss Roberts."

"Okay, if the building is 10 feet tall, what would the volume be?" She felt sure that he would not be able the answer this question.

Again, he was quick to answer, "Fifteen hundred feet, Ma'am."

Miss Roberts was pleased. "Very good, Billy! You are brilliant with numbers. Someday, you will make a very good businessman if you stick to numbers and do less fighting!"

The students laughed.

Miss Roberts reprimanded them. "That is enough boys and girls!" She looked at Billy, waiting for a reply.

"Yes, Ma'am," he said looking down at his desk.

The children ate lunch outdoors because it was such a sunny day. Katie, Billy and Matthew found a spot in the shade under a tall oak tree. Katie told Billy, "I saw what you did to Jenny's hair, but I won't tell Momma. When she sees Miss Roberts note, you will be in trouble enough."

"Maybe, I shouldn't give your momma the note," Billy said as he looked at the ground and fidgeted with the grass on the ground.

"Miss Roberts will surely discuss it with Momma and

Pa at church, and they will be sore at you for not giving them the note," she said.

They ate their lunch, and Billy thought about his predicament. He was not on particularly favorable terms with Mrs. Martin as it was, and he was worried about making her cross. "I am in a real pickle. What would you do if you were me, Matthew?"

Matthew enlightened Billy, "I would talk to Pa. He'll be a lot easier on ya'."

Billy smiled and looked up at Matthew, "I am not the only brilliant one in this family!"

The children walked home after school. They had worn a trail across the low-land fields and crossed the bridge at the creek. Their shortcut went through the trees and back out over the meadow before reaching the farm. When they arrived at the farm, Billy saw Mr. Martin in the barn yard. He ran to him immediately. It did not take him long to agree that Mr. Martin was much more lenient than Mrs. Martin. He asked Mr. Martin, "Can I talk to you, man to man, Sir?"

Mr. Martin put down his pitch fork, took his hat off and wiped his forehead with a handkerchief that he had pulled from his pocket. He sat on a wooden bench, "Yes, son. You can talk to me anytime, about anything."

Billy told Mr. Martin about the fight at the school, "I was just defendin' my honor, Sir."

"I would have done no different, Billy." Mr. Martin patted his back. "The people in town don't ever have anything new to talk about. They will soon forget all about the incident. Don't worry yourself about it too much." He noticed the worried look that Billy still had on his face, "Don't you worry about Mrs. Martin either. I will talk to her."

"Oh, thank you, Mr. Martin!" Billy smiled widely.

Matthew came running into the barn yelling, "Come on, Billy! We gotta' do our chorin'!"

Mr. Martin found his wife working over the cupboard, kneading bread for supper. "Mmmm, it smells mighty fine in here."

"Why thank you, Mr. Martin, what do you want?" She knew Mr. Martin exceedingly well by now and knew he wanted something, so she was smug with him.

"The boy got in a fight today, defending his honor, and I want you to let it be. Do you think you can do that?" He was extremely careful and spoke with the utmost respect.

Mrs. Martin looked at her husband with admiration, "Yes, I can do that," and kissed her husband on his cheek. It was a rare occasion.

"I am gonna take the boys huntin', Mrs. Martin," he grinned. He took the rifle and powder from where it hung above the doorway. It was Mrs. Martin's father's gun, and it had hung there since the house was built. It was a Brown Bess long rifle used by her grandfather in the Revolutionary War. He gathered some hardtack from the cupboard and stuffed them in his pockets as he went out to get the boys.

As Mr. Martin opened the barn door, he could hear the boys yelling, "Get 'em! Get 'em!" Just then a piglet ran out the barn door into the corral with both of the boys chasing it.

Mr. Martin laughed out loud as Billy threw his whole body over the piglet in an attempt to catch it. He landed smack dab in the middle of a mud puddle in the corral. The piglet squealed wildly and eluded him, slipping right out from underneath him. Billy looked hysterically funny with his face pitch black from mud. He stood and paused with his mouth open and his arms held slightly away from his body, dripping with goo. The piglet trotted in front of Mr. Martin and slipped into her pen through the hole where she had escaped.

Matthew stood surprised with his mouth wide open, just for a moment, and then finally broke into roaring laughter. Eventually gathering his composure, he said, "Momma's gonna be mad at you. We better take ya to the well and clean ya up!"

Mr. Martin and the boys walked, for quite a ways, until they reached the head of a spring that flowed down a draw. The draw was shadowed by two steep hillsides that were covered with trees. They scooted the dead leaves aside, below a large oak tree, and sat with their backs resting against it. They sat for a long time in silence, waiting for movements or noises.

Mr. Martin, seemingly in deep thought, finally spoke in a whisper. "When I was a young boy my father drank too much. I took a lot of beatings from him and finally ran away from home when I was very young. I worked hard, moving from farm to farm. That is how I met Mrs. Martin. I worked for her on our farm. It took a long time to get to know her, and at first, I didn't like her much"....

Matthew giggled and nodded his head up and down enthusiastically.

"...but we fell in love, and I married her. I am a very happy man and would not change anything about my life since I met your Momma."

"There is one thing I want to tell you boys. Never give up on your dreams," he continued. "There is a big world out there ready to be explored. Many riches waiting to be plucked for the man that is not afraid to go and get them. Never get stuck in a rut. Never settle for less, and seek and make your fortunes before settling down and making a family. Then, and only then, will you be able to offer something more to your wife and children." He paused for a moment. "One final piece of advice. Always be good to your children."

Billy's eyes lit up as he realized that there was promise in his future. "It's an honor to know you, Mr. Martin!" He could hope now that his future might be brighter. Living with the Martins showed him a different way of life, hard work would lead to happiness. Listening to Mr. Martin speak of riches gave him a dream of his own. His outlook and attitude would change, and he would make something of his life. He would have more than his destitute parents.

Mr. Martin put his hand on Matthew's knee and whispered, "Shhhh." He heard some rustling in the trees in front of them. He lifted his rifle and pointed it in that direction. A large, whitetail buck walked out of the trees, pausing and sniffing the air with his ears perked forward. "Kaboom!" Mr. Martin shot, and the loud boom echoed through the valley. The smoked cleared, and the buck laid motionless on the forest floor. "There, my dear boys, is the family meat supply!" Mr. Martin boasted.

They field dressed the deer and drug it home.

Mrs. Martin and Katie finished her dress. It was ankle-length with a full skirt. It was tight around her tiny waist, and had a white, ruffled petticoat to go underneath. Katie modeled it for her mother then hugged her, "Thank you, Mamma. I love it! I can't wait until Sunday, so I can wear it!"

Her mother put her hands on Katie's shoulders and stepped back to look at her, "You look so grown up, Katie. I still think of you as my little, baby girl. I guess I am going to have to face the fact that you are almost a woman."

"I promised Maggie that I'd show her," Katie giggled.

Mrs. Martin rolled her eyes and shook her head. "You and that darn cow!"

Katie went out to the barn to show Maggie. "What do

you think of me, Maggie?" Maggie lifted her head from her manger and looked at Katie. The foal in the other stall peeked from behind his mother and snorted. Katie giggled, "Do you like it too, baby boy? I love it. I am going to pick some flowers to wear in my hair too!" She twirled around to make the skirt flare. "What would I do without you, Maggie?" She twirled once more and went back to the house to change.

Mr. Martin and the boys had come into the house to tell Mrs. Martin about their kill. As Katie walked into the house, Mr. Martin looked at her and said, "Oh my, Kit, you look beautiful!" He looked at Mrs. Martin. "I guess that I should clean this rifle right away, so I can discourage the suitors!"

"Thank you, Pa," Katie twirled around for him. "Do you really like it?"

"Yes, Katie," he said. "You look almost as pretty as your momma did when she was your age. You two did a wonderful job with the dress. It's beautiful!"

"She is much prettier than I was, Mr. Martin!" Mrs. Martin was blushing.

Billy stood and stared at Katie. He had never seen a girl so beautiful as Katie was. Matthew hardly noticed and said, "Did you see the big buck Pa shot, Katie? You should have been there. Kaboom! He got 'em good, Katie!"

"I'll go up and change and come see him!" She climbed up the ladder as Billy watched her go.

After changing her clothes, Katie ran out to the barn as Moe pulled the deer up to the rafters by a rope. He was an enormous buck with full, beautiful antlers. "Wow, Pa! He's a biggin'."

Mrs. Martin watched with one hand on her hip and the other on her forehead to block the evening sun. "I guess we'll be having tender loin for supper!"

"I'll skin him and bring them into you right away, Mrs. Martin. That sounds wonderful! I am as hungry as a bear!" Mr. Martin tied the rope and put Moe back in the field. "Good boy, Moe."

Matthew jumped up and down, "Me too, Pa! Can I help you cut him up?"

"Uck!" Billy wrinkled his nose.

Mr. Martin laughed as he sharpened his knife on a leather strap, "I reckon so, son. If ya promise not to cut yourself and bleed all over it!"

Mrs. Martin and Katie headed for the house to prepare supper. Mrs. Martin turned and shouted, "Fetch some wood for me, Billy."

"Yes, Ma'am," he shouted back and ran to the wood pile.

Katie was walking backwards, facing her mother. "I can't wait to eat some venison, Momma! It has been a long while since we ate venison. It is so good!"

"We'll eat our fill while it's good, and we will make jerky out of the rest, so it will keep longer." Mrs. Martin listed all of the things that she had planned to do with the meat. We can have tenderloin tonight, liver tomorrow, roasts and stews, tongue and tripe! None will go to waste!"

"Uck tripe! Do we have to have tripe?" Katie wrinkled her nose.

"It is all good Katie." Her mother opened the door, and they went inside. "Waste not, want not!"

Chapter Five
The Bull Frog and The Peeper

Katherine stretched, thinking about how the world has changed since 1849. She thought about how hard their life was compared to hers, but how delightful it was. Things were so much more pleasant and simple back then.

It was late morning when she climbed out of bed and thought about what she would do today. Curious about what happened to Katie, she was not ready to go home. "Why did they sell their farm?" Something happened.

After breakfast, she fixed a coffee to go and went to the Library. She spent the day there looking at old photo's and newspapers. There was not a lot of information dating back that far, but she did learn about the surge of migration to the west. She wondered if they went west with the Gold Rush.

She asked the Librarian, "Do you know where the old school house would have been located?"

The Librarian thought for a moment, "Follow me." She took her to the balcony and through the long free-standing shelves filled with books. On the far wall, was an old photo, "I think it was just west of town. At the time, it would have been on the outskirts of Masontown, but now there is a subdivision there."

Katherine looked at the photo. "Can I take it down for a moment?"

"Sure, I suppose that would be fine," she said.

She held the photo, and it took her back to her dream. The school yard in the photo was exactly the same as the one in her dream. There was a buckboard that looked just like the Martin's on a path that meandered through the field in front of the school. It was uncanny. It seemed that she possessed an unbelievable, wonderful gift.

She left the library and walked down Main Street to the end of town. She imagined the wooden boardwalk in front of the sheriff's office and Sweeny's General Store across the street. When she reached the end of town, she saw the subdivision and just past it, she could see the meadow where the children walked home after school.

She went to bed early that night. She could not wait to fall asleep.

XXXX

Spring was in full swing this Sunday morning. The farm was full of the scent of freshly bloomed flowers, and the barnyard was full of new born babies. There were small chicks fluttering behind hens; piglets running and playing on the tips of their tiny hoofs; and a small, deer-like foal nudging Mary's teats, and stumbling on his not yet steady legs.

Katie had finished milking Maggie and let her out in the field. She was collecting eggs for breakfast and still had to wash the clothes from the day before and put them on the line. She could hear her mother shouting from the front porch. "Hurry, Katie! I need those eggs now!" The biscuits were ready for breakfast, and Mrs. Martin needed the eggs.

Katie ran to the house with a basket of fresh eggs and the pail of milk and delivered them to her mother. "Here you go, Momma."

Mrs. Martin snatched up the eggs. "Ring the bell for breakfast, Katie so your Pa and the boys can wash up."

"Yes, Momma, right away," Katie was breathing hard and in a rush.

Mr. Martin was out in the field behind the plow, conditioning the land for the corn crop that would be planted next week. He waived to Katie, "I'll be right in, Kit." It would take him a few minutes to unhitch the team and re-hitch them to the buckboard.

Katie rushed back into the house, and Matthew and Billy ran past her almost knocking her over. They were playing cowboys and Indians, chasing each other and screaming at the top of their lungs. "Bang! Bang! I gotcha! You're dead!"

Katie screamed, "Settle down, and stop being so rough in the house." She noticed lately, that Matthew was entering an awkward age. His voice and body were changing. She could tell that he was confused as to whether he was a boy or a young man. He was still always getting into trouble and playing pranks. He never stopped to listen and was constantly under foot, running through the house and screaming like a wild Indian. Other times he was so grown up, like when he helped Pa in the fields or hitching the horses.

Everyone was in a rush because after church there was a picnic that was to double as a celebration for Katie's sixteenth birthday. It was a very exciting day, and the house was in chaos.

Mr. Martin had dressed the best two pullets, and Mrs.

Martin roasted them and baked a fresh, warm blackberry pie for the picnic.

The house smelled so delicious when Katie opened the door that she stopped and took a deep breath and smiled. "Mmmm, Momma, it smells so good in here!"

"There will be plenty of good food at the picnic today, but let's eat breakfast first." Mrs. Martin placed the venison and porridge on the table. "Wash up, boys!"

Mr. Martin came in and closed the door. He checked the bottom of his boots, "clean and dry," he said looking at his wife for approval. He washed his hands and sat at the head of the table. Blessing the food for the family, he thanked the Lord for providing the big buck that they had been gorging on for the past week.

Mrs. Martin passed the venison. "Thank you, Mr. Martin. How are the fields coming?"

"We're fixin' to finish real soon, thanks to the extra help from both the boys!" He noticed a bit of boyish competition going on between them and was careful not to complement one more than the other. "Are you excited for your birthday party today, Kit?"

"Yes, Pa! I can't wait! Wait until you see my dress now! Momma did such a good job on it. It looks store bought!"

He glanced at his wife and smiled, "I bet it does, Kit!"

Each member of the family ate quickly and quietly, so they could finish their chores and not be late for church.

After breakfast, Katie helped her mother with the dishes. It was a touching moment. Her mother was rarely emotional, and Katie saw through her stern, outer shell. Mrs. Martin was proud of her daughter and was slightly teared up about her coming of age. She dried her hands on the hand towel and held Katie's face in her hands. She took a moment to study her and then kissed her on the forehead.

Gently turning her around, she playfully slapped her on her butt, "Go, get to work!"

Katie filled the old iron wash tub with several buckets of water that she had brought up from the well. On the back porch, she scrubbed the clothes with lye soap against the washboard. After rinsing them in clear water, she wrung them out and hung them out on the clothesline. All that was left to do was wash up and dress for church.

Her chore dress was well worn and had been patched in many places, but that did not matter because no one ever visited during chore time at the farm. After filling the pitcher for the wash basin in her room, she was ready to change. She washed using the lye soap that she and her mother had made the previous fall after the hog was butchered.

Billy was sneaking up the ladder with huge bull frog that he had found near the pond. He tipped toed to the curtain quietly and peaked to see where Katie was, so he could scare her with the frog. He stopped and could not help but stare as Katie slipped her dress off. She pulled the dress slowly up her long, curvy legs and over her head. As her long, thick, wavy, blonde hair was released from inside the collar of her dress, it fell, bouncing off the top of her butt. Her back bone and muscles curved in slightly at the small of her back and narrow waist, and bowed back out sharply to form her hips and full, rounded butt. Katie moved the wash cloth over every curve of her body. Her body was perfect in every way. He could see her plump breasts as she leaned over to wash her smooth, ivory legs.

He knew it was wrong, but it was impossible not to watch.

Katie looked up and saw his reflection in the cloudy, old mirror of the wash basin. She screamed with embarrassment, snatching her new dress up off the bed and covering herself with it.

Billy dropped the frog and hurried down the loft ladder.

Katie screamed at him, scolding him through the curtain, "Billy Sternwall, you are a childish peeper." After pausing for a moment until she was convinced that she was once again alone, she dismissed the incident and finished washing. She put on her new dress, twirling once in the mirror to admire it. Instead of wearing braids, she decided to put her hair up, after all, she was turning sixteen. Keeping some of her curls loose, to fall back over her head, she swept her hair up in a French roll. She adorned her hair with the flowers that she had picked, placing them randomly among the curls. Peering into the smoky mirror, she pinched her cheeks to make them pink. She was beautiful.

Katie came down the ladder, and her father put his arms around her. "I can't believe that you are a grown woman already. I think, I will just lock you up here and keep you all to myself! Next thing ya know, you'll be meeting a fine, young man that will want to take you from me. I won't know what to do!"

Katie started to speak, "But Pa..."

Mrs. Martin interrupted, "That is not going to happen for a while, Mr. Martin. Katie is going to teach school for a while. She will have something to fall back on if she needs it. This world is changing everyday, Mr. Martin."

Katie did not mind too much that her mother was planning her life for her. She did not, at least not until lately, have any interest in boys.

Mr. Martin and the boys went out to get the buckboard from the barn, so the women did not have to tread through the dirt. He helped his wife and Katie up on the bench seat. She rode in front of the buckboard with her parents this Sunday, while the boys rode in the back and the foal trotted behind them.

When they arrived at church, they lined up as usual, greeting Pastor Robinson, "Happy birthday, Miss Martin," he said as they entered the little, white church. Her excitement grew as many of her friends greeted her and wished her a happy birthday.

They took their seats in the same order and in the same pew. Even before the Pastor began, Katie was eager for the sermon to end and the picnic to begin. Just as she thought the Pastor was going to stop rambling, he would start again. His tone was always stern and serious, and his voice was loud and deep as he sent his message screaming through the small, white church.

Katie was bored and fidgeting as she glanced over the crowd. All at once, the Pastors voice became muffled, and the crowd seemed to disappear as she became distracted. It was him, the stranger that she had seen on the beautiful horse. He looked like he was in his early twenties with very sharp and chiseled features. His complexion was dark, and his hair was black. He glanced over at her, and smiled as if he knew that she was staring at him, and her breath almost stopped. His smile was bold and confident, and it made her heart beat wildly in her chest. She felt a strange tingle move down her back and into her stomach, making her tremble. His eyes were almost gray and seemed to pierce right through her heart. She quickly moved her eyes back to her hymn book, and her face felt fiery red. She was confused by the feelings that just rushed through her body. She wondered if he knew.

The picnic was a monumental event, and everyone attended. All of Katie's friends were there, and she looked forward to visiting with them, dancing and eating. It was a potluck, and each family brought their favorite dishes. There were roasts, stews, fresh, early spring vegetables, and deserts of every kind. The food was all arranged banquet style on tables covered with white linen cloths and topped with centerpieces full of freshly picked wildflowers.

Aunt Alice grabbed Katie's arm and showed her the beautiful cake that she made for her. It was vanilla flavored and covered in pink and white flowers made of light and fluffy butter frosting to match her dress.

"Thank you, Aunt Alice! I love it!" Katie kissed her on the cheek.

"You are very welcome, Katie," she said. "You are my only niece, and I love you!"

She was not actually Katie's Aunt. She was just an old friend of the family, and she just called herself Aunt Alice.

The breeze blew a delightful fragrance across the churchyard and cooled the warm spring sun. Katie looked over the crowd to see if the handsome, young man was there. She did not see him.

Katie's mother pulled her aside and introduced her to the new couple in town. "Katie, this is Mr. and Mrs. LaShea. They just moved to Pennsylvania from New York City."

They were absolutely charming and dressed in the latest fashions from Paris. They had immigrated from France and had heavy, elegant French accents. It was apparent that they were very influential citizens.

Mrs. LeShea was beautiful. She wore a frightfully expensive hat and dress made of heavy, dark-green velvet that was adorned with thick, silky fringe. "Very nice to meet you, Katie," she did a slight curtsy.

"Charmed," Katie replied as if she were practicing her "tea time" manners.

Mr. LeShea was handsome with a tall but well proportioned body. He reached out and put Katie's hand in his. It was easy to tell that he did not work in the fields because his hands were not rough and chapped, and his face was not leathery from the sun. He was dressed in a silk suite and tie, and wore a thin, dark mustache. "Pleasure, Miss Martin."

"The pleasure is mine, Mr. LeShea," she said with a smile as he kissed her hand.

Mrs. LeShea was in the midst of explaining, "My son, Jack, is twenty, and he helped us move here from New York City. We moved into the Smith estate, and after settling in, Jack will be leaving with the cavalry."

Katie realized that her son was the dashing, young man that smiled at her in church.

Two of Katie's friends approached and tugged gently on her arms, pulling her from the LeShea's.

Katie politely excused herself, "It was very nice to meet you both."

"The pleasure was all ours. Happy birthday, Katie. We hope to see much more of you," Mr. LeShea said as he gently grasped his wife at her elbow.

Katie left with her friends who were giggling and whispering about boys and dancing.

June asked, "Has anyone seen Johnny? I wonder if he will ask me to dance."

Katie stopped, and pulled June toward her with both hands, stopping her in her tracks. "Tell me how you felt when you first knew that you liked Johnny."

"I just think he is handsome. I don't feel anything, why?" June looked confused.

Katie looked into her eyes, "Do you feel like your insides are going to explode when you see him?"

June lowered both her brows and wrinkled her nose,

"Are you asking if I feel sick when I see him?"

"No, June, do you feel all tingly inside, like when the cold wind gets into your coat in the winter!" Katie tried to explain.

"I don't think so, Katie. I don't think I do. Why, am I suppose to?" June laughed at her.

Realizing that June was oblivious to true love, Katie gave up on the subject. She tried to join in on the girlish fun, mingling through the crowd, but she found herself inconspicuously scanning the area for Jack. People were gathering to offer their congratulations to her on her birthday. She halfheartedly thanked them, not even taking the time to recognize who was speaking to her. Jack was all that she thought about since the moment that she saw him, and she was eager to see him again.

The party was in full swing. There was a line forming at the banquet tables, but Katie had lost her appetite from all the excitement. The local fiddlers cheered the crowd to a happy roar as they started playing their music. Mr. Martin and the rest of the men who had been discussing the gold rush and traveling west were sneaking whiskey from their flasks.

Mr. Martin took a sip. "I sure would like to join the adventure. Word has it, men are earning their fortunes in Virginia City. The city is overflowing with money."

"Well, Mr. Martin, you should. Thanks to men like my son, the cavalry is gaining control over the hostiles and have been able to subdue them," Mr. LeShea said convincingly.

Mr. Sweeney popped into the conversation, "I hear, there are over thirty thousand people in Virginia City and plenty of money to go around!"

Mrs. LeShea approached and squeezed in next to her husband. She overheard part of the conversation and said,

"They are just completing the construction of a grand opera house and only allow the best entertainers to perform. I would love to see it!"

Mr. LeShea said, "They have discovered the largest deposit of ore in the world there. The most educated engineers and builders are running the show with the latest technology available. It is quite contrary to the wild, uncivilized place you might think it would be."

Mr. Sweeney was excited to add, "They have over one hundred saloons there. Can you believe it!"

"Quite advanced fashion too!" Mrs. LeShea became bored with the conversation. "Mr. LeShea, this is our song."

"Excuse me, gentlemen," he said as they left, walking toward the dance floor, Mrs. LeShea was swaying back and forth to the music.

"Excuse me. I must dance with my daughter," Mr. Martin said as he looked for Katie.

He found her and insisted that she dance with him. "It isn't often that there is the opportunity to dance, and it is your sixteenth birthday."

She was reluctant, but eventually welcomed the distraction. "Alright, Pa! Alright!"

There were several boys that wanted to dance with her, and she danced, but she held little interest for any of them. To her, they were more like brothers than suitors. One right after another, she danced until way after dark.

Mr. Martin found his wife sitting with the other women and talking after they had finished their meal. With his left hand behind his back, he leaned toward her extending his right hand to her. "Would you do me the honor of dancing with me, Mrs. Martin?"

She took his hand and stood. "Why yes, Mr. Martin. I would love too!"

He led her out through the crowd and held her tight

under the stars and the moon. He stared into her eyes as he danced with her. He loved her so.

When the dance was over, Mr. and Mrs. Martin sat on a bench and watched their daughter dance. Mr. Martin looked at his wife and said, "You know, it won't be long before our daughter will pick one of those young men out there, and we will lose her forever."

"I know Mr. Martin. I am not ready for that day. I don't think, I ever will be. It just seems like yesterday when she was just a toddler running and playing in the yard. Time slips away so quickly."

Katie was exhausted and extremely thirsty, so she walked to the tall tree where a table was situated with jars of punch. As she sipped her punch, she heard a deeper than expected voice coming from behind the tree, "Happy birthday."

Katie turned and realized it was him. His accent was not as strong as his parents but still, very romantic. He was tall, and the muscles on his arms stretched the sleeves of his shirt then spanned thick up his shoulders and neck. He had a chiseled waist that she could see through the white, starched shirt that he was wearing.

"Come for a walk with me," he insisted confidently.

She opened her mouth but could not speak. It was absurd for him to ask her. It was impossible for a young lady to be with a young man without a chaperone. She finally gathered her composure and spoke. Her voice was shaking as she explained abruptly, "I most certainly will not!"

Jack reached over and grasped her hand firmly, pulling her quickly behind the tree. He lifted her by her tiny waist and rested her up against the tree with ease. He pressed his body firmly against hers and kissed her on her lips. She could feel the hardness of his body, and her body shuttered as she felt a tingle deep inside her.

It all happened so fast that she could not resist his advances. She wanted him to kiss her again, but she knew that she had to escape his grip and return to the party. She could not get caught. It would devastate her mother to see her so close to a boy. Deep down, she wanted to stay, but she knew she should not be having these feelings. It was not the proper way for a young lady is to act.

She managed to pull away and slap him firmly on his face. He released her, and she rushed back toward the party, straightening her hair and smoothing out her dress. She stopped and turned to look behind her.

He was leaning up against the tree, watching her with a smile. He tipped his hat and said, "Happy birthday," as he turned and walked into the trees.

As she returned to the party, she could not stop the smile that appeared on her face.

Chapter Six
The Hero and The Cake Walk

"I was right! The wagon train! I bet they go west! Katherine sat straight up in bed.

Excited for Katie and Jack, she turned her laptop on and caught up on her notes. Jack was a dashing, confident man, and he captivated her with his romantic accent and bold attitude.

Katherine did not go down to the lobby until mid-morning. When she finally did, the manager had saved her a plate of breakfast, and she returned to her room with it and some coffee. After she had eaten her breakfast, she crawled back in bed and fell back to sleep.

XXXX

Friday was the last day of school, and Miss Roberts arrived unusually early. She cleaned the slates that the younger children had used and put them up. After cleaning the desks, she stacked them along the walls of the room, making sure to label anything that the children had forgotten to take home. She swept the wood plank floor and packed the books away, putting them up so the mice would not get into them over the summer. She cleaned out her desk and the inside of the wood stove.

Miss Roberts had an exciting day planned. All testing and grades where done, and it pleased her that all the students made standard, having enough points to move on to the next level. To reward the children for their hard work, she thought the last day of school should be a fun one.

Her apron was dirty, so she went out to the well and lowered the bucket to get some water. She cleaned herself up as well as she could and waited for Sheriff Jenkins. He promised to come early and move the outside tables closer together, so they could place the food on them. He had also agreed to bring some venison. The sheriff had shot a large stag, and being a single man, it was much more than he could eat.

Miss Roberts talked to each and every parent and arranged for the pot luck, good-bye party at the school house. Every parent had agreed to attend and bring a dish. That is, except for Mr. Johnson.

When Miss Roberts approached him, he exclaimed, "I don't need to go to any damn school picnic! I don't have time for that kind of nonsense! There's too damn much to do around here to be goin' off doing nothin!" Mr. Johnson was almost too drunk to stand when Miss Roberts visited him. He claimed that he had too many chores to do this time of year. Living up in the hills in a make shift cabin, he survived off trapping and hunting. He had no animals to feed or crops to tend, and the family was terribly poor. Everyone knew that the little money he made with his traps was spent on whiskey. He drank too much. Other than what the children were forced to do, nothing got done at Mr. Johnson's place. Miss Roberts felt sorry for Tom and Jenny.

She knew their life must be exceedingly difficult.

She had a speech planned that mentioned every child and his or her achievements. Katie was the oldest child attending the school and this would be her last school year. She was only required to attend until she was fourteen, but she was able to stay and earn her teaching paper. She helped Miss Roberts and earned a certificate showing her skill to teach.

Sheriff Jenkins arrived, "Mornin', Miss Roberts. How are ya this morning?"

"Very good, Sheriff, very good!" She blushed a little.

"You looking forward to havin' the summer off?" He was making small talk and seemed to be a little smitten with her.

She looked down at the ground, and with her hands behind her back, she swayed from side to side like a shy school girl. "It will be a nice break, but I will miss the children."

"Where would you like this table moved to, Ma'am?" He said politely.

She looked at him a little dazed, thinking about the sudden feelings that she had for him.

"Ma'am?" he asked again, trying to get her attention.

"Oh, yes. Sorry, right over here," she said.

He moved the table for her, and she put a linen cloth over it.

Bending over to gather some stones for his fire, he told her, "I am going to set a campfire over yonder, Miss Roberts. If ya need me, you just holler. Ya hear?"

She unintentionally batted her eyes at him. "Thank you, Sheriff." As she turned to walk away, she tripped and started to fall. Sheriff Jenkins caught her in his arms, or she would have fallen to the ground. As he held her up, their eyes met, and their faces were very close together. He looked into her eyes, and she looked into his. There was a long silence.

Finally, the sheriff spoke, "You alright, Miss Roberts?"

She gazed into his eyes, and then at his lips but was too embarrassed to speak. Quickly, he kissed her on her lips and looked at her eyes for her reaction. Judging from the expression on his face, he was just as surprised as she was that he had kissed her. Without moving her eyes from his, she smiled at him and slowly moved her fingers up to her lips, touching them lightly. Her face was red, and she did not know what to say or do. After being totally lost for words, Sheriff Jenkins finally glanced away and lifted her to her feet.

She stepped back from him and straightened her hair and her dress. She looked down at the ground, but still smiled. "I am fine, Sheriff."

With an awkward stance, Sheriff Jenkins said, "Good, Ma'am, good!" He cleared his throat and took his rocks to his cooking sight.

The children arrived anxiously dragging their parents behind them. They were excited to show off the achievements that they had accomplished during the school year. The women put their side dishes down on the linen-covered table and started their own conversations as the children went on to play among themselves. Placing her molasses cakes on the table, Mrs. Martin gave Miss Roberts a hug. "Oh, Miss Roberts, I sure hope our children were good to you this year!"

"Oh yes, Mrs. Martin, they were wonderful. Katie was such a big help, and Matthew is so well behaved. Even Billy was good after his first day." She laughed. "He just had to establish himself, that's all!"

"Yes, he really is a good boy. He has just had some

bad luck," Mrs. Martin agreed.

Miss Roberts looked up at the tree line. "Speaking of bad luck, I am so surprised that Mr. Johnson let the children come today!"

Tom and Jenny were coming through the woods and out into the opening toward the school yard. She put her arms around them and welcomed them to the picnic. "I am so glad you could come, children!"

Tom pulled away and ran toward the other children. Jenny said, "Thank you Miss Roberts, but we didn't bring any food."

"That's alright, child! You just go and have fun with the other children!"

Miss Roberts walked back to where the other women were standing. "I sure feel bad for those youngins! They don't stand much of a chance without their mother." Mrs. Martin and the other women sadly nodded in agreement and watched as Tom and Jenny joined the other children in play.

All the children played in the schoolyard, knowing that this would be the last day of play for the summer. The rest of the summer would be filled with hard work which did not seem to bother any of them.

Miss Roberts called all the children and their fathers around the table where the women were gathered. "First of all, I want to thank you all for coming today. I felt the need to reward the students and thank them for being so good. Every one of you worked hard and completed the lessons I had for you. You all earned enough points to pass standard, and next year we will all move on to the next level. So, I want to thank you all for making it so easy for me. I look forward to teaching all of you again in the fall." Leaning over, she picked up a stack of papers and continued, "I guess you all know that Katie will not be back. She has passed all her requirements to teach her own group of children, and it is my honor to give her the paper which allows her to do it."

The crowd clapped and cheered for Katie as she stepped forward to receive her paper. "I will miss you, Miss Martin," Miss Roberts hugged her. She looked at Katie's parents, "You should be proud of her, she really did work hard for me."

"We are very proud," Mr. Martin said as he clapped for her.

Katie stepped back over to her parents, letting them hug her and inspect her paper.

"For the rest of you students, I have your honorary certificates of completion for the standard, and I will read them in alphabetical order." She read them off, one by one, and Matthew and the other students came up to receive them while the audience cheered and clapped for them. Billy stood sadly, wishing he was able to get an honorary certificate.

"Billy Sternwall," she called his name, and he looked up with a surprised expression. "Yes Billy, I know you were only with us for two weeks, but you surpassed the qualifications in that short amount of time, and you qualified!"

As he received his paper, he shook Miss Roberts hand wildly. He was so excited. He ran to Mr. and Mrs. Martin and hugged them. They both teared up, holding him tightly. Mr. Martin picked him up off the ground and twirled him around with excitement.

"Now, last but not least, I would like to thank the parents of these wonderful children. I know times are hard, and there is a lot of work to be done at home. I know life would be much easier if you had your children at home to help. Because of their education, your children will have an easier life, and I am glad you let them come. Now, with that said, please, everyone eat! We have games to play after dinner!"

Sheriff Jenkins cooked the venison over the fire, and everyone stood waiting to get some from him. The line continued along the tables, and everyone filled their plates with fresh vegetables, stew, potatoes and dessert. Everyone stood, ate and visited with one another.

As Miss Roberts held her plate out in front of Sheriff Jenkins, he said, "I saved these special pieces for you, Ma'am."

She smiled and blushed. "Thank you, Sheriff, that was very nice." She wanted to talk to him, but she was not accustom to getting attention from a man, and she was taken by surprise.

After dinner, Miss Roberts again gathered the crowd, "It's time for games!" She passed out gunny sacks and pitted the children against their parents. The crowd laughed as they watched the adults clumsily and comically stumble and fall in the bags. Everyone had such a lovely time. After the gunny sack race, Miss Roberts organized a cake walk. She gave cakes and baked goods that she and the mothers' made as prizes. Each child won a cake, one way or another.

Tom Johnson ran to the Sheriff and stood behind him when he saw his father riding down through the wood. Mr. Johnson rode down at a lope, and he was swaying from side to side on his horse. It was obvious that he was too drunk to ride properly. In fact, when he stopped his horse in front of the sheriff, he fell off onto the ground. He grabbed on to his horse's leg and cussed as he pulled himself up.

"God damn children! I told you to stay home and do the chorin'! Ya weren't suppose ta come down here to this useless schoolhouse for this no good, damn picnic!" He pulled Tom out from behind the Sheriff and pulled his arm back and let his son have it right on the nose. Tom fell to the ground unconscious.

"Get up, damn it! Get up!" he slurred.

The sheriff grabbed Mr. Johnson by his arm and twisted it behind his back, pushing him over, and he fell to the ground. He tied his hands together with a rope. "Mr. Johnson, you are under arrest."

"You can't arrest me for hittin' my own kin, damn it!" he cussed.

The sheriff pulled him to his feet. "You watch me, Mr. Johnson!" He boosted him up on his horse and reached down to check on Tom who was starting to stir.

"I am sorry about this, Miss Roberts, but I have to go. See if you can get the boy up and moving. I will check with you when I get Mr. Johnson locked up." He got his horse and led Mr. Johnson to town.

Tom was regaining consciousness, and his nose was bleeding profusely. Miss Roberts took her apron off and sat on the ground, scooting under him and putting his head on her lap. She held her apron over his nose trying to stop the bleeding. "Mr. Martin, could you get my wagon, please?"

"Yes, Ma'am." Mr. Martin pulled the wagon up next to them, and he and the other men lifted Tom into the back. Mr. Martin was going to ride into town with him, but Billy grabbed his arm. "Let me do it, Mr. Martin."

"Alright boy," Mr Martin said. "I'll pick ya up in town."

Miss Roberts drove Tom, Jenny and Billy into town, and Mr. Martin followed in the buckboard with Mrs. Martin, Matthew and Katie. They helped to get Tom and Jenny settled at the Roberts' place.

Mr. Martin called Billy. "Its time we head home, Billy."

Tom grabbed Billy's arm. "I reckon I owe you an apology."

"It's alright, Tom. Don't worry about it," Billy said.

Still holding on to Billy's arm, Tom looked him in the eye and said, "Thanks for helpin' me."

"Anytime, Tom Johnson, anytime." Billy smiled. He left the house and got into the buckboard. They headed for home.

When Sheriff Jenkins reached Miss Roberts house, the doctor was just leaving. "Doc, how is he?"

"He will be just fine, Sheriff. He took quite a blow though." The doctor was concerned. "He doesn't have to go home to his father, does he?"

"That depends, Doc. I have his father in jail, and the boy is safe for now." He shook his head. "I am going to see what I can do about it."

"You do that Sheriff. He can't go through much more of that. The man could kill him," he said and stepped up into his buggy.

The sheriff knocked on Miss Roberts door.

"Hello, Sheriff, please, come in." She was not quite as shy at this point because of the serious matter at hand.

"How's the boy, Ma'am?" he asked as he took his hat off.

"He is doing better. He is in bed, and his sister is upstairs with him. You can't let them go back, Sheriff!" She had a serious tone. "I know, I am not a married woman, but I want to keep them here with me. I can give them a good home. Can you make him give them up?"

"It's not that easy, Miss Roberts." He looked down at the floor. "Let me work on it. He will be in jail for a while. Can I see the boy?"

She smiled and tilted her head in admiration. "Of course." She showed him upstairs to the room. Tom was laying in the bed, and Jenny was sitting beside him in a chair with tears in her eyes. The sheriff stopped and stood at the foot of the bed with both hands on the brim of his hat in front of him. "How ya feeling, boy?"

"I'm alright, Sir," he said. "I've taken worse."

Sheriff Jenkins looked at Miss Roberts with concern. "Listen, boy, I don't want you two to have to go back there. Would ya be willin' to press charges on your Pa?"

Tom sat up with the look of excitement in his eyes and then his excitement faded when he realized, "We have nowhere else to go, Sir!"

Miss Roberts sat on the edge of the bed and put one hand on Tom's and held Jenny's hand with the other. "I want you both to stay here with me!" Tears started to roll down her face. "I don't want you ever to take a beating like that again."

The excitement returned to Tom's face. "You would do that for us, Ma'am?"

Jenny stood and hugged her, "You are my hero, Miss Roberts!"

"Yes I would, children." She wiped her eyes with her apron. "Nothing would make me happier."

Sheriff Jenkins cleared his throat and batted his eyes. He walked toward the door and quietly eased out. As he walked down the steps, Miss Roberts called to him. He stopped to let her catch up. She walked him to the door and outside. "Do you think we have a chance?"

He turned to her. "I am gonna go talk with the man. If the children press charges against him, I am hoping he will let them go." He stood there for a minute looking at her face and said, "Miss Roberts?"

"Yes?" she replied.

"After all this is over," he said, "Can I see ya. I mean personally?"

She blushed and looked down at the ground with a smile. She looked back up into his eyes and said, "Yes,

Sheriff."

"Ya bolt your doors, and I'll be back," he said.

Sheriff Jenkins open the door to his office, and Mr. Johnson shouted, "You let me out of here, damn it! You can't keep me here for hittin' my own kin!" He rolled out of the cot that was in the corner of the cell and stood.

"You listen to me, Johnson," the sheriff said, standing confidently in front of the cell with his arms crossed and his feet spread wide apart. "Your youngins are pressing charges against ya'. You'll be here a long time."

Mr. Johnson took two sloppy steps forward and grasped the bars of the cell to brace himself. "To hell with them damn youngins. They ain't no good for nothin'!"

"If you let 'em go and agree to let 'em be, I'll let you go, but ya gotta leave town and never come back." The sheriff waited for a reply and hoped for the best.

Mr. Johnson thought for a long while. He looked at the sheriff and could tell by his eyes that he was not bluffing. He glared at him and said, "Good riddance to the little devils!"

The sheriff got his keys and unlocked the door. He took Mr. Johnson by his collar and said, "If you ever set eyes on those kids again, I won't hesitate to use my gun on ya!" He pulled him out the door and set him on his horse. He pointed the horse to the west and slapped him on his rump. The horse jumped and ran through town with Mr. Johnson hanging on with all his might. He could hardly keep his seat.

Miss Roberts watched through the curtains of her window. When she saw him ride by, she felt fear move through her body as he passed but was relieved that he did not stop.

Soon, the sheriff rode up and tied his horse on the hitching post. She opened the door and ran out to greet him, anxious to know what happened.

He opened the gate and put his arms around her, squeezing her tight, he lifted her up off the ground. She did not have to say a word. Knowing that she and the children would be safe, she had never been happier.

Jenny and Tom watched out the bedroom window upstairs and smiled at each other. Jenny was crying with happiness. "We are free, Tom! We are free!"

"Yes, Jenny, we sure are!"

School had been out for three days, and Katie and the boys had adapted to their summer routine. Katie looked after the kitchen garden, the chickens and took care of Maggie. She did the laundry and helped her mother in the house.

Matthew and Billy helped Mr. Martin in the fields. They had finished the plowing and were planting the corn seed. The ground was good and warm. Mr. Martin was happy. "Things are going good this spring, Mrs. Martin." He passed the beans down the table.

She smiled and said, "I talked to Miss Roberts in church today."

"I heard that she had offered to take on the Johnson children," Katie said.

"Yes," Mrs. Martin continued. "The sheriff kicked Mr. Johnson out of town and let her take the children."

Mr. Martin smiled at his wife. "Rumor has it, Sheriff Jenkins is courtin' her now!"

Matthew choked on his beans.

Billy said, "Uck!"

Even though Billy had a serious crush on Katie, neither of the boys had any serious interest in courtship.

Katie swallowed the food that she had in her mouth and said, "Well, I think it's very romantic."

Mrs. Martin looked at her daughter a bit surprised. "And just what do you know about romance young lady?"

"Nothin', Momma," she replied quickly.

Mrs. Martin looked at her husband. "I am happy for both of them. I hope they marry and raise those children together. They are both getting on in years and are a little old to start a family of their own."

It was evening, and the stars shone bright in the sky. The moon was out and a breeze blew, cooling the evening air. As Sheriff Jenkins came up on Miss Roberts steps, the porch swing moved with the breeze. It was a beautiful night. Sheriff Jenkins knocked on the door, and Miss Roberts opened it.

She was surprised and smiling. "Hello, Sheriff."

"It's a beautiful evening, Miss Roberts. Would you like to come out and sit for a spell?"

He took the wildflowers from behind his back and showed them to her. She opened the screened door and took the flowers slowly from his hand. She was almost teared up because no one had ever shown her such a romantic gesture. Lifting them to her nose, she smelled them.

"They are beautiful, Sheriff Jenkins!" She looked at the porch swing. "Let me put these in some water. Won't you have a seat? Would you like some tea?"

He removed his hat and held it to his chest. "Yes Ma'am, that would be nice."

"I'll be right out." She went into the house and put the flowers in a vase with some water and hurried out to the porch with the flowers and some tea on the tray. Placing the tray on the table, she asked, "Would you like some honey, Sheriff Jenkins?"

"Yes, Ma'am," he said rubbing his hands on his pant legs.

She gave him a cup of tea in a beautiful china tea cup and saucer and sat on the other side of the porch swing. They both sat in silence for a while, looking up at the stars.

Finally, Sheriff Jenkins broke the silence, "It's a beautiful night, Miss Roberts." He scooted closer to her and held her hand.

She stiffened her body, "Yes, Sheriff, it is."

XXXX

When Katherine finally woke, it was afternoon. She went down to the cafe and ate lunch. After that, she decided that she would go back out and visit Mr. Wrigley.

He was excited to see her. "You are still here! You find what you need, Sweetie?"

"It has been a wonderful journey, Mr. Wrigley. Listen, I want to ask you a favor," she said.

"What can I do for you," he yelled.

"I was wondering if I could have some copies made of the pictures you have?"

"Well, I suppose that would be alright," he said. "Come on in, Sweetie. I will let you get the albums down."

She opened the screen door and went into the house. She opened up the brown album again and thumbed through the pictures. "There are just a few, Mr. Wrigley." She noticed another photo that she had not noticed before. It was a photo of a group of people at the schoolyard. It was everyone that was at the picnic on that last day of school. "Sheriff Jenkins, Miss Roberts, Tom, Jenny, Mr. and Mrs. Martin, Katie, Matthew and Billy!"

"I'll be damned. How'd you know that!" Mr. Wrigley asked.

She looked at him and then back at the photo. "I don't know, Mr. Wrigley. Can I bring these back tomorrow?"

"Yes, Ma'am, you sure can," he said with a confused look on his face. "I will sure look forward to it!"

Katherine drove straight to Pittsburgh and found the nearest photo shop. She took the photo's inside and asked for duplicates.

"It will be a few hours," the clerk told her.

Katherine did not want to take a chance that she might lose the old photos, so she waited.

It was late when she returned to the Bed and Breakfast and climbed the steps to her room. She would be taking the photo's back to Mr. Wrigley tomorrow, so she went to bed.

Chapter Seven
True Love and Lost Crops

Two weeks had passed, and Katie had not seen Jack. She obsessed over him. Maggie was the only one that she could confide in, and she told her about the feelings that she had for Jack. She looked and listened to make sure that no one was in the barn.

"I can't stop thinking about the way his body felt while he was pressing up against me," she whispered. He is haunting me, Maggie. Momma would be cross with me because she raised me to be a lady. I know that what I feel is wrong, but I can't make it stop." She was not prepared for what she was going through. "My friends never talk about feeling this way. Am I going insane?" She was in complete agony. She asked Maggie, "I wonder why he is hiding. Why has he not gone to church? I just can't believe that he is not thinking of me. Doesn't he want to see me as much as I want to see him? I wonder if he knows that he is torturing me. Maybe he is staying away to make me feel like this."

She would not dare share her feelings with her mother. She would forbid her to see him again. Sometimes she wished that Maggie could talk so she could get advice from her, but she was glad that she had her as a confidant.

"I wonder what I would do if he kissed me again. Would I be able to resist the spell he has on me?"

She finished her milking and put Maggie back in the stall. She hugged her neck, "Good night, my dear friend."

The next morning, Katie took her father's riding horse to town to pick up her mother's order at the general store. It was another beautiful morning. Dew was on the ground, and the birds were singing as she mounted the old gelding.

"It's a beautiful day, old boy!" She closed her eyes and took a deep breath of the fresh spring scented air. She smiled for the first time since she had seen Jack. She seemed to be more like herself today than she had for a long while. Taking her time, she lazily enjoying the quiet time to herself. She was just to the edge of town near Wrigley's Livery Stables when she saw him.

Jack was leading a small herd of horses to the livery stables. She realized that he must have been away getting those horses for the cavalry. She felt a little sorry about the terrible thoughts that she had about him. It made sense now. The soldiers were building forts along the Oregon Trail to protect the wagon trains. She remembered what Mrs. LeShea had told her about Jack joining the cavalry. None the less, she was still mad at him. She could not help it.

He smiled at her and then tipped his hat and said, "Madam".

Glaring at him, she lifted her chin and looked the other way as he passed. Her legs were weak, and she struggled to keep her composure as she dismounted the old gelding and entered the store. Her hands were shaking and moist when she took the paper list out of her string tie purse and gave it to Mr. Sweeney.

He read the list out loud and asked, "Will that be all,

Miss Martin?" He paused for a moment, waiting for her to answer and then finally, repeated himself, "Miss Martin, will that be all? Miss, are you alright?"

Katie looked startled when she finally gathered her wits and realized Mr. Sweeney was talking to her. "I am sorry. What did you say, Mr. Sweeney?"

He repeated himself again.

Katie acknowledged, "Yes, Sir, that's all."

He gathered the items from the store shelves and charged them to Mr. Martin's account. The storekeeper loaded the two small packages in her saddle bags.

Katie noticed that the wind was blowing and some clouds were gathering. She looked around, hoping to see Jack but there was nothing. Reluctantly, she turned her horse toward home.

She was cross at herself. After all this time, she worried about him, and now after seeing him, she did not even speak to him. Looking down every street, she hoped to see him. She passed the livery stable, and he was not there.

It started to sprinkle on her as she rode out of town slowly.

She spoke out loud to herself, "Why didn't I speak to him! That was my chance, and I ruined it. I am such an idiot!" Just when she thought that she might be able to put him behind her, he penetrated deep into her heart and soul once again.

The road home meandered across two small hills and a small patch of trees in a valley. A bridge spanned the river that flowed under it. Katie reached the top of the first hill, and she looked back. She noticed a horse coming behind her at full speed. It startled her, and she kicked her horse into a full run. Her father's horse was old and slow, and the rider behind her was gaining on her. Her heart raced with adrenaline. As she topped the second hill, he was already at the bottom of the hill behind her. She took the downward slope at full speed.

The rain was coming down harder, and the wind was blowing it in her face. When she came to the bottom of the next hill, she looked behind her, but the rider was not there. Maybe he stumbled, or maybe she out ran him. She took the corner, and all at once, the horse and rider came up out of the brush beside her. It was then that she realized that it was Jack. She kicked her horse, hoping to out run him, but he came up beside her and plucked her off her horse. His horse slid to a stop as quickly and smoothly as it ran. Jack slipped off his horse with her in his arms, and before she could think, he kissed her. Her mind was spinning. She felt as if she should slap him for being so bold, but she could not bring herself to do it.

The rain was pouring down on them, and the wind blew it almost sideways. He carried her down under the bridge and kissed her again. This time she did not stop him. She could not stop the spell he had on her. Wanting to feel his muscular body, her hands began to move down his neck and across the muscles in his back. They were firm and moist from the sun's heat. Still kissing her, he let her slide down on to her feet. He moved his hand across her cheek and neck and pressed her lips tight to his.

Lightening flashed, and thunder cracked loudly.

She froze with emotion as he moved his hands down her back and pressed her body into his. A chill moved down her spine, and her insides began to flutter with a tingling sensation. She moaned slightly, and he knew that she wanted him. Since the first moment that she saw him, she knew that she wanted him. She was not reluctant, nor afraid. He picked her up again and laid her down in the grass under the bridge. As he rose up, he effortlessly slid her body under his.

They hardly even noticed the raging storm that was descending down upon them.

Her hands moved further down, past the curve in his back and his butt flexed as he pressed deeply into her. She was eager for his touch. He pressed against her firmly until she almost exploded. The pressure of his body against hers, made her heart throb rapidly, and now, when he pressed against her, she pressed back. Jack unbuttoned her dress and kissed her neck. She pressed her hand on the back of his head and grasped his hair, pressing him into her. She knew that what she was doing was wrong, but she did not stop him. She ignored the shame that she felt. She wanted him more than she had ever wanted anything. She moved herself closer, and he slowly and gently caressed her. She wanted him to take her and to know that she loved him, wanting no other. They made passionate love, and then they laid under the bridge entangled, looking into each others eyes and sharing gentle kisses. For Katie, it was emotional bliss. It was truly love at first sight for both of them.

They spent the afternoon planning their future. Jack was sure and confident when he spoke, "Marry me!"

Katie looked up at him. "It is not that easy. Momma expects me to"....

Jack interrupted her, placing his finger up against her lips. "We will marry when I get back with the rest of the cavalry horses. Then, I will send for you when I get stationed."

"But, you don't understand"...

"Your mother will just have to understand." It was apparent that Jack was accustom to getting what he wanted. Katie did not mind. She wanted what he wanted, and she was madly in love with him.

He kissed her again, "I will return in two weeks and will ask your father for your hand."

Katie stood and buttoned her dress. While putting on her petticoat and straightened her hair, she watched Jack as he dressed. His body was amazing to her. His muscles were bulging and glistened with rain drops.

The rain turned into hail and was beating down on the bridge above. The horses took refuge in the water under the bridge to keep from being stung by the jagged balls of hail. Jack held Katie tight as she flinched at the loud rumble and lightening that struck so near that it deafened her. The wind was fierce and got so strong that Jack had to hold Katie up to the berm of dirt against the inside edge of the bridge. Tree limbs and debris flew through the air, and he shielded her from them. Entire trees were falling.

It was then that Jack realized. "Tornado!"

Katie shouted over the loud roar, "I have to go home, Jack! My family!"

"You have to wait until it is over, Katie. You can't go out there!" he said. "I will take you when it is over!"

The storm subsided as fast as it came. The air was perfectly still and quiet. Jack retrieved the horses and handed Katie's reins to her. "I will take you home, Katie."

"No, Jack!" She was frightened. "I don't want you to come. I don't want them to know we have been alone together!"

"I want to make sure you and your family are safe before I leave." He lifted her chin up and looked at her face. "It is alright, Katie. They will not know."

They rode together to the hill that overlooked Katie's house.

The fields were torn to pieces, but the house was still standing. She stopped her horse and could see her father saddling Moe and her mother standing next to him. "He is coming to look for me, Jack. I will go from here."

He dismounted and pulled her down from her horse.

He kissed her and held her body close to his. "I love you, Katie Martin, and I will think of you often while I am away."

She looked into Jack's eyes, "I love you too, Jack LeShea. I'll be waiting for you."

Katie rode down the hill and out of the woods.

Her father handed Moe's reins to his wife and ran to her. "Kit! I am so glad you are alright! I was so worried about you!"

Katie could see the fear in her fathers eyes, and she heard the worry in his voice. "I'm alright, Pa. I hid under the bridge. The fields are gone, Pa! Our crops! They are all gone!"

"I know, Kit." He looked toward the house. "The important thing is that we are all alright. Just a little closer, and we would not have made it."

Mrs. Martin came up with Moe. "Oh, Katie," she hugged her. "I was so scared!"

They all walked to the barn where Matthew and Billy were. Mr. Martin had sent them out to check on the animals.

Matthew ran up to meet his family shouting, "All are accounted for, Pa!"

"Thank God," Mrs. Martin said.

They stood and looked over the ravaged crops in the fields.

"Will we have to plant 'em again, Pa?" Matthew asked.

"I don't know what we will do." He was seriously worried, but wanted to keep up a strong front for his family. "I will think of something, son." Mr. Martin put his hand on Matthew's shoulder.

Billy shook his head from side to side and sighed. "That sure was a lot of hard work gone to waste."

"Come on, Katie, lets fix some dinner," Mrs. Martin

said, and they walked to the house.

Mr. Martin and the boys followed, loading some wood in their arms as they went in the house. Mr. Martin put some wood in the cook stove and Mrs. Martin put a pot of beans on the stove and made some biscuits. They were all sad, exhausted and quiet. Katie set the table and churned some butter while the beans were cooking. Mr. Martin and the boys sat at the table in silence.

"Momma, are we gonna be alright?" Katie asked.

Her mother turned and said, "Listen to me, children. We have been through worse, and we have always made it through the bad times. Do you remember the drought? And the fire? And the locus?"

"Oh, I remember the locus, Momma!" Matthew was eight when the locus came. "They ate a path across our fields!"

Mr. Martin scooped up the beans and passed the bowls down the table. "We'll be alright!"

Katie scooped some fresh butter into a bowl for the biscuits. They all sat quietly and ate.

After supper was over and the dishes were done, Katie went out to the barn and called Maggie. She came trotting around the corner. Putting the stool on the ground, Katie washed her teats. "Oh, Maggie, it seems like a lifetime has gone by today. So much has happened. Where do I start?"

She put the rag up on the wooden rail next to her and started milking.

She told Maggie about her trip to town. She lowered her voice to a whisper when she told her about her time with Jack. "I am so much in love, Maggie." I never thought I could feel this way about anyone. I would die for him, Maggie. Everything just happened."

"Then the storm, Maggie! You saw the storm. I hope your weren't scared. I know that I wasn't here, and I am sorry about that." Katie rubbed her and patted her shoulder. "I was worried about you, and Momma, and Pa, and the boys. I don't know what I would have done if something happened to you. I would have never forgiven myself for not being here to save you."

She squeezed Maggie's teat one more time and put her in the stall. Fearing the possibility of another storm, she chose to leave her inside for the night.

Everyone was finally tucked away in bed, and Mrs. Martin crawled in with her husband. "Oh, what a day, Mr. Martin."

"Yes, it was a frightening day. It will be a long time before I forget it." He pulled the covers up over her and tucked them under her neck.

She turned on her side and looked into his eyes. "What will we do, Mr. Martin?

"I don't know, Mrs. Martin," he replied. "We don't have the money to replant. I don't know what we will do. I reckon we have two choices. We can sell everything we own and replant, or we can sell everything we own and go west."

"Maybe we should consider it." She raised up on her elbow and propped her head up with her hand. She looked at him with an intensely serious expression. "Are you absolutely sure it's safe? I almost lost my daughter today, and I don't want to go through that again!"

Mr. Martin was surprised that she was even considering it and took her hand into his, "That goes to show you, Mrs. Martin, it is just as safe out there as it is right here at home."

"It would be so wonderful to go there and have a better life, but I have spent my whole life here, fighting for this little farm. My mother and father spent most of their life fighting to keep this little farm. It is so hard for me to give up and leave! I don't know if I can do it. The farm is ours, free and clear. We always have it for sure. What if we don't find our dreams out west? What if we fail our children? I will think about it, Mr. Martin. Don't say anything to the children. I don't want them to get all excited about it yet."

She blew out the lamp and put her head down on her husband's shoulder.

Mr. Martin smiled, "Yes, Ma'am!"

Mrs. Martin fell into a deep sleep and had a beautiful dream. In her dream, she was in Virginia City. The city was nestled in a valley with hills that were covered with juniper trees and sagebrush. It was a beautiful, sunny morning, but it was cool and crisp. The aroma that the sagebrush released into the air was blissfully tranquil. There was a church steeple standing up high, looking over a cluster of buildings and beautiful houses. The hillsides were dotted with mines, employing thousands of men.

As her beautiful carriage drove into the city, she could see stores lining the main street and women dressed in beautiful clothing. She could see the hotels, many of them. There were clothing stores and a haberdashery. A fine restaurant on a corner was crowded with people. The men dressed in silk suits and the women wore beautiful, colorful dresses and hats, and they carried parasols.

She looked up the hill and saw the Opera House. It was a beautiful, tall building with stone arches that beckoned patrons in to see the magnificent performances given by famous actors and singers.

Down the street, south of town, she saw a stately, white hospital with a porch shaded by a balcony that was covered with ivy and supported by white columns.

Her Carriage stopped, and her husband came to the door, and opened it. He was dressed in a silk suit with a handsome black hat. She had never seen him so handsome and happy. He took her hand and helped her out.

They walked into a glorious, white, two story, wood frame house. The front porch had a crystal chandelier hanging from the ten foot ceiling. He opened the front door for her, and the entry was almost as large as the entire house that they lived in now. There was a mirror hanging on the wall with two elegant, upholstered arm chairs on either side.

He extended his arm and invited her to sit in one of the chairs, and he sat in the other. Opposite the entry stood a regal staircase that spiraled boldly up to the second floor of the house. She watched as her children and Billy came down the stairs.

Katie was beautiful. Her hair was up, and her dress was store bought. It was full and hung so low that her shoes could barley be seen. A wide ribbon was wrapped around her waist and tied into a bow, dangling over a bustle. She wore a feathered hat that was particularly suitable for her age.

Matthew and Billy both looked so handsome and proper as they politely walked Katie down the staircase. They wore black silk suits with white linen shirts and black shoes. They were wearing white gloves.

She smiled as the children reached the bottom of the stair case.

She stood and looked at herself in the mirror. She was surprised when she saw herself. She was well groomed, and her hands were soft and supple. The skin on her face looked well rested and firmer and not reddened by the sun. Her clothes and her hat were exquisite. She looked down at her shoes. They were brand new and the most beautiful shoes that she had ever seen.

There was a knock at the door. It was not a knock made by knuckles. It had a ting to it. It was a knock made by a large brass knocker fastened on the door. Her husband took her arm, and they stood in the entry next to their children as a servant came to open the door. It was Mr. and Mrs. Sternwall. The servant bowed slightly and swung his arm wide as he opened the door inviting them into the house.

They entered, and the group walked into the parlor that was surrounded by bay windows covered in beautiful, heavy, velvet drapes. The floor was finished with polished wood, and the room was filled with expensive furnishings. They sat, and the servant poured cocktails from a crystal glass pitcher into pristine stemware.

Soon, the dinner bell rang, and everyone stood and walked, arm in arm, into a large dining room with a long, wooden table. The table was surrounded by eight chairs and a prodigious candle chandelier that hung over it. The table was set with white china on white linen. A large bouquet of fresh flowers spread over the center of the table, and a feast lay on a sideboard, waiting to be served.

After dinner, a glass of liquor was served in the parlor, and then the driver entered the room, "Your carriage awaits."

Mrs. Martin woke to her husband kissing her forehead. "Oh, I don't want to wake up, Mr. Martin. I had the most wonderful dream."

"Then don't, Mrs. Martin. I will fix our breakfast this morning," he said.

Mrs. Martin teased, "No, I will get up. No sense burning the house down too!"

XXXX

Katherine woke and stretched. "Poor Katie," she thought. She is so in love and unable to talk to her mother about it. Katherine knew how she felt. Not that she was ever in love, but that she had never been able to talk to her mother about things like that. She hoped that Katie was not in for a heart break.

She thought about her dream and how real it felt to her. She could feel the romance, smell the flowers and hear the rain and the terrible wind when it blew under the bridge.

Thoughts of Mrs. Martin's dream raced through her head. She wondered if they came true for her. She hoped so, but she knew that money would not substitute for Katie's love for Jack.

She got up and showered. After eating breakfast, she went out to Mr. Wrigley's to deliver the photos. "Thank you, Mr. Wrigley, it was very nice of you to trust me with them."

"Your welcome, Sweetie," he said. "It was my pleasure! I don't get many visitors. Certainly not any that are interested in the good old days. I just don't meet many young folks that are interested in the past. Please come see me again, alright? Those old pictures just sit up there getting dusty, and I enjoyed looking at them with you."

"I will, Mr. Wrigley. If I ever get back to Masontown, I sure will!" She kissed him on the cheek and left.

After driving out to the bridge, she stood under it. She sat and looked at the trees for evidence of the tornado that tore through them. There was none. It was astonishing how Mother Nature heals herself. Everything was beautiful and pristine. People are born and raised to live wonderful, rich lives and then they die. All is forgotten; pushed back into the pages of time.

She closed her eyes and remembered the steamy romance that took place under the bridge and smiled.

Chapter Eight
Bed Rolls and The Chariot

Katherine spent the rest of the afternoon writing in her room. She thought about returning home, but she could not leave yet. She needed to know what happened to Katie and her family. She knew that there was more than what she has found here in this town.

She wanted to know what happened with Jack and the romance that he and Katie shared. Katie was so in love, and so was Jack. She could feel the passion they shared. Passion like that only comes once in a lifetime.

Margaret's life was peppered with tragedy and hardship. Is this the reason that she sold her farm? Was the destruction of their crops, the straw that broke the camels back?

What was to happen to Billy? The Martins saved him, and his life would be changed forever. He had new direction and focus.

Would Sheriff Jenkins and Miss Roberts marry and raise the Johnson children? She wondered.

There was too much left unsolved, so Katherine could

not yet leave.

She unwrapped a sandwich that she had bought at the grocery deli and turned on the television in her room, falling asleep.

XXXX

The Martin family spent the entire day cleaning up the debris that was left by the tornado. They cut up trees that were knocked over and stacked the wood for next year's fire. They gathered the smaller limbs and burned them in a pile. Mr. Martin and the boys used some old, left over lumber to patch the hole in the barn roof that was peeled up by the wind. They repaired paddock fences and gates. Katie and her mother worked in the kitchen garden. There was little left intact after the tornado ripped through it. They were able to salvage some cabbage for supper. There were some potatoes left in the ground, but they were green and the plants were gone. They dug them up and left them on top of the ground, hoping they would ripen enough to eat them.

Mrs. Martin and Katie prepared dinner at dusk. They made a pot of beans, some biscuits and boiled some cabbage. The family sat around the table quietly eating. They were sad and hungry and exhausted. After dinner, they all helped to clean up and went to bed early.

Mr. Martin thought about the crops and wondered, "How am I going to salvage the growing season. I will have to work fast." He wondered what he could sell. He did not possess anything of real value. Everything that he owned was needed to operate the farm.

He looked at his wife and began to speak. He was going to ask her what she thought they should do, but she was sound asleep. Through all his anguish, he smiled. He still had his family that he loved so dearly. That is all he needed to give him hope and courage.

The next morning, Mrs. Martin watched as the children came down the loft ladder. She remembered the dream that she had two nights before and imagined them descending the spiral stair case in elegant clothing. She wondered, if she agreed to go west, would her dream come true? Would it put an end to the constant struggle that they endured on the farm? Would she be doing the best thing for her children? It would give them a chance to live a much better life than she did as a child. If she did not, would they struggle and toil their whole lives just as she has had to do? Would that be fair to them?

The children went outside to do their morning chores, and she started a fire in the cook stove. Mr. Martin was pulling his boots on, getting ready to go outside when he heard a knock on the door. He opened it, and it was Mr. and Mrs. Sternwall and Audrey. "Hello, come in!"

Mrs. Martin placed her hands on her cheeks. She thought to herself, "It is just like my dream. The children coming down the stairs. Mr. and Mrs. Sternwall knocking on the door. Is this a sign? Should I agree to go?"

The relief on Abby's face was unmistakable. Mr. Sternwall said, "We heard about the tornado and came as fast as we could. I am glad everyone is alright! My son, is he alright?"

"Yes, Mr. Sternwall, he is fine! Mr. Martin pulled out two chairs. Please sit down and have some coffee. I am sorry you had to come all this way. We had a little clean up to do yesterday, and we lost the crop, but we are all just fine."

Matthew went into the barn to feed the chickens when he overheard Katie talking to Maggie. He stood real still and quiet, and he heard her say, "Maggie, I sure will miss you when I marry Jack. He will be back soon, and we will be getting married."

"I am telling Momma!" Matthew shouted.

Katie stood and said, "No you won't, Matthew Martin, or I will never speak to you again! Do you hear me!"

Just then Billy came running in the barn. "Ma and Pa are here! Ma and Pa, they are here!"

Matthew and Billy ran into the house.

Billy hugged his mother. "Ma, Pa, what are you doing here?"

"We worried about you, son!" she said.

Mr. Sternwall looked at Mr. Martin, "I am real sorry to hear about your crops. Are you going to replant?"

Mr. Martin looked at his wife, "I don't know, Mr. Sternwall. I don't know what we'll do."

The words burst out of Mr. Sternwall's mouth as if he could not hold them inside any longer. "We are going west. We are here to fetch our son, and we are going west on the next wagon train. Why don't you join us?"

Mrs. Martin saw her husband glance at her, and she thought of her dream again. It was too much of a coincidence. She looked back at her husband, "We will, Mr. Sternwall! We will!"

Matthew and Billy hugged each other and jumped up and down. "Really? Really? Are we really going?"

"Yes, boys," Mrs. Martin said. "We are really going."

Mr. Martin hugged her, lifting her up off the ground and twirling her in a circle. He was elated. He could not believe that she would allow it. He put her down and, moving the hair from her forehead, he looked into her eyes. "Are you sure, Mrs. Martin? Are you sure you are not going to change your mind?" He searched her face for reassurance. His eyes filled with excitement and hope.

"I am sure, Mr. Martin," she laughed knowing his happiness.

When Katie opened the door and came in with the bucket in her hand, her family and the Sternwall's gathered around the table. She froze with fear when she walked in the door and wondered why they were all there. Did Matthew tell them about Jack? The looks on their faces sent chills of fear through her body.

Her father motioned her to join them. "Sit down, Kit. We have exciting news for you!"

She looked at Matthew, and the excitement in his eyes told her that the meeting was not about what she had done. He squirmed in his chair, hardly able to sit quietly.

She took her place at the table in a tall-backed, wooden chair and glanced from person to person wondering what was going on.

Her father must have seen the concern in her eyes. "Don't worry, Kit. I assure you that I bare good news."

There was a long pause as Katie's father glanced at his wife, waiting for her to take charge like she always did. But this time, it seemed, she was giving him full control of the situation.

Finally, as tears were about to fall from Katie's eyes, Matthew exploded. "We're goin' west on the wagon train!" He started jumping up and down with excitement. "We're gonna be rich! We're gonna be rich!"

Katie's mouth fell open. She could not speak and could hardly breathe. She stuttered, trying to relay her unwillingness to go. "But, Pa, we can't!"

Her father put his hands on her cheeks and looked at her with those loving eyes. "There is no reason to worry. The cavalry has the bandits and Indians at bay."

She still could not speak. She could not tell them what she had just done.

The move excited him. "I have wanted to go for some time now. The Sternwall's are joining us. I can finally offer this family more than the living we have squeezed out of this farm while it squeezes the life out of your mother and me. We barely make enough money to keep it. The only reason we have not gone before was because of the danger. Now that the cavalry is involved and protecting the trail west, your mother has finally given in to my persistence and is allowing us to go!"

"When, Pa?" Katie asked.

"We don't have to wait long! The train leaves in five days! Isn't this exciting?" he said.

Katie's eyes were filled with tears as she looked at her mother. "We couldn't possibly go, Momma!." She could not tell them why. She began to cry and climbed up the ladder to the loft and fell on her bed sobbing.

Mr. Martin looked at his wife. His face was filled with confusion. "I thought she would love the idea of traveling west." Saddened by her reaction he asked, "What can I do?

"She is sixteen, and her life has always been here," Mrs. Martin said. "She has life-long friends here. I don't think she has ever thought about going far. She was planning on taking a teaching job close to home. She thought that she would marry and raise her own children here some day."

He shrugged his shoulders and shook his head back and forth. "She has always liked adventure."

Mrs. Martin poured some more coffee into her and Abby's cups. "She will be fine once we get started."

Abby looked at Mrs. Martin, "You have done so much for me. Is there anything I can do to help?"

Mrs. Martin looked up at the loft with confusion. "She is getting to that awkward age. I will talk to her tomorrow."

Matthew looked at Billy. "Lets go pack our things!"

Mrs. Martin scolded Matthew. "Oh, no you don't. I will be supervising the packing! We will have to be particular about what we take because we won't have very much room!"

With disappointment, Matthew conceded. "Yes, Ma'am."

Maggie stood perfectly still for Katie that evening as she cried and asked, "What will I do? My love is here, and I can't go. I just can't. The wagon train is leaving in five days, and Jack won't return with another herd of horses for thirteen days. How will I let him know where I have gone? Oh, Maggie, will I ever see him again?"

Katie looked at Maggie and dried her tears. She gathered her wits and made a pact with herself. "I will see him again, no matter what. I will figure out a way. We have made plans to marry and be together forever." She dried her tears and, with her mother's determination, she held her head high and went to the house with her eggs and her bucket of milk.

Mrs. Martin was sitting in her chair by the fireplace knitting a scarf. She called Katie and motioned her to sit in Mr. Martin's chair. "I know this is going to be quite a change for you, Katie, but you will like it out west." She reached over and touched her. "You will see. There are plenty of settlements where you can teach, and plenty of promising men with fortunes to provide a bright future for you. It is the best thing for you."

"But, Momma"...Katie paused. She could not tell her mother about Jack. She knew that she would not approve of her settling down at such a young age.

Her mother gave her the raised eyebrow, and Katie said, "Yes, Ma'am."

Every moment during the next five days was filled with tasks. The Martins had to decide what to keep and what to sell and pack all their belongings into the small wagon. There was a lot to do in such a short amount of time.

It was agonizing for Katie. All that she could think of was Jack and their short time together. She told Maggie, "I know he loves me as much as I love him. It is the way he touches me and kisses me. I can't bare the thought of leaving him behind. He will find out where I went, and he will follow me. I will see him again!" She nodded her head and said, "I know he will."

"Oh listen to me, Maggie," she sighed. "Here I am rambling on..." She thought about poor Mary. She was going to lose her foal. Mr. Martin had found a buyer and the gentleman was going to pick him up the day before their departure. Katie did not have the heart to tell her.

First thing the next morning, after breakfast, Mr. and Mrs. Martin went to the Land Office to sell the farm. Mr. Williams worked there and bought everything that he could acquire at a discounted price. Mr. Martin told his wife, "Mr. Williams is going to try to steal the farm if he knows that we are anxious to sell it."

"Let me handle it, Mr. Martin," she said.

They entered the door, and Mr. Williams greeted them. "What can I do for you today, folks?"

Mrs. Martin said, "What would I pay for sixty acres if I wanted to buy, Mr. Williams?"

"Well let me see, Mrs. Martin, where do you want it?"

"Somewhere close to our place," she replied.

"Well I have 80 acres out by your place, and I am askin' $5.00 an acre."

"Does it have a house or a barn on it, Mr. Williams?"

"No, Ma'am, just the land." he said. "Are you looking to buy some more land?"

She looked him in the eye. "Is it cleared or wooded?

Did it get hit by the tornado?"

"It is wooded, and yes, it has a trail in it as wide as a tug boat!' he said.

"That seems awful expensive for a wooded piece of land with a big mess on it, Mr. Williams."

Mr. Martin looked at his wife. She was brilliant, and he was amazed.

Mr. William's eyes got bold, and he moved closer to her. "Well, that's what wooded land is goin' for right now!

She asked, "How much is cleared land going for then?"

"I got some over there for $7.00 an acre," he said.

"Alright then, you will give us $7.00 an acre for ours?" she replied.

"Now, Mrs Martin, you know I am not in business to lose money," he said. "I gotta make a profit!"

"Yes, Mr. Williams, but there is a house and a barn. The crops are gone, but the tornado repairs are made."

Mr. Williams got out a slate and a piece of chalk. He went to his desk back behind the counter and scribbled. He spit on the slate and wiped it with his sleeve, and he scribbled some more. Finally, he spoke, "Alright, Mrs. Martin, $7.00 an acre, but you are robbing me!"

Mrs Martin said, "Fine then, the deal is done!"

"You'll have to follow me to the bank, folks." He got his sweater off the hook and opened the door, extending his arm, "After you."

That night, when Mr. Martin tucked his wife into bed, he told her, "I was so proud of you at the Land Office today. You sure know how to handle people, Margaret!"

"It was nothin', Mr. Martin," she said smiling. She turned to him and kissed him on the cheek.

The next day, the Sternwall's helped the Martin family pack their furniture into the buckboard and haul it to

Sweeney's General Store. Mr. Sweeney bought a building in town that he used as a used furniture store. There were so many people moving in and out of town with the wagon trains that he was beginning to acquire quite an inventory.

Mrs. Martin decided what to keep and what had to go. She directed the men and the boys telling them what to load in the wagon. Room by room, they emptied the house, leaving only bedrolls and cooking supplies.

As Mr. Martin and Mr. Sternwall drove down the lane with all of the old furniture loaded to the brim in the buckboard, Mrs. Martin thought about her dream and all of the elegant new furniture that was in her new, two story, white house. She smiled and wiped the sweat from her brow. She told Abby and Katie, "Come on, lets sit down on the step and have a cup of water and rest.

Soon the men returned and loaded the things from the barn.

When night finally fell, everyone had laid out their bedrolls on the floor in the empty house. Mrs. Martin did not care that she did not have her feather mattress. She slept like a baby.

Only three days left, and the train would be leaving. There was still a lot to do. Mr. Martin and Mr. Sternwall ate their breakfast early and hitched the team. They were taking the buckboard to Uniontown to trade it for a covered wagon. It would take them all day and into the night to get there and back.

"Can we go, Pa? Please!" Matthew pleaded.

Mr. Martin looked at Mrs. Martin and shrugged his shoulders.

"I suppose it will be alright," she said. "You stick close to your Pa and don't get lost."

Mr. Sternwall put his hand on Billy's back, "Come on, boys, load up!" They jumped up on the back of the buckboard and the men climbed up in front. Mrs. Martin handed her husband a basket with some hardtack and biscuits for the trip. "Hup," they headed down the lane.

It was still early, and the women and Katie ate their breakfast. Katie was still quiet, and Mrs. Martin was too busy to spend much time trying to console her. The women cleared the dishes from the table, and Katie went out to milk Maggie.

Abby washed while Mrs. Martin dried the dishes. "I hope she gets over her disappointment about this move," Abby said.

"It will take time, but when she gets to Virginia City and gets settled in, she will like it. I know she will." Mrs. Martin dried the last dish and put it in the wooden chest that will go in the wagon. "What will we do with ourselves all day, Abby?

"I don't know," she said.

Katie was quiet as she milked Maggie today. Her life was turning upside down. Maggie seemed to understand. She stood quietly and ate her corn.

It was a lazy day for the women. They worked in the kitchen garden for a while and picked up some potatoes to have with supper. They sat on the step and watched the chickens peck the ground. Then, since they knew the men would not return until late, they went to bed early.

The next morning the boys slept late. They had gotten home terribly late, but there were not many chores to do. Mrs. Martin and Abby got up and fixed breakfast while Katie milked and fed Maggie. Mr. Martin and Mr. Sternwall fed the rest of the animals and drank coffee while the women prepared their breakfast. They loaded the wagon and prepared a list of supplies they would need to purchase at Sweeney's the morning after next. Tomorrow, Mr. Wilcox was coming to purchase the foal, the pigs and the chickens.

It was the big day, and Mr. Martin whispered to his wife waking her up, "Your chariot awaits!" Mrs. Martin smiled and opened her eyes. Perhaps her dream is coming true! They woke the children and packed their bedrolls into the covered wagon. Mrs. Martin cried as they drove down the lane. She would never see the farm again.

It was day break five days from when Katie learned the terrible news and all the wagons gathered in town. There were twenty-eight in all, the biggest train yet.

There were not any children Katie's age. There were two boys Matthew's age including Billy. The boys were in the street playing cowboys and Indians.

The Martins had packed their wagon with just enough supplies to last until they arrived at the nearest settlement. They tied the Jersey cow and Mr. Martin's riding horse behind the wagon.

"At least I still have you, Maggie." She said patting her on the shoulder.

Mary and Moe pulled the wagon filled with supplies. It would take months to cross if there were no problems along the way. The train would stay together, no matter what, and everyone in it would help the others along.

The excitement was intense among all who were traveling, and Katie could see the sadness in the eyes of the people left behind. She looked at the crowd.

She saw the sheriff with Miss Roberts on his arm and Tom and Jenny by their sides. It made her feel happy to know that their lives would be turned around. It must be so different for them now that they have a normal life with people that care about them.

She saw her friend June. She thought out loud, "That's it!" She waved her arms and shouted, "June! June!" She darted through the crowd. People were stopping her and hugging her.

112

The Pastor stopped her, "We will miss you, Miss Martin."

"Thank you, Sir," she said. "I will miss you too."

Mr. Sweeney said, "It has been a pleasure to know you, Katie. You be careful now, you hear?"

"Yes, Sir," she said, pushing through and dodging in and out and finally reaching June. She had been Katie's best friend, and even though she was a bit silly, Katie knew that she could count on her.

June screamed loudly over the crowd, "Katie, I wish you weren't going! I am going to miss you so much!" Tears were forming in her eyes.

"I need you to do me a favor, June! Listen to me carefully! You can't tell anyone! Do you promise?" Katie held her by her arms and looked her in the eye.

"I promise, Katie. What is it? She put her hands on Katie's elbows. I will do what ever you ask!"

"Remember the young man in church" She looked around and whispered in June's ear. "The new family in town?"

June shouted over the crowd, "Yes, the handsome one. I remember!"

"Shhhh. His name is Jack. He is away gathering horses for the cavalry. He will be returning next Saturday," Katie said.

June pulled Katie closer. "How do you know, Katie?"

"I just do." She moved closer to June's ear. "You have to promise me that you will go to the old Smith place on Saturday and tell him where I have gone. Do you promise?"

June looked as if she felt deceived. "You didn't tell me that you liked him, Katie!"

"Come on, Katie! It's time to go!" Mrs. Martin was standing on the wagon and waving for her to come.

"Just promise me, June!" Katie became irritated.

"Alright! Alright, Katie, I promise! June hugged her.

"I will miss you, June!" Katie ran back to the wagon.

"I will miss you too, Katie!" June shouted.

Katie knew all the people that were traveling among the train, but there was no one to whom she felt particularly close. There was nobody that could comfort her. There was no one that could make her want to go. Jack was the only one that could do that. She would gladly go if Jack were going. He would be going west with the cavalry, and she hoped that he would find her and marry her. She would just have to be patient and keep her secret to herself just a little longer.

The train left town at seven that morning, and if luck permitted, they could average twenty miles a day.

Chapter Nine
The Pinkerton and The Slave Boys

Katherine woke filled with excitement. She just knew that the Martins must have gone west with the gold rush.

She booted up her laptop and studied the trail west. She plotted out the route closest to the way that they would have gone. She wanted to go during the daylight, so that she could see the land and what it would have been like as they traveled.

She packed her bag, except for what she would need tonight and in the morning, and then went down for breakfast. While she was eating, Katherine got a call on her cell phone. "Hello."

"Is this Katherine Hampton?"

"This is she," she said. "Can I help you?"

"This is Dr. Gates. I am the Human Resource Director at the Mayo Clinic in Los Angeles, California. I have a copy of your transcripts, and I must say, I am very impressed."

Katherine's heart pounded in her chest. This was a tremendous opportunity for anyone. "Thank you, Sir."

"Would you be able to come to Los Angeles for an interview? Say, in a week or two?" he asked.

Katherine paused. She thought about how unorganized she was. She had not thought about her career in some time now.

"Miss Hampton, are you there?"

"Yes, Sir, please forgive me, my mother just passed away." She did not want to pass up the interview. "Yes, Sir, I would love to interview."

"I am sorry about your loss." He did not want to lose the opportunity to hire her. "Take as much time as you would like."

"Two weeks will be fine, Dr. Gates," she said. "What day would you like me to come?"

Dr. Gates set an appointment with her and hung up the phone.

Because Katherine was following the path of her dreams, she had become distracted from her career. If she followed the Martins west, she might already be in California in two weeks. If not, she would stop her journey and go to the interview. She hoped that if she stopped, the dreams would not.

XXXX

It had been two weeks, and other than some reports of bandits dressed as Indians, the trip had been safe and calm.

Katie rode with Mr. and Mrs. Martin in the wagon, and Mr. and Mrs. Sternwall and Audrey were in the wagon behind them. Abby was still extremely timid and shy to everyone except for Mrs. Martin. To everyone else, she was quiet most of the time and relied on her husband, Dirk Sternwall, to give her direction.

Mr. Sternwall had a serious nature and, being a man of

few words, he kept to himself. Katie thought that he probably had a temper and seemed to have a dark side that she did not understand.

Katie walked most of the time. This kept her in shape and gave her time alone to think about Jack and daydream of what their life together might be like. He should have returned and learned of her absence by now. She spent all of her time thinking about him and still believed, with all her heart, that he would come to get her as soon as he could catch up to them.

Matthew and Billy absorbed every second of the trip, making it an adventure of a lifetime. Katie laughed as the boys ran, explored and played as if they were indispensable scouts for the train. Sometimes, Matthew was such a boy, and others he seemed terribly grown up. Once in a while, their parents allowed Matthew and Billy to use the riding horses to venture up and down the train. They visited and checked with all the travelers to relay messages. It was times like these that Katie could see the man blossoming from her baby brother. He looked so grown up riding the horse with the wind blowing in his sandy, blonde hair. He had gotten so tall, and his shoulders were broadening. Even though he was a nettlesome boy, he had such a caring and loving side to his soul. He had always been highly emotional for a boy, and his feelings were easily hurt. He was a faithful and loyal friend to the other boys and also to Katie. She imagined the day that he would be all grown up and independent. She wondered what he would do with his life. If he would be a soldier or a politician. Maybe, he would be a doctor or a lawyer.

The wagons came to a stop, and Matthew and Billy rode up to see what was going on. Katie reached up and took Audrey from Mrs. Sternwall, so she could play for a while. Audrey was adorable with brown coils of hair falling down to the bottom of her back. Since recovering from her illness, she seemed so happy and playful.

They all took advantage of the break and filled their canteens, ate some biscuits left from the night before and checked the horse's hoofs for any rocks that may have gotten lodged.

The wagon master rode up with a tall man dressed in a black suit and hat with an extra horse tethered to his saddle.

Katie thought to herself, "Could it be Jack?" Her heart was pounding in her chest. As he rode closer, she realized it was not. This man was older, but he was clean cut and wore an unusually thick, long mustache. His hat brim was flat and pulled down, so his eyes could hardly be seen.

Billy and Matthew were riding behind them, and as the men passed, the boys stopped next to Mr. Martin. Billy said, "He is a bounty hunter. A Pinkerton man."

Mr. Martin asked, "What does he want?"

They watched as the two men stopped at the wagon behind them. It was the Sternwall's wagon.

The Pinkerton man called out, "Mr. Sternwall?"

Mr. Sternwall replied, "Yes." He had a nervous look on his face and was studying the area as if he were looking for an escape.

The Pinkerton man drew his six gun. "I wouldn't do that if I were you. Step down from the wagon." Being careful to keep his eyes and his gun on Mr. Sternwall, he stepped off his horse.

Mr. Sternwall took a deep breath and gave the reins to Abby.

"Slowly, Mr. Sternwall." The Pinkerton man cocked his gun.

Dirk Sternwall stood and slowly crawled down from the wagon.

Everyone stood silently in disbelief as the Pinkerton man tied Mr. Sternwall's hands and helped him up onto the spare horse. The Pinkerton man mounted his own horse and clucked at it, touching it with his spurs.

Billy broke the silence and screamed, "Wait!" He ran to his father's side and grabbed his boot. "What's happening, Pa? What'd ya do?"

"Listen to me, boy. I will be alright. You take care of your mother and your sister. You are going to be the man of the family now. You work hard to make me proud. Ya hear me, boy?"

The wagon master turned and rode back toward the head of the train, and everybody watched in silence as the bounty hunter rode off with Mr. Sternwall behind him.

An unstoppable river of tears flowed down Abby's face. Billy tied his fathers horse to their wagon and climbed up with his mother. He put his arms around her as she cried.

The wagon train started to move and Mrs. Martin climbed down from her wagon and up onto Abby's, taking the reins from her hand. Mr. Martin helped Katie and Audrey up into his wagon. "Hup."

When the sun began to set, the wagon master gave the order to circle the wagons for the evening. As usual, the children gathered wood, while the women prepared supper, and the men repaired wagons. Abby and Mrs. Martin worked silently as they prepared the meal. Mrs. Martin knew that Abby needed some time to get over the shock that she had just endured.

At supper, Katie and the boys ate on a blanket by the fire with Audrey. Katie and Matthew sat in silence until Billy finally spoke, "Momma said that Pa took some money from the man he was working for. I am really worried about Momma. I don't know what's fixin' to happen to us without Pa. We don't have enough money to move on. I've done

119

learned my lesson. It's not worth the trouble, breakin' the law."

Katie worried about Billy because, although he was exceedingly outgoing, determined and self-reliant, he was like his father and frequently his judgment was not the best. Hopefully, he had truly learned his lesson.

Mr. and Mrs. Martin sat alone with Abby when she finally spoke. "I suspected my husband of steelin' from that farmer. I knew he couldn't have made enough money to go out west, but I was hopin', somehow, that I was wrong. I wanted to ask, but you don't just go stickin' your nose into Mr. Sternwall's business." She started to sob, "I don't know what we're gonna do."

At bedtime, Mrs. Martin climbed into bed with her husband. "I tried to console her, but she is in a terrible fix. She has Billy and Audrey to take care of. She has just a small amount of money. Not enough to finish the trip."

Mr. Martin suggested, "Maybe she could stay on at Independence, Missouri. It is our next stop, and the train will be staying over a couple of nights. It is a very busy place, and we can help her find work and a place to stay."

Abby was in her wagon, and Katie could hear her sobbing as she fell asleep that night.

Two days later, Abby had calmed down and gathered her composure a bit as the wagon train circled outside Independence, Missouri. Independence was a bustling town. It was the beginning of the Oregon Trail, and people came from all directions to join the train. Mr. and Mrs. Martin promised Abby that they would accompany her into town. They knew how shy and timid that she was, and they knew that she had no idea how to approach a potential employer. They took her to the Independence Hotel where they inquired about possible employment. It was an exceptionally large, stately establishment.

The man at the hotel desk looked interested. "We have been looking for help. Let me fetch Mrs. Brown."

Mrs. Brown came, hurrying around the corner. Grabbing Abby's arm, she swooped her up. "Thank you, Lord! I prayed someone would come to help us out!" She was a loud and boisterous woman, and she was in a rush. She pulled Abby along as she gave her orders. "I'll give you room, board and pay in exchange for housekeeping and laundry services. Let me show you where you will be stayin'." Mrs. Brown was dragging Abby along. She could not get a word in edgewise as she looked behind her at Mr. and Mrs. Martin who were lagging behind. "We have been very busy and have been waiting for someone, just like you, to fill the position." Mrs. Brown took Abby and Billy to a room downstairs. It was small but nice and comfortable. "I trust that this will do."

"Yes, Ma'am," Abby replied looking at the room furnished with a wood stove, two beds and table.

"There is a bath house down the hall," Mrs. Brown said. "Now let me show you to your duties." She was a pushy woman but seemed to make Abby feel at ease with her instantly. Abby preferred to be told what to do.

Mr. Martin and the boys took Abby's wagon and team to the stockyard to sell them for her. When they arrived, they weaved through the crowd and watched as the auctioneer was selling slaves. Slavery was not legal in Pennsylvania, and Matthew and Billy had never even seen black people before. Matthew looked up at his father, "What are they doing to 'em, Pa?"

"They're sellin' 'em, son. It's a darn shame what they do, treaten' folks like animals." Mr. Martin did not believe in slavery. He placed his hands on each one of the boys and turned them around. "Come on."

"Can't we stop 'em, Pa?" Matthew asked.

"No, son, there ain't nothin' we can do about it. It's legal in Missouri." He found the horse sale and was able to get a fair price for Abby's horses and wagon. They kept Mr. Sternwall's riding horse for Billy.

Mrs. Martin could see the relief on Abby's face as she thanked them. "How can I ever thank you for helping me the way you have? You are truly Christian people."

The wagon train camped outside town for two days. This gave the Martins time to stock their supplies and rest their horses.

The sheriff came out the night before they left and went from wagon to wagon, asking if anyone had seen some "blacks". He said that two young men had escaped in the night. Nobody had seen any, and almost everyone there probably would not have told if they did. Most of the people on the train were from the north, and they did not take kindly to slavery.

After a sorrowful farewell, Abby, Audrey and Billy walked back into town, and the train headed west.

That evening after the wagons had circled, Mr. Martin was helping to repair a wagon directly in front of theirs. The wagon belonged to a young couple, Jake and Katherine Jones. Mrs. Jones introduced herself to Mrs. Martin. Her skin was pale, and she was dainty and small. She was plain but pretty and was in her mid twenties. Her hair was sandy blonde, and she had freckles on her face. She was very polite.

Mrs. Martin liked her instantly. "Would you and your husband like to join us for supper, Mrs. Jones?"

"We would be thrilled," she said. "What can I do to help you?"

"There are some dishes in that box," she said, pointing to the side of the wagon. "You could take those out if you would like. There will be six of us."

"Alright." She took the dishes out and stacked them on the blanket that Katie had laid out on the ground. "Where are you from, Mrs. Martin?"

"We are from a small settlement in southern Pennsylvania called Masontown." Mrs. Martin was stirring the beans that she was warming over the fire. "Have you ever heard of it?"

"No, Ma'am, we are from northern Ohio," she said. "It is far colder there than here. I am glad to be out of it. My husband and I are newlyweds, and going west has always been both our dreams."

"You don't have any children yet?" Mrs Martin asked.

"No, Ma'am, not yet, but we will. We want a bunch of them!" They prepared supper together and visited.

Mr. Jones crawled under his wagon and was surprised by a young, black boy who had lodged himself in the rigging. The boy fell to the ground unconscious. He was thin and bloody and looked as though he had been badly beaten. Mr. Martin and Mr. Jones pulled him out from under the wagon and called for the women.

Mr. Martin wadded up his shirt and put it under the boys head. "Mrs. Martin, could you get the boy some water, please?" Could you get some wet cloths to dress these wounds, too, please?"

"Of coarse, Mr. Martin." Mrs. Martin and Mrs. Jones hurried back with some food, water, some wet cloths and a medicine box that Mrs. Martin had packed for the journey.

A crowd was gathering around the boy.

Mr. Martin rolled the boy over on his side. His back had been badly whipped and had blood and puss dripping from it. He wet the cloth and dabbed it on his back. Appling some ointment to his clean wounds, he tore strips from the linen that was in the box. He propped him up and wrapped the linen around his entire torso and leaned him up against the wagon. After lifting his head and blotting his forehead with a wet cloth, the boy began to wake. He moaned with pain. Mr. Jones pulled a flask of whiskey from his wagon and put it up to the boy's mouth. The boy took a small drink and choked and coughed.

The wagon master approached and asked, "What is going on here?"

"It seems as though we have a stow away," Mr. Martin said, looking up at him.

Mr. Martin stood and went to his wagon, pulling out a bedroll. He rolled it out by the fire that Mrs. Martin had started. Asking Mr. Jones to help him, they carried the boy to the bedroll and laid him on his side.

The men stood and looked at the boy. Mr. Jones said, "How could they beat a young man almost to his death just because his skin is black?"

"God forgive them," the wagon master said. "He doesn't look but fourteen!"

He is surely not old enough to be away from his parents, but it doesn't look like he had much of a choice," one of the other men said.

The boy opened his eyes and said, "Charlie? Where is Charlie?"

The wagon master walked over to him and knelt, "Who is Charlie, boy?"

"Ye'sir, Charlie's my brother. He's under the wagon behind me."

The men looked at each other and then at Mr. Martin's wagon. They walked over to it, and Mr. Martin laid down on the ground and looked under it. There was a small boy. He was possibly ten years old. Being frightened, his eyes were wide, "Please don't beat me, sir!"

Mr. Martin's heart sank. He felt awful for the boy. "Please come down. We won't hurt you, son."

He moved slowly, crawling down, inch by inch.

Mr. Martin extended his hand to the boy, and Charlie flinched. "It is alright, boy. I promise, I won't hurt you. I will crawl out of here, and you can come on out and take care of your brother. You are not in trouble here."

The boy crawled out from under the wagon and ran to his brother. He took his hand and held it tightly. His eyes darted from person to person as he feared for his life.

Mr. Martin told the older boy, "I don't want to scare your brother. Will you ask him if he is alright? Does he have any wounds that need to be dressed?"

"Ye'sir. Don't worry, Charlie. We's gonna be alright. You alright? "

"I'm alright, Jep. I'm hungry," he said.

Mrs. Martin jumped up, "I'll get him some food and water." The women tended to the boys and Katie and Matthew stood and watched with curiosity.

The men gathered around the fire. The wagon master said, "What are we gonna do with 'em?"

A vulgar man, with a strong southern accent, picked up a stick from the ground. "I say, one of us ride back and get the sheriff and let them deal with 'em."

Mr. Martin said, "They are just children. We can't turn them over to those heathens to be beaten and tortured."

"Slavery is the work of the devil," Mr. Jones shouted.

"Yeah! Yeah!" The crowd shouted, raising their fists. Everyone started to speak at once, and nobody could be heard.

"Bang! The wagon master shot his six gun up in the air. "I am the law on this train, and I say the boys stay."

The man with a strong southern accent shouted, "Well, I don't like it one bit!"

"Me neither! We don't need no damn niggers on this train," said another.

"How many opposed?" the wagon master said. "Well, put up your hands and let's see ya!"

All the men looked around. The two men put their hands in the air. There was a long pause of silence while they all looked around at the crowd.

"Is that all? Anyone else?" the wagon master shouted. "Looks like you two are out voted. You can pull your wagons to the rear!"

The man from the south threw the stick down on the ground and walked to his wagon, and the other one followed.

"Now, who's gonna take care of these youngin's?" the wagon master asked.

Mr. Martin and Mr. Jones raised their hands. They looked at each other and smiled. "We'll watch over 'em!" Mr. Jones shouted.

Mr. Martin and Mr. Jones returned to their wagons and joined their wives and children.

"Looks like we have guests!" Mr. Martin put his arm around his wife and the other around Katie. "Is that alright with both of you?"

"I am proud of you, Mr. Martin," Mrs. Martin said as she kissed him on the cheek.

Katie looked at her father. "How could those men be so cruel, Pa? They are just young boys. They are scared to death! Has the devil got them ruined?"

"I don't know how, Katie." He kissed her forehead. "It seems we live in two different worlds, the north and the south."

Mr. Jones knelt down next to the boys and took their hands. He said, "You won't have to worry anymore. We're gonna take care of you. From this day forward, you are free. Nobody's gonna beat you anymore."

The older boy looked up at his younger brother, "Ya

hear that, Charlie. We free!"

Charlie hugged his brother. "I wish Mammy and Pappy were here, Jep!"

Mr. Martin cleared his throat and wiped a tear from his eye. He looked at his wife and shook his head. "It's a darn shame, Mrs. Martin."

She put her arm around his waist. "At least they are safe now, Mr. Martin."

Mrs. Jones brought another bedroll from their wagon and laid it out next to Jep. "Here you are, Charlie. You can sleep here next to your brother."

Mrs. Martin helped her children with their bedrolls.

"We'll be sleepin' here, next to y'all," Matthew said to Charlie. "If'in ya'll need anything, ya just ask, that's all."

Mrs. Martin smiled at her son, and they all went to bed.

Early the next morning Mr. Jones woke Jep early. He dressed his wounds with fresh linen and helped him into a bed that he made for him in the back of his wagon. Charlie rode with Jep that day, sitting at the back of the wagon and looked out with curiosity. He watched everything from the back of that wagon, and by that evening, Jep was sitting up and looking out too.

Matthew rode Mr. Martin's riding horse and stayed right by the boys. Every once in a while, he would ask, "Y'all alright? Ya need anything?"

They just nodded and smiled.

When the wagons circled that night, the two boys climbed down out of the wagon and stood, waiting for instruction. Mr. Jones said, "If you're up to it, you can help Matthew gather some buffalo chips for the fire." By this time, the train was crossing prairie land and wood was scarce. The children circled wide to find enough buffalo chips for the fire.

The man from the south approached them on horseback. He had an evil look in his eye when he said, "You boys better watch yourselves. I'll put a rope around your necks and drag ya across this prairie."

Matthew was scared and looked over at the wagons. His father was watching. Seeing Matthew look, the man looked over and saw Mr. Martin and he turned and rode off.

The boys gathered their buffalo chips and ran back to the wagon. Matthew told his father and Mr. Jones what the man had said.

Glaring over at the man on his horse, Mr. Martin said. "You boys stay close to these wagons and don't stray off. Ya hear me?"

"Ye'Sir," the boys said in unison. They felt safe with Mr. Jones and the Martins and gladly agreed.

That night, after everyone was tucked into bed, Jeb told Matthew about his parents and how they were captured in Africa. He told them about what his life was like as a slave on a Virginia plantation, and how he and his brother were sold to slave traders.

Matthew felt sorry for the boys, and they sealed a brotherly bond that night.

Chapter Ten
The Buffalo and The Feast

The sun was just peaking into the window when Katherine woke. She had not set an alarm because she did not want to take a chance that it might wake her from her dream.

She took pride in the fact that her distant relatives had strong moral standards and did not approve of slavery. She wished that she could have known them personally. She thought about it for a while and in a way she did.

After getting out of bed, she typed in the journal that she had saved as "dream.wps". She was careful to included every detail because she did not want to forget any of it. She showered and dressed and then packed her bag.

Katherine checked out of the Bed and Breakfast and thanked them for their hospitality.

Breakfast, across the street in the cafe, was especially good this morning, and she thanked the waitress for her help. Filling her thermos with coffee, she started for Independence.

She stopped many times along the road and looked at

the land. She knew Katie and the Martins had seen the same trees and the same hills. She closed her eyes and smelled the wildflowers and the breeze that blew gently on her face.

When she reached Independence, Missouri, she stopped. She had crossed four states, and it was late, but she had a lovely day. She checked into a hotel and ran a bath in the jetted tub in her room. She opened the bottle of white wine that she picked up after filling her gas tank. Unwrapping the plastic cup from the tray on the counter, she poured some wine into it. She slid down into the jetting water, resting her head on the back of the tub and sipped her wine. As the steam rose off the tub, she thought about the extended family that she had been dreaming about and was fascinated that it was happening to her. Wondering why it was happening to her, she pondered, has she always had the power to dream of the past? What triggered it to happen now? Did she open a deeply seeded ability when she started to research her heritage? What ever it was, it was a gift, and she felt blessed to have it. After finishing her bath, she put her night gown on and climbed into the huge bed. The remote was next to it, and she turned on the television. Trying to stay awake long enough to watch a movie, she could not. She slipped into a deep sleep.

XXXX

It was mid-morning, and the wagon train crossed a vast prairie. The land was flat, and Katie watched the horizon curve, leaving nothing but the sky in every direction. There were no hills or trees to block the view. The prairie was full of grass and wildflowers. The ground was dry and dusty, but the breeze carried an aroma that made her take full, deep breaths. It gently blew against her face and cooled the heat of the sun as she walked beside Maggie behind the wagon.

It was a beautiful morning, and Katie was full of hope that this would be the day that Jack would finally catch up to her. She thought about the day his arms would hold her again, and she smiled. The memory of his face and body were etched deep in her mind. She could almost feel the muscles on his neck and shoulders and the way his body felt against hers. She thought about his masculine chest and the way his waist became narrow. Remembering how it made her feel when she moved her hands down his waist, and when he pressed himself against her, she could feel the passion that they shared and it made her tremble.

The sound of barking dogs interrupted the wonderful daydream in which she was immersed. She passed behind Maggie and could see a settlement of Indians that were camped along the trail. She ran up to the front of the wagon and reached for her mother's hand. Mrs. Martin pulled her up. "Indians, Pa! Indians!"

"Yes, Katie, don't worry. Just stay calm," he explained. "They are friendly Indians."

Indian women and children were standing at the edge of the camp and watched, motionlessly, as the train rode by. More women and children were running to catch a glimpse. A few old Indian men slowly stood and watched from within their camp. There were ten or fifteen teepees and several small fires. The smell of meat cooking on the fires tempted Katie's taste buds. It had been a long time since she had eaten meat and it smelled so delicious. Hides were stretched out and staked down to the ground. Six or seven dogs were standing on the edge of the camp barking as the train slowly went by.

Matthew was riding his fathers horse and trotted up next to the wagon, "I think they are as curious as we are, Pa!"

"I believe so, Matthew," Mr. Martin said. "Looks like a hunting camp. The young men must be out hunting. It looks like they have been killing buffalo!"

"It smells like it too, Pa. What I wouldn't do for some!" Matthew said.

Katie scooted close to her father on the bench of the wagon, "They scare me, Pa."

Mr. Martin smiled. "That's just because you've never seen them before. There is nothing to be afraid of Kit. They are friendly Indians. They won't bother us if we don't bother them."

"Just the same, can I ride up here with you and Momma for a while?" Katie asked.

"I reckon that'll be just fine, Kit," He giggled.

They watched as the Indian camp faded into the horizon behind them and two towering rock formations started to take shape in front of them. Mr. Martin told them, "That is Courthouse Rock, and just past it will be another one called Jailhouse Rock."

Matthew was curious. "Why do they call it that, Pa?"

"When we get closer, you will see that it looks like a courthouse with a jailhouse next to it," he said.

The entire wagon train marveled at them.

"It will take two days to reach the base of them," he explained. "Then it will take two days 'til you can't see them anymore."

Katie said, "How do you know so much, Pa?"

"The rocks are important landmarks," he said. "People remember things like this and tell others, so they know they are going the right way."

"Your father was born smart," Mrs. Martin teased.

Mr. Martin laughed and added, "If the settlers don't reach them by June, they wouldn't pass the Rocky Mountains before the winter snow makes it impassable."

Two days later, the train took their noon break in front of them and some of the men, including Mr. Martin, Matthew and Mr. Jones, rode up to the base. Even on horseback, it took a frightfully long time to reached the base. The men carved their names in the rock along side some others that had been carved there.

The women watched as the men mounted their horses to ride back. Mrs. Martin made a sudden jolt as a rifled fired. They watched as Mr. Martin's horse reared, making Matthew fall to the ground. He scrambled to his feet as a bear charged at him. Darting from side to side, he held his arms wide, trying to find an escape from it. The bear raised up on its back feet and roared.

Mrs. Martin gasped and screamed, "Shoot it! Shoot it!"

Mr. Martin dismounted from his horse and shot him. The bear kept moving toward Matthew on it's hind legs. By the sound of his roars, Mrs. Martin knew he was angry. Another shot sounded, and then another, and finally the bear dropped to the ground and Mr. Martin ran to his son who was frozen in his tracks. The bear was only a few yards away from him.

"Are you alright, son?" Mr. Martin put his arms around him and hugged him tight, crying, "Oh, Dear God, thank you for making my shot fire straight!" He pulled his sons hat off and kissed his head and held him, thanking the Lord.

After several minutes, Matthew came out of his shock, "I think I'm alright, Pa. I was so scared!"

Mrs. Martin sighed with relief and put her face in her hands while her heart slowly lowered it's pace.

The wagon master rode full speed toward the men. They all dismounted and field dressed the bear, dragging him back to camp. The men cut the bear into quarters and put the meat on a handmade spit over a fire made of buffalo chips.

When Mr. Martin returned to the wagon, he said, "That was close, Mrs. Martin. Your son was almost that bear's dinner instead of the other way around."

Mrs. Martin held her son in her arms. Tears rolled down her face as she squeezed him in silence.

The aroma of meat roasting on an open spit filled the camp. It was a marvelous smell, and everyone ate their fill of meat. None went to waste.

That afternoon Katie's fear for the Indians passed, and she jumped down off the wagon and walked beside it. The breeze had faded, and it was hot and dry. They were traveling through a vast stretch of prairie that seemed never ending.

Matthew was riding his fathers saddle horse, and Mr. Jones watched as Jep and Charlie walked beside him.

The boys were barefoot and wore torn trousers with a rope tied around them to hold them up. Their shirts were old and had holes in them, and the sleeves were torn half way off. The back of the shirt that Jep wore had slashes cut into it as a horrid reminder of his hideous beating. They were sturdy boys and with a proper diet they would grow to be strong and healthy.

Mr. Jones saw that they had trouble keeping up with the Matthew's horse. "You boys ever rode a horse before?"

"No, Sir, we ain't," Jep said with an excited look of hope on this face.

Mr. Jones smiled at them. "Would ya like to?"

"Oh, ye'sir, ye'sir, we sure would," Jep said.

Mr. Jones handed the reins to his wife and jumped down off the moving wagon. He waited for the wagon to pass and untied his horse from the back of it. Tightening the cinch first, he boosted Jep up on him. The boy hung on tight as Mr. Jones led him along next to Matthew.

Mr. Martin elbowed his wife and pointed as Matthew started with the riding instructions.

"Now ya take the reins in yer hands. Yup, like that," Matthew said patiently. "Now, take up the slack a bit. If ya want him to stop, ya just pull back on 'em. Real slow like, don't jerk!"

"I got it!" Jep said.

"Now, if you want him to go, just kick him a little with yer heels." Matthew laughed as the horse jumped and started to trot.

Mr. and Mrs. Martin were proud of their son and smiled as they watched him. He was a staunch friend to the boys, and they were good for him too.

"Not so hard! Just a little!" Mr. Jones said as he pulled the horse back.

"Alright...." Jep was hesitant and had a scared look on his face. He had a hold of the reins in one hand and was hanging on for dear life to the saddle horn with the other. The reins were too long and uneven.

Mr. Jones stopped the horse and helped him fix his reins. "Alright, just calm down. The horse will stay up here with Matthew's. If he starts to stray, you just pull back and stop him, and I will help you."

Jep learned quickly while Mr. Jones watched carefully, and Charlie ran behind, jumping up and down with excitement.

Mrs. Jones watched her new husband with love in her eyes. She felt lucky that he was so gracious with the boys. She had not talked to him about it yet, but she wanted to keep them.

When Mr. Jones felt that Jep had the situation under control, he told him to stop the horse. "That went well. Good boy!" Then he put Charlie up behind Jep. "Alright now, give him a little kick." Jep kicked a little too hard, and the horse jumped forward, and both boys came tumbling off to the ground.

Matthew loped up to retrieve the horse, and Mr. Jones ran to help the boys. "Y'all alright?" He picked them up off the ground and checked them carefully for broken bones.

They both broke out into roaring laughter. "Ye'sir, we fine, Mr. Jones!"

He smiled and dusted them off. "So this is what fatherhood is gonna be like, huh?"

"Here ya go, Mr. Jones," Matthew laughed, handing the reins to him. "Y'all are more fun than a barrel of monkeys!"

Mr. and Mrs. Martin were watching. "This is wonderful entertainment, Mr. Martin," she said.

Mr. Jones teased, "Well, you have the 'stop' down, Jep, but you need to get the 'go' down."

Jep was still laughing, "Ye'sir, Mr. Jones."

Mr. Jones put the boys back up on the horse and gave him a little tug to get him going. He watched for a while until the boys caught up to his wagon, and he felt that they would be safe. He ran and jumped back up on the wagon. "You keep an eye on 'em, Matthew!"

"Yes, Sir," he replied.

Mr. Jones was a kind, young man. He was tall and lean and had shoulder length, light-brown hair. By the way he handled the boys, Katie thought he must be good with children.

As Mrs. Jones handed her husband the reins, Katie noticed that he kissed her on the cheek. She was envious. They were so happy, and she wanted so to share that kind of love with Jack.

Looking at the horizon to the south, Katie saw an immense cloud of dust rumbling over it. She ran up close to the wagon and shouted to her father, "Pa! Pa! Is that a dust storm? Over there, Pa!"

He shouted back, "Sure looks like it! Matthew... Jep! Look up yonder! Now, I want you to run up quickly and tell the wagon master."

"Yes, Sir!" Charlie crawled down from behind Jep and jumped into Mr. Jones wagon, and the boys kicked their horses into a lope and rode toward the beginning of the train, alerting the wagon master. By the time he returned, the train had stopped, and everyone started to prepare for the storm. Just then, Matthew shouted, "Pa! Look!"

Mr. Martin looked and shouted, "Everyone, get in the wagon!"

A massive herd of bison were coming straight for them at full speed. Their numbers were so large that they looked like ocean waves and had created a vast cloud of dust.

"Stampede! Stampede!" echoed down the train.

Matthew and Jep got down from their horses and tied them to the wagon. They jumped into the wagon with their parents.

The bison were headed straight toward the wagon train. Families watched in suspense, braced for the worst, as they got closer and closer. The sound of their hooves pounding against the ground became louder and louder. It sounded like thunder. The ground rumbled under them. The herd got about a hundred feet from them, and like a turn in a river, the mass moved to the east. Some just missing them by ten or twenty feet.

Excitement intensified thourghout the train as everyone shouted, "Haw! Haw!" and the men stood outside their wagons waiving their arms, attempting to divert them. As the last few buffalo rumbled past, Mr. Martin watched them fade into the distance. Taking off his hat, he wiped his brow with his handkerchief and looked at Mrs. Martin with a look of desperation and relief. "Whew!"

As if that were not enough, as the dust settled, a group of Indian men stood sitting horseback where the bison had passed. There were fifteen or twenty Indians standing in a bunch looking at the wagon train.

Blocking the sun from his eyes with his hand, Mr. Martin peered toward the front of the train. The wagon master mounted his horse and rode toward the Indians. Riding twenty feet or so, he stopped and raised his hand in the air with his palm facing forward.

Mr. Martin looked at his wife, "Y'all stay in the wagon!" He slowly walked to the back of his wagon and retrieved his rifle.

The Indian leader rode to the wagon master as the train waited silently in suspense. The anxiety lifted as if it were a cloud of smoke when the Indian man raised his hand up in front of the wagon master. Mr. Martin let out a deep sigh of relief.

They spoke for a while and then the wagon master motioned for the wagons to circle. The wagon master rode up to the train and asked Mr. Martin, Mr. Jones and a few others to go with him.

When he returned, Mr. Martin told his wife, "It looks like the whole train has been invited to supper!"

She looked at him curiously, "What ever do you mean, Mr. Martin?"

"The Indians have several bison down, and they are going to contribute one for our supper!" he said.

She looked a little confused and alarmed. "Are you sure that they are friendly, Mr. Martin?"

"Yes, Mrs. Martin, I am sure!" He put his arms around her and gave her a hug of reassurance.

"Meat, two meals in a row!" Katie was excited.

Matthew tugged on his fathers shirt. "Can we help, Pa! Please!"

"Absolutely not!" Mrs. Martin interrupted. "You stay here and help me set up camp for the night!"

Mr. Martin rode off with the other men, and the women circled their wagons along with the rest. They set up their camp and started a fire from the chips that the boys had gathered. Katie got some water from the barrel tied to the back of the wagon, and warmed it on the fire so that everyone could wash. They were especially dusty from the stampede.

The remaining men built a massive fire in the middle of the camp where the buffalo meat would be roasted. They were waiting for the coals to form, so the meat could be cooked. When the men returned with the Indians and the meat, all of the children were excited and wanted a chance to see them. The women were excited to feast on the fresh meat for supper.

The Indians knew sufficient English to communicate. They also used their hands a lot to communicate. Smiling and laughing with them, they seemed to have an appreciation for children and welcomed their curiosity.

A young Indian brave looked at Matthew and reached down, taking a buffalo chip from the pile by the fire. He tossed it out like a Frisbee. Again, he looked at Matthew and smiled, pointing down at the pile of chips. "Come!"

Matthew looked at his father, "Can I, Pa?"

"Sure." His father walked over to the pile with Matthew just in case. Jep and Charlie and some other children followed.

Matthew picked up a chip and tossed it, making it fly for a good distance. Jep and Charlie picked up a few and ran out further into the prairie. They threw one toward Matthew, and he caught it. He laughed out loud, and so did the Indian brave. Soon, all of the children were out on the prairie playing and laughing while the meat cooked on the fire.

Katie sat back with her mother, who was a little apprehensive about the situation. "They seem friendly, Momma. They are wonderful with the children."

The men each carried a large piece of meat to the fire and gave it to the wagon master's wife to prepare it. One of the Indian men opened a neatly packed package made of leather and took out a heart and the testicles from the Buffalo that they had field dressed.

Mr. Martin told his wife, "They took great care when removing these pieces from the carcass."

The Indian man handed the organs to the wagon master's wife. She hesitated. She looked at them and then at the Indian. She was frightened and did not want to offend him, but she was confused as to what to do with the meat.

The Indian pointed at the organs and then pointed at the fire, "Cook!."

She stood there, not wanting to touch them. He put them in her hands, and she held them out, far from her body, with her lip crinkled. Everyone was watching, and laughter filled the camp. Laying a large rock in the middle of the coals, he took the organs from her hands and laid them on it. He looked at her and smiled. She seemed a little more at ease than she had been, but still was a bit scared. She held her bloody hands out looking at them. The crowd roared with laughter while she washed her hands with the water that was warming in the pot by the fire.

The man picked up a stick and poked at the meat turning it over on the hot rock. He handed her the stick. She stood with the stick in her hand. He looked at her and then looked at one of the other Indians wondering what was wrong with her. The other Indian raised his eye brow with confusion. The Indian took the hand that she was holding the stick in and poked at the meat with it, turning it on the rock.

The crowd was watching and still laughing loudly. When they noticed the Indian was not laughing, they stopped. They looked at him, waiting for a reaction. They were afraid that they might have offend him. All were silent and stood perfectly still. The moment was tense.

Finally, the wagon master's wife took the stick and poked the meat, turning it on the rock. The Indian burst into laughter and the crowd, feeling relieved, laughed along.

After the game of toss, Matthew and Jep sat right next to one of the Indians for supper. Katie leaned over to her mother, "I don't know how they can eat with Matthew staring at them like that."

Mrs. Martin looked up and laughed. She watched her son who was sitting next to one of the Indian men. Matthew was chewing his meat and just stared at him. Mesmerized, he did not even take his eyes off him to look at his plate. Every once in a while, the man would just glance at him and smile.

The Indian man, who was giving cooking lessons to the wagon master's wife, pulled the pieces of meat from the hot rock. He stabbed them with the stick and then put the other end of the stick into the ground. He left the meat up in the air to cool.

A few minutes later, he took the heart down and took a bite from it. He passed it to the woman and motioned for her to take a bite. The look on her face was priceless. She did not want to taste it, but she did not want to offend him. The laughter started again.

Her husband laughed, "Taste it, Belle!"

Taking a small bite, she slowly chewed it. She tilted her head and raised her brows while the Indian watched, waiting for a reaction.

"Good!" she said, nodding at him. She looked at her husband, "Good!"

The Indian man laughed and took it from her. He passed it around, and everyone tasted it.

That night, after the Indians left and the crowd dwindled for the night, Mr. and Mrs. Jones climbed into bed. Mrs. Jones asked her husband, "You are getting quite attached to them boys, aren't you, Jake?"

He pulled the covers up over them and turned toward her. "I am, Katherine, did you see them today? They have never had moments like they had today. They have never known any good in their lives. It is truly wonderful to see them happy. I mean really happy, and I am proud to give that to them."

"Would you like to keep the boys?" she asked.

"I would, Katherine. Would you?" he asked.

She looked at him and smiled as she rubbed her stomach. "Yes, I think they would make wonderful brothers for our baby."

"Baby?" he whispered. "Are we gonna have a baby?"

She sat up and nodded her head. "Yes, Jake, we are going to have a baby!

He sat up and put his arms around her and held her tight swaying her from side to side. He crawled to the rear of the wagon and stuck his head out. "We're gonna have a baby!" he shouted.

"Hurray! Hip Hip Hurray!" Cheers echoed through the camp.

Chapter Eleven
The Raging River and The Renegade

Katie's life was such an adventure. Katherine thought about how glorious it was to experience her life. A life that people in our time can only read about or watch on television. With our modern technology, she wondered what Katie would think about our generation. If she were born in our time, she would be able to text Jack on her cell phone.

Katherine powered her laptop and searched Independence, Missouri, history. She found several historical sites in Independence, but only one building that was built prior to 1849. It was the first court house and was where our forefathers had planned the city of Independence.

Searching for "Sternwall" in the phone book, she found two listings and one was William Sternwall. She jotted down the address and the phone number and then searched his name on the computer. She found out that William Sternwall was a wealthy man. He owned a chain of hotels and motels in the area, including the one where she was lodging. He also owned an enormous cattle ranch outside of town. She decided to give him a call. Dialing the number, she received his secretary.

"My name is Katherine Hampton," she said. "I am looking for William Sternwall."

The secretary paused, "Please hold."

Katherine waited a moment and the woman returned to the line. "Mr. Sternwall is in a meeting. Can I have him call you back, Miss Hampton?"

"I am in the area for a short time." Katherine paused to think about how long she would be in Independence. "I am researching my ansestory and my great, great, great grandmother knew a Billy Sternwall that lived here in the 1840's. I just wanted to visit with him to see if he knew anything about them."

"One moment, please." The woman was all business and seemed to be put out by Katherine's request.

"This is William Sternwall. Can I help you?" The man was a bit irritated and apprehensive when he spoke.

Katherine explained her request again.

"I am sure that I don't have any information for you, Miss Hampton." He seemed to be a busy man. "That was a very long time ago!"

"Yes, Sir, it was, and I am sorry to bother you." She waited to see what his response would be.

"It's quite alright." Mr. Sternwall hung up the phone.

She packed and went downstairs to check out of her room and find the dining room. Shortly after ordering some lunch and a glass of wine, she saw a door swing open that was labeled "Administration." A man dressed in a suit came out holding a briefcase. Katherine lifted her hand, calling the waitress to her. "Excuse me. Do you know who that man is?"

She lifted her head to look and nodded. "That is Mr. Sternwall. He is the owner of this fine establishment." Her tone was a bit sarcastic as if she did not like him very much.

Katherine was puzzled. William Sternwall was of oriental descent and Billy was not. "Maybe, it was a different family?"

She ate her lunch and purchased a coffee from the Starbucks that was located in the hotel lobby. Thinking, she sipped her coffee and got into her car, "If I lived in 1849, I would miss Starbucks the most."

Katherine drove into downtown Independence and stopped at the old court house. It was a delightful place. It was a small, building made out of squared logs with white chink in them. She thought it was a shame that more of this historic town had not been preserved. Anxious to see the prairies where the Indians shared their buffalo with Katie and her family, she drove toward Nebraska. Staying close to the original trail, she stopped and looked across the vast prairies. She closed her eyes and remembered her dream. She was lucky to have been able to experience it twice. She continued her drive until the daylight was about to fade behind the horizon. The sun was setting, and it cast a golden hue over Courthouse Rock and Jailhouse Rock. The rock formations could be seen for miles and miles. The towering landmarks must have been a formidable site for the settlers on their westward journey. They just popped out of the ground like lonely monuments inviting them further into the unknown. The prairie was so vast. When she stepped out of her car, she remembered the feeling of beating hoofs on the prairie during the buffalo stampede.

After seeing the sites, Katherine ate dinner and checked into a Hotel in Bridgeport. She slipped into her bed and turned the television on until she fell asleep.

XXXX

The wagon train came upon a river, and the wagon

master stopped the train, so that everyone could prepare to cross it. It was a large river, and the endeavor would be difficult. Mr. Martin tied everything down tightly and checked the rigging and the harnesses. Wanting to make sure the wagon wheels were sturdy, he checked them and the under pinning.

Mrs. Martin and the children were nervous. The river was high and swift, so the men strung a strong rope from a tree on one side to a tree on the other side. The men helped their wives and their children across, one by one.

Once the women and children were safely on the other side, they rode their horses across. Mr. Martin rode his old gelding across with Maggie's lead tied to his saddle horn. Katie was scared for her. She swam across with the whites of her eyes showing and her head barely above the water. Mr. Martin's gelding struggled to pull her safely to the other side. The weight was more than the gelding could handle, and he swam as hard as he could swim but got nowhere. Mr. Martin slid from his back and hung on to his tail.

Katie stood at the edge of the river and held her breath until the gelding finally found solid footing and scrambled out of the water. She took the horse by his reins and pulled him out of the river. When they were safely out of the water, she untied Maggie and tied them both to a tree while Mr. Martin crawled out of the water exhausted. The men rested, and Katie ran her hands over Maggie to make sure she was alright. "It's, alright girl. It's over. You are fine."

After the men had rested, they crossed back over and began to bring the wagons over, one by one. They screwed a pin into the side of the wagon and fed the rope through it to keep the current from pushing it down the river. Then they tied the rope back to the tree on the other side. The draft teams pulled as the men pushed and tried to keep the current from tipping the wagon over. One by one, they worked to get them across. While slowly being pulled across, the fifth wagon broke loose, snapping the rope with a loud ping. The current took a hold of the wagon and turned it over on the men that were guiding it across. Women were screaming, and the other men were in a panic. They were diving under the water, looking for them. One by one, they bobbed up and swam with the current, finally making it to the edge of the river. The current broke the wheels from the wagon, filling it with water and sending it down the river. The horses struggled to keep their footing and tried to pull the wagon to the other side, but they lost ground as the wagon pulled them down the river. The frame of the wagon tore apart, spreading its contents from one side to the other and freeing the horses, allowing them to reach the river's edge. Too exhausted to move any further, they stopped. The wagon was ruined beyond repair.

Knowing that everything they owned was in that wagon, the poor family was devastated. Thankfully, they were traveling with other family members who shared their wagon with them. Everyone pitched in to supply them with bedding and clothing.

The men repaired the rope and finally got the rest of the wagons safely to the other side. It was afternoon before they got the train back together, and there was a steep, rocky hill that the wagon master wanted to pass before dark. Some wagons made the climb and others did not. Several wagons lost wheels on the steep, rocky slopes.

Several men were hoisting a wagon up to put the wheel back on it when it slid on the shale, pinning a man under it. The women stood frozen with panic on top of the hill and watched. They could not see who the man was. Mrs. Martin finally spotted her husband and Mr. Jones struggling to lift the wagon, so they could drag the man out. She was relieved, but she was concerned for the injured man. The women ran, scrambling down the hill to help. By the time they reached them, they had released the man from under the wagon. He did not seem to be breathing, and the wagon master had him propped up, trying to revive him. The man finally gasped for air and held his chest in pain. His wife ran to him in a panic, wanting to help. Making sure he had no broken bones, the wagon master and the man's wife felt his body. As they pressed down on the man's ribs, the man jerked and moaned. The wagon master asked, "Can anyone find some strips of cloth that I can use to wrap this man's chest?"

A couple of women ran to one of the wagons on top of the hill. They ran back to the wagon master and gave the strips of cloth to him. He wrapped the man's chest tightly with the cloth and called out to recruit some help, "Can someone help me get this man to his wagon?"

"Right here!" Mr. Jones and the wagon master slowly took the man up the hill and to his wagon where his wife had made a bed for him.

"Thank you, Sir, but I am fine." He tried to rise and gasped for air.

"You have some broken ribs, young man." The wagon master asked the man's wife, "Do you have any whiskey?"

"No, Sir, we don't drink." She said.

"It's in the box over there," the young man said. His wife looked at him surprised.

The wagon master lifted the lid to the wooden box and took out a flask, "You'll need this for the next day or two. Then you'll be fine."

He and Mr. Jones left the couple and returned to the broken wagon. "Alright, boys, lets get this wheel fixed and get this wagon up the hill!"

The wagon trains before had paved a trail to follow,

making it much easier than before, but the trails were still rough and, several times a day, it was necessary to stop and repair wagons. One by one, they trudged over the hill, and finally, they were all over the top.

The sun was setting, and the train had barely gone a mile all day. Dusk was settling in, and the wagon master decided that the train would stop here for the night. They circled the wagons and the women fixed supper. While the boys gathered wood, Katie milked Maggie, and the men did some more repairs to the wagons.

Katie was hot, dirty and tired. Her feet were sore, and she had to re-bandage the blisters from the day before. Tomorrow, she would ride in the wagon and rest her feet.

Supper was late. Because it was such a struggle crossing the river, Mr. Martin was exhausted. "I just want to get into bed and get some rest," Mr. Martin said as he took one last bite of beans and stood.

"Go ahead, Mr. Martin, I will clean up and be right in." Mrs. Martin and Katie picked up the dishes and washed them in the bucket of water that Matthew had brought from the river.

Katie was sweaty and dirty. "I am very tired, but I would do anything to take a bath in the river, Momma."

"I know, but it is too late and we need to get some rest. Tomorrow will be here too soon." Mrs. Martin wiped her hands on her apron. The sun was already down, so Katie's mother helped her and Matthew make their beds outside the wagon.

Katie laid down in her blankets but could not sleep. It was still hot, and her feet were still burning. The camp was silent, so Katie quietly took a lantern and slipped down to the river. She thought that she would take a swim and soak her feet, so that she would be able to sleep better. She found a calm spot away from the swift current and slipped off her night dress. She left her under garment on and slipped her feet into the water. It felt so good on her tired and blistered feet. The water was still brisk enough to refresh her, and she slipped down into it, soothing her hot, tired muscles. She leaned back into the water to wet her hair. She felt refreshed and cleansed from all the dust and soreness. Now, she would be able to sleep.

Suddenly, Katie felt something grab her ankles and pull her under. She screamed, but she was not heard. She was already under the water. Struggling to free herself, as soon as she could get to the surface and get a breath of air, she was forced back under the water again. She was being drug down the river. She grasped at anything that she could find but only found gravel and moss at the bottom of the river. Just as she would reach the surface to get a breath of air, she was forced back under. Finally, she was pulled out of the water by her feet and gasped, struggling to get her breath. She realized that a man had her feet and had pulled her down the shallow part of the river. She kicked and screamed. He jumped down on her and pinned her to the ground. Pulling a handkerchief out of his pocket, he gagged her mouth with it. Her screams became muffled. The handkerchief was dirty and smelled and tasted like sweat, whiskey and tobacco. It made her gag. The man was so tall and strong that she did not stand a chance. His hands were enormous, and he was able to carry her under one arm as he mounted his horse. He threw her over the saddle in front of him, and she dangled like a sack of flour as he rode off down the river. Water was splashing up on to her face. She could not see. It was as dark as pitch with no moon, and she could not tell which direction they were riding. She did not know how far they rode but it had to have been several hours, first at a run, then a lope and finally a fast walk. Her ribs were throbbing with pain from bouncing against the saddle. The pain was unbearable.

The horse finally stopped, and the man dismounted, pulling Katie down off it's back. She struggled but was unable able to escape. The stench of body odor and fire ash surrounded his presence, and his breath smelled of whiskey and tobacco. He turned her away from him and picked her up by her waist with his arm, and his gigantic hand was holding her off the ground. His other hand grasped a hand full of her hair on the back of her head. Katie was scared. He was so strong that she could not move. He said nothing, only drunken grunts. She realized what he was going to do and kicked him. Hitting him mid shin, he gasped and then walked forward a few steps. He held Katie with one arm, not once letting her feet touch the ground. He took some leather straps from his saddle bags and carried her to a fallen tree stump. Pressing her up against the stump that came a little higher than her waist, he lifted her up and bent her over it. He pushed her tight against it with his body. His breath was heavy on her neck, and it reeked, gagging her. He had her hair in his hand, and as he held her in place, he tied her there, so she could not move. She was helpless as he pulled her undergarments down, exposing her. This time, both of his hands were free, and she heard him grunt with satisfaction that he was able to see her nakedness and touch her freely. She struggled trying to break free again, but the more she moved, the more the tree stump cut into her hips.

The man untied his trousers and let them fall to the ground. He rubbed himself against her. He was limp. Leaning over her body, he put both of his hands on her breasts and pressed against her, rubbing back and forth. He was still limp. Katie could tell he was angry because he could not penetrate her. Stumbling back to his saddle bags, he took a drink of whiskey and mumbled. He pulled up his trousers, laid down in the dirt and passed out.

151

Katie cried and pulled on her bondage until her wrists were bleeding. Her body throbbed with pain.

When the man woke the next morning, it was just breaking dawn, and as he stood up, Katie saw him. He was a towering man with a bald head. His muscles protruded everywhere, and he had strange tattoos all over his body. He had a scar that went down his forehead and all the way down his face to his chin. He was not an Indian and matched the description of one of the renegades that were raiding the wagon trains.

Katie wished she had listened to her parents and not separated herself from the wagon train. If she would have only listened to her mother, she would have been safe with them right now.

Katie's parents woke and started breakfast. Her mother asked Matthew, "Where is your sister?"

"I don't know, Momma. I think she went down to the river," he said.

Mr. Martin was just crawling out of the back of the wagon and over heard the conversation. "I will get her and some water." He grabbed the bucket and headed to the river.

When Mr. Martin reached the bank of the river, he found Katie's night clothes. "Kit...Kit, where ya at?" He called out again and walked out into the shallow part of the river. He looked both ways and called her name. She did not answer. There was nothing but silence.

He frantically jumped in the water, diving under for as long as he could hold his breath. He searched the river bed, swimming back and forth. He ran back to the wagon train. Soaking wet and in a panic, he called for help. He gave Katie's clothes to Mrs. Martin. "I can't find her! I can't find Kit! Get help!"

A crowd gathered and people walked up and down the

banks of the river calling her name, "Katie!...Katie!"

Mrs. Martin tried to stay calm, and Mr. Martin was hysterical. He swam down stream, calling for her. He got out of the river and ran up and down the bank, screaming her name. The wagon master formed a search party, and all of the men, women and children began searching.

The renegade went to the creek and wet his face. After saddling his horse, he left. Katie kept pulling on her bondage but could not free herself. She was bleeding at her wrists and ankles. She prayed that someone would find her before he returned. She was exhausted, dirty, naked and had not slept.

The huge, bald man returned with a rabbit that he must have killed. He was drunk again and swayed when he got off his horse. He built a fire and cooked his meal without offering any to Katie. He sat by the fire and glared at her with a dirty, sinister smile on his face.

After finishing his meal, he stood and walked toward her. Her undergarments where still down at her ankles. She wished she could speak, so she could beg him to stop. This time when he pulled his trouser down and rested against her, he was hard. He penetrated her, and she screamed, but her screams were muffled by the handkerchief that covered her mouth. He thrust into her slamming her up against the tree stomp and her insides felt as if they were ripping apart. Katie cried and continued to scream as he pounded and pounded into her, ramming her hips into the tree and sending pain through her insides. Finally, with a moan and a jerk, he stopped. He reached down and grabbed her breast with his huge hands and pulled on her tightly as he pushed deep inside of her. She could feel liquid run down her legs. He held her there for a long moment. Shivering as he pulled out of her, he slid to the ground and collapsed. He slept there into the night as Katie wept and tried to find a way to escape.

The search party had combed the river bank on both sides for hours. The search went on all day and into the night. There was no trace of Katie, and her parents and brother were up all night, calling for her.

The search went on again in the morning. Because the renegade rode down the shallow banks of the river, there was no evidence of a struggle, or of his horses tracks.

The wagon master pulled Katie's father aside and with his head held low with sorrow, he said, "I don't know how to put this, Mr. Martin, but your daughter must have drown. I am very sorry, but the wagon train must keep moving. Would you like me to perform a service?"

Mr. Martin was direct with his answer. "No, Sir, I can't be certain that Katie is dead, and I won't leave her."

With an emphatic but stern tone, he warned them, "It is not safe to stay out here alone. You should at least go as far as the nearest fort. You are risking your wife and son's lives by staying. At least if you went to Fort Kearny, you would insure their safety.

Mrs. Martin insisted, "I won't lose my whole family, Fred." Mrs. Martin loved her husband with all her heart and would not dream of blaming him for this tragedy. He was already blaming himself, but she could not help but think about the safety of their home on the farm. If they had stayed, none of this would have ever happened.

Mr. Martin gave in to them both and a glimmer of hope lit his face when he said, "That's it! They will help us! They will send out another search party!"

The renegade forced himself upon Katie over and over again. She became weak and was unable to struggle. She closed her eyes tight and thought of Jack, wishing he would save her.

The brutal renegade walked up behind her and rubbed himself against her until he was hard. He spit on his hand and wiped it on her, so he could penetrate her easier. He was a vulgar man and had no mercy on Katie. He left her for hours at a time, returning to cook his food on the fire and drink from his whiskey bottle. He did not feed her or give her water. He raped her over and over for days. On the fourth day, Katie was lifeless. He lifted her head and let it fall lifelessly. He grunted with contentment, packed his horse and left her there to die.

Katie's parents accompanied the wagon train to Fort Kearny, Nebraska. The landscape transformed into low, rolling hills that were sparsely sprinkled with large oak trees possessing branches that sprawled their wide canopies over the ground.

The fort was just being developed and had a few adobe mounds, some framed quarters, some tents and several outbuildings. The fort was located on a narrow fork of the Platte River.

Mr. Martin went directly to the headquarter office and pleaded for help. "Please, help us! It is your job to protect the people! Our tax dollars pay for it! She needs your help. What if she is lost! She doesn't stand a chance out there by herself." His heart was torn in two and tears fell from his face.

"Alright, alright, Mr. Martin. You can have five soldiers and search the area for two days. That's all I can spare." The officer put his hand on Mr. Martin's back, "I have a daughter myself. I'll do what I can."

Mr. Martin and the soldiers returned to the river where Katie had disappeared. The search resumed for two days, and still, nothing was found, not a clue. Her Father was forced to return to the fort.

The officer approached Mr. and Mrs. Martin, "The wagon trains have stopped coming for the winter. All I can offer you is a tent, but you are welcome to stay on here. You will never make it over the Rocky's before winter hits."

Mrs. Martin looked at her husband, thinking that he might be disappointed. She realized that, because of the delay, it was to late into the summer to move on, and they would not be able to continue their journey until the following spring.

To the contrary, Mr. Martin was adamant, "My daughter's body has not been found, and I will not continue without her. Thank you, Sir, it's mighty hospitable of you to let us stay."

They accepted the offer to use the temporary home and moved into a small tent. The tent was stocked with three cots, and it had a wood stove to keep them warm and cook over.

Mr. Martin would hunt and fish for food. He and Matthew would help with the construction of the fort, and Mrs. Martin would help with cooking and laundry. All members of the family would help to pay for their keep at the fort. They were not the type to be free loaders.

Chapter Twelve
Lost to Some and Found to Others

Katherine sat up in bed, trying to catch her breath. Her heart was pounding. She had been trying to pull herself out of her dream but could not. She was fighting her nightmare, and sweat was dripping from her forehead. Still dreaming, she screamed out loud, "Katie, no! She can't die! She can't be dead!" Finally, she forced the dream from her mind and woke. Her stomach was sick, and she ran to the bathroom. Bent over and holding her stomach, she vomited in the toilet. She washed her mouth out with the sink water and wiped her face with a wet cloth. Looking at her pale reflection in the mirror, she noticed a resemblance to Katie. She backed up to the doorway and slid down the edge of it, bursting into tears.

The renegade frightened her, and she was afraid to go back to sleep. "Is this what Katie wants me to know? Is this why I am having these dreams?"

She booted her laptop and searched for more information about Katie. She searched all morning, and finally, she found a death record. Mary Kate Martin

Standing Bear died in 1879. "She was forty-six! She didn't die!" she said. "Standing Bear? That sounds like an Indian name."

Katherine ordered room service and recorded her dream. She Googled the history of Fort Kearny, Nebraska. Fort Kearny was an outpost for the U.S. Army established in 1848. It is located near present day Kearney, Nebraska.

Katherine finished her breakfast, showered and packed her clothes. Driving to Kearney, Nebraska, she found the location where the fort once stood. Still present, were the bare parade grounds and several cottonwood trees that were planted around where the fort once stood. Disappointed, Katherine drove back to Kearney and purchased a room for the night.

Again, she ordered room service. She was uneasy about falling asleep that night but was concerned about what had happened to Katie. She turned the television on and slipped into bed.

XXXX

Katie woke to a strange but soothing aroma. She tried to open her eyes, but they seemed to be almost sealed, and her sight was so blurry that she could not see. She tried to sit up but could not because she was dizzy and disoriented. She realized that she was no longer bound and remembered the bald man and what he had done to her. In a panic, she struggled to pull herself up.

As she stood, a woman spoke to her in broken English and touched her shoulders. "Do not worry, young girl. You are not in danger."

Her voice was comforting, and Katie laid back down. Her sight began to clear as the woman placed a clay cup in her hand.

"Drink." The woman dabbed Katie's eyes with a warm cloth, and Katie sipped while her eyes began to focus.

The woman's hair was gray, and she was terribly old. Her skin was brown and wrinkled like leather, and she had a dozen or so course, black hairs growing on her upper lip and her chin. She looked wise and kind. Her hands were small but crooked and swollen, and she was short. Katie realized that she was an Indian woman. She asked, "Where am I?"

"Shhh, drink, rest." The woman pulled the hides up over Katie and tucked them under her.

The room was hot, and Katie was sweating. She pushed the covers off, and the woman pulled them back up. "You must keep them."

The small, log, hut where she was recovering had cracks stuffed with clay to keep the wind and weather out. The doorway was covered with a buffalo hide. The bed that she laid on was also made of animal hides. There was a small, open fire in the middle of the hut, and the woman was chanting and holding an idol of some sort. Smoke came from the idol, and the woman waved it slowly in the air over Katie.

The Indian woman had cared for Katie for several days before she had the strength to sit up in her bed. She seemed to be a doctor, and she fed Katie tea made from wild herbs and bark. As she dressed her wounds with the muck left over from steeping the tea, Katie spoke, "My name is Katie, what is yours?"

"Winona." The woman said it slowly.

Katie watched her as she dressed the wounds, and she saw that she had scars on her wrist and her ankles and her hips. She shuttered when she thought of the renegade that made them.

Katie did not know where she was or how far away her family was. She was thankful to have been rescued and was glad to be alive. "Thank you for saving me."

The woman pulled the covers back up over Katie. "I could not let you die, child."

Katie thought about her parents and knew how hard this must be for them. They must be looking for her, and they would not have moved on without her. She wondered if she would ever see them again. She wondered if they would ever find her. She was sick with worry. She should not have wondered off on her own.

Mr. Martin still rode out to the river and searched for Katie. He thought maybe someday, she would return to the place where she was lost.

Mrs. Martin, being more practical, had slowly accepted her loss and tried to move on with her life. She believed that God had a reason to take Katie, and she was in a better place.

Matthew missed her, and the whole incident seemed to transform him from boyhood to manhood. Jep and Charlie had moved on with the train and, because he had no young friends at the fort, he pushed his childish ways aside and spent endless hours with his father hunting and helping at the fort. They were constructing a large hall to be used for many purposes such as church services, meetings and even parties.

During Katie's time in bed, she slowly became close friends with Winona. Winona began to open up and speak more freely with her. "Winona means little girl." She pointed at Katie, "What does Katie mean?"

Katie thought for a moment, "I really don't know? Where am I Winona?"

"We are Wa-Zha-Zhe," she said. "White men call our tribe Osage."

Katie realized that Winona would not be able to describe her location. She only knew that this was her home. She learned a lot about Winona and her tribe.

Winona told Katie about her tribes spiritual beliefs. They believed in a force that they called Wakonda. "We pray to the spirits. They help us sometimes, and sometimes they punish us. Itsike is also a force. He is a trickster. He can make life very hard sometimes. One day, I will take you to see our 'little old man'. He prays and teaches our ways."

"What does he teach?" Katie asked her.

"He teaches about Wakonda and the spirits. He prayed that you would not die. All things die, child, but you are too young to be taken from this world."

Katie was curious about Wakonda. "Is he your God? Do you go to his world when you die?"

"No, child, Wakonda is not a man, Wakonda is a power and people do not go anywhere when they die, they just die. The only part of you that lives on is your children. That is why it is very important to have some."

"Do you know about our God?" Katie asked.

"I have heard about your God, child," she looked doubtful and confused, "I do not understand him. He says that if you deserve it, you will live again after you die. There is no life after death."

Because Katie had gone to church her whole life, she believed in Jesus. She knew that she would go to heaven. She knew that Winona had been raised all of her life believing in Wakonda, so she was not going to argue with her, but she asked, "Would you like to learn about our God anyway?"

"You can tell me if you think that you must." She went on with her chores.

One day, Katie pulled herself out of the fur bed and peered through the opening of the hut. It was so bright outside that it nearly blinded her. Squinting and shading her eyes with her hand, she looked out across the land. It was beautiful, flat and full of grass as tall as a small child. It was very late in the summer, and the grass across the prairie spread for as far as the eye could see, swaying gently in the breeze. There were twenty or thirty huts spread over the land. Children were playing, and women were working together in a circle.

The women wore deerskin dresses with leggings and moccasins. Their hair was black and long and tied into braids. Their clothing and hair were decorated with colorful beads. Their life seemed primitive, but it was a happy and peaceful place.

The old woman saw her and smiled. She had very few teeth and looked comically sweet. "Come! Come!" She was always happy, friendly and caring to everyone. She waved to Katie, "Come! Come!" They were slicing the fat from the skin of some hides.

A dozen children stood and ran to Katie, taking her hand. They were laughing and tugging on her. She hesitated, looking back into the hut. She had come to feel so safe there. Turning back to Winona who waved to her again, she went.

The women surrounded her and touched her blonde, wavy hair and spoke strange words. When the old woman spoke to them in a stern voice, they stopped and went on with their work. Katie sat with them and watched, basking in the sunshine that beat down on her and made her warm. Women spoke to each other in the Osage language, and Katie wondered what they were saying. They ignored her, as if she were not there. Winona looked up at her from time to time and smiled.

After a while, Winona gave Katie a tool and showed her how to tend the hides. It resembled an oversized arrowhead but was dull on one side. She showed Katie how to scrap the hides without tearing them. It was tedious work, but when it was finished, there was no meat, fat or anything on the hide. It was smooth and soft and moist. When they finished, they stretched the hides out on the ground and put sharp stakes through the edges of them to hold them in place. They picked up the ones that they had stretched out the day before and worked the stiffness out of them, then staked them back out again.

After all the work had been done, they took the children to the river and bathed them. Katie stood in the water and bathed. It had been a long time since she had taken a bath. Winona helped her clean herself in her bed, but bathing in the water felt especially good. The water was warm, and she immersed herself in it, swishing her hair back and forth to cleanse it. She felt so much better now that she was clean.

The children played and swam, laughing and splashing one another. One of them approached Katie and touched her. She said words that Katie did not understand. Winona explained that the girl wanted to know why her skin was so pale compared to their skin. Winona was remarkably patient with her as she explained that Katie was from another nation. She told the young girl that many people came from Katie's nation, and soon they would be everywhere. She told her that Katie did not speak the Osage language.

The child spoke again, and Winona told Katie, "Asheke wants to know if you can tell her what your words mean. She said that she would tell you what her words mean."

Katie smiled at the girl. "I would like that very much!"

Winona put her hand on the girls shoulders and

pointed to Katie. "Katie!"

The little girl smiled and sweetly said, "Kat-ie!" and she laughed.

The children began to scream and laugh, pointing toward the horizon. Katie saw some riders coming fast and was startled. She ran back to the hut and hid, watching behind the hide that covered the doorway. There were twelve or fifteen of them. They were screaming back to the children and coming at a hard run. She hid under the fur blankets that covered her bed. She listened for a while and realized that it was the men of the tribe, but she was filled with fear.

Winona came to her hut later that evening. She sat by Katie on her bed and started to speak. "You do not have to worry, child. The Osage Indians are gentle people. We are good hunters, and we grow crops. We are not warriors. We do not kill people." She paused with a real serious look on her face.

After being in deep thought for a moment, Katie saw a smile crack slightly on her face.

"We do have war sometimes, but not like your people. We do not fight over possessions or land. We fight mostly with the northern Kiowa tribes. We fight to prove that we are more brave than they are. When we fight, we fight with clubs and no one is hardly ever killed. We use our longbow and spears to hunt. We do not use them to kill people."

Katie smiled at her and was glad that she knew her.

The following day, Katie waited until the men left before she came out of the hut. She peered through the opening and watched their backs as they rode out of the camp. The men wore deerskin loincloths, leggings, arm bands and moccasins. Their heads were shaved except for a scalp-lock that spanned from their forehead to their neck. Their straight, course hair stood up three or four inches.

They wore no shirts, had tattoos, and she could see that they were tall, dignified, lean and strong. They jumped onto their horses at a run with ease and rode with skill.

She knew that they would be back again in the afternoon after their hunt. She would spend the day with the Winona and retreat to the hut when the men returned.

Sitting next to Winona, she asked, "Can I help?"

"Yes." Winona handed Katie a thin strip of leather and a sharp needle made from a bone. Katie threaded the needle, added a bead and then sewed it into the moccasin. She listened as they spoke their language and began to pick up some of the words. Katie felt at home with them. She was aware that the old woman knew what had happened to her, but if she had told the others, Katie could not tell. They did not look at her with pity like the old woman did.

Summer turned to fall and then fall to winter. As time went on, Katie did not lose hope that she would be found and returned to her family, but she felt comfortable with the old woman.

She learned how to tend the hides and sew robes out of leather. She learned how to find and pick the wild herbs that the old woman used to doctor her and the others. Making cake out of cornmeal, she learned how to cook over an open fire. She gathered wood for the fire and water for drinking. Warming water on the fire, she bathed near the river with the Indian women and children. Her favorite thing was teaching English to the young children.

At the fort, Mr. and Mrs. Martin answered a knock on the door of their quarters. A handsome young man entered and introduced himself, "I know you probably don't remember me, but my name is Jack LeShea. I have just been stationed here, and I heard about Katie."

Mr. and Mrs. Martin remembered him, "Please come

in, Jack, how is your mother and father?"

He said, "They are doing fine in Pennsylvania and wanted to make sure that I sent their greetings."

"Well, thank you, Mr. LeShea," Mrs. Martin said. "Would you like a cup of coffee or something to eat?"

"No thank you, Ma'am," Jack was nervous and fidgety. "I want to tell you something."

"What can I help you with, son," Mr. Martin asked as he pulled a chair out for Jack.

"Sir," he paused. "Before you left Pennsylvania, Katie and I spent some time together, and we fell in love."

Mrs. Martin interrupted, "But that is impossible. She never mentioned it."

"That is because I was going to ask Mr. Martin for her hand in marriage when I returned with the cavalry horses," Jack said, looking down to keep the tears from forming in his eyes.

Mrs. Martin looked at the ceiling, "Oh, my God," she paused, fighting the tears from her own eyes. "She tried to tell me, and I didn't listen." She started to cry.

Jack stood, "I am sorry, Ma'am. I am truly sorry."

Mr. Martin put his arms around his wife.

Jack stepped back. "Mr. Martin, could I ask a favor of you?"

Mr. Martin said, "Yes, Jack, what is it."

"Could you take me to the place where she vanished?"

Mr. Martin eagerly agreed. He was excited that he had found someone that would spend the time to help him. He still hoped that he would find a clue explaining what had happened to her that night.

Mr. Martin and Jack LeShea left the next day at daylight. Although it was mid winter by this time, Mr. Martin easily found the location where he had found Katie's night clothes. Jack knelt there and took a moment to pray.

166

As he lifted his head, he had tears in his eyes. "Dear Lord, please help us find Katie today."

Both men rode up and down the river banks, looking for clues, hoping that they would find something that would prove her survival. The grass and bushes had dried and withered in the winter weather exposing the area more clearly. It was even more apparent that nothing was to be found. They camped there that night and sat beside a fire in silence. Finally, Jack spoke, "I want you to know, Mr. Martin, that I loved your daughter more than anything. I still do."

Mr. Martin wiped a tear from his face. "So do I, Jack, so do I."

The next morning was a cold, ugly, gray morning. The men's breath was steamy as they saddled their horses. It was a depressing time of the year, and their moods were grim when they rode further up and down the river. Mr. Martin to the east and Jack to the west. They rode for hours and then crossed the river and returned. The two men met back where they started and sadly and quietly rode back to the fort, returning to their quarters.

Mr. Martin retired to his bed without speaking a word, and from that day forward, came to grips with the fact that his beloved daughter was gone forever.

Katie was out gathering wood for the fire. She heard the dried, wrinkled, brown leaves crunch on the ground behind her. She was startled and turned around quickly. A young Indian man was standing there watching her. "My name is Sequoya." He was smiling.

She was startled and ran. Hiding behind a tree, she peered out from behind it.

He stood with a curious look in his eyes and watched her. His eyes were kind, but she was frightened. He walked toward her.

She lifted her hand and shouted, "Stop!" and he did.

He was still confused as he watched her for a minute. "I will not hurt you." When he saw the fear in her eyes, he backed away to reassure her that he was leaving and was not going to harm her.

As he left, she watched him. She guessed that he was a few years older than she. He was exceedingly handsome, and even through the thick fur hide that covered him, she could tell his body was lean and hard. She noticed that he had no hair on his face, but his body was extremely masculine. His nose was long and sharp, and his face was lean and dignified. He looked kind, but the brutal memories of the renegade were still etched deep in her mind, leaving her fearful.

She hurried back to her hut with as much wood as she could carry. She laid it down by the fire and put a stick of wood in it. Crawling into her bed, she laid there, thinking about the Indian man and about Jack and how safe she felt in her bed protected by the old woman.

Chapter Thirteen
The Waterfall and The Massacre

When Katherine woke, she was happy for Katie. Although, she was still in shock that Katie had endured such a horrid torture, she had been saved. Even though she had been separated from her parents, and she missed them terribly, Katie seemed at peace with the Indians, and they treated her well.

She felt sorry for Katie's mother, brother and especially her father. She did not have any children, but knew it must have been unbearable to lose one. The pain they must have felt not knowing whether she was dead or alive. How painful for Katie knowing that her parents would be going out of their minds, trying to find her.

She thought about the Indians. Growing up in New York City and the coast of Maine, Katherine had never given much thought to Indians. She learned about the Pilgrims and their encounters with the Indians in Elementary School. She learned of the Indian wars in High School, but she never gave the matter much thought. Television always portrait them as savages. She thought about how naive it was to think they were all unfriendly savages. If her dreams were indeed a true replay of the past, then they were wonderful, loving and clean people. Not at all what she pictured them to be. Their clothing was beautiful. The bead work was fantastic and colorful. The young man in the woods was remarkably handsome. "I wonder if he is Standing Bear?"

XXXX

It was very early spring, and the grass on the prairie was thick and green. Flowers were pushing their way up through the dark, loamy soil under the unusually warm, spring sunshine.

This afternoon, when the men returned, Katie did not hide. She stayed next to the old woman. She felt safe there and knew that Winona would not let anything happen to her. When the men approached, the wise, old woman held Katie's hand. She knew her fear and wanted to reassure her.

The men dismounted. There was laughter and joking among the hunters, as they delivered the bounty from their hunt to the women to tend. Their laughter eased Katie's fear, and she smiled slightly, but her posture was stiff because she was frightened and nervous.

The young man that Katie encountered in the woods was among them and noticed that Katie was there. He stopped laughing, and his face lit up as he smiled at her. Her face turned serious as her eyes locked onto his, and she could not move them. His eyes were bright, black and shiny like his hair lock. They were hypnotic, and there was something about him that mesmerized her.

He came and sat beside her near the fire. She did not know what to do. Her eyes were still locked on his, but full of fear. Several of the women, realizing what was about to happen, picked up their tools and left. Katie was holding tight to the old woman's robe, secretly pleading with her to stay. The young man put a leather lace around Katie's neck with a stone on it. She did not move her eyes from his as he stood and walked to his hut.

The old woman stood, "Come." She walked with Katie back to the hut and sat with her. "Sequoya is the young brave that found you. You were almost dead when he brought you to me. He is very brave, protective and strong, and you are very lucky. He has been in "Little Old Man" training since he was a child, and he is destined to be a great leader of his tribe. The leather lace is an invitation to courtship. He is an honorable man, a good hunter and will make a good husband for you." Hunting was a vital skill that proved a man's ability to provide for his family and his people.

Katie tried to explain, "But Winona, you don't understand, I am already spoken for! I am in love with another man."

The woman did not seem to acknowledge it.

The following day, Katie was standing thigh deep in the sparkling river water, helping to bath the children. It was a calm, sunny day, and they were laughing and playing in the warm water. Katie heard an arrow whiz by, very close to her head and pierce the muddy water in front of her. She turned around quickly and looked behind her. Sequoya was sitting on his horse holding the empty bow. She trembled with fear and turned quickly, looking at the arrow in disbelief. When she saw the arrow, she realized that he was not shooting it at her. The arrow had severed a water moccasin on the bank of the river in front of her. He had saved her life again. When she turned to look at him, he was still holding his bow, and he smiled. He clucked at his horse and moved toward the arrow, bending over his horse to pick it up. He turned his horse and rode up beside her, offering his hand to her. She looked at the old woman who gestured her to go. Katie gave Sequoya her hand, and he pulled her up behind him on his horse.

They rode lazily for hours, enjoying the beautiful day. Katie had her arms firmly around his waist, and he was holding her arm with his hand. His waist was firm, and the muscles on his shoulders, arms and neck were strong and glistened dark brown in the sun.

Sequoya had saved her life twice, and she felt a deep affection for him. She suddenly found him to be irresistible. Thoughts of Jack still haunted her, and she struggled with her feelings for both men. She silently wondered, is it possible to love two men in one lifetime?

From that day forward, Katie was not afraid of the Indian men and did not hide from them. She spent much time with Sequoya, teaching him how to speak English, and he taught her how to speak his language.

She taught the children English lessons and how to read and write. She took part in all of the sacred rituals of the tribe, including the ritual that cleansed the earth and the village for spring corn planting, child naming, mourning, and her own wedding ceremony.

Her marriage to Sequoya was beautiful. They were married in colorful costumes that had been handed down to them. The celebration lasted for three days. Many ceremonies took place over that period and each had a distinct meaning. Katie felt blessed to be Sequoya's wife. He was not only a loving husband but also a devoted friend.

After the last ceremony had ended, Sequoya boosted her up on his horse and jumped up behind her. They rode a long time, and finally, they came upon a beautiful waterfall. It was an magnificent sight. The water must have dropped a hundred feet from the top of the cliff and splashed down, forming a mist at the bottom.

Sequoya dismounted his horse and tied him up to a tree beside the river. He helped Katie slide down off the horse. He took her hand and led her down the bank and across a tree that had fallen across the river and on to the fall. A rainbow formed and danced across the mist that cooled them from the heat of the day. The noise was intense as the water rumbled off the cliff and hit the rocks at the bottom.

As Sequoya disappeared under the falling water, Katie watched for him to return, but only his hand appeared. She put her hand in his and he pulled her into it. As they walked under the fall, they laughed and refreshed themselves in the water.

Sequoya looked at Katie with loving eyes, and she gazed into his. He touched her cheek and followed her cheek bones with his fingers. He gently pulled her close to him and kissed her. His strong hand turned soft and gentle and moved behind her neck. She remained silent and could not take her eye away from him as he placed his other hand around her waist and pulled her closer. He kissed her lips and held her tight.

So many feelings rushed through Katie's mind and body. She wanted him with all of her heart and every inch of her body. She thought that she would never feel those feelings again. She still loved Jack, but the feelings that she felt for Sequoya were like no other, not even Jack. He made her feel safe. He made her feel loved.

She kissed him back and showed her willingness for him to touch her. The cave was illuminated by a dull, moving strobe of light that reflected through the water. He picked her up and took her deeper into the cave behind the water fall. Gently laying her on the cool cave floor, he effortlessly pulled her body close to his. He watched her body as he undressed her and touched her lean muscles with his fingertips. She let him explore her body as she watched his eyes. His hands moved from her neck to her breasts. He kissed her lips and her neck. She moaned softly, and he pulled her body closer to his. Making her hips rotate toward his body, he pressed back against her applying more pressure. He lifted his body and moved her under him. She quivered and moaned lightly. The bulging muscles on his neck and shoulders excited her, and she kissed them. Her hand moved down across his back and waist. She felt his muscles pressing into her, deeper and deeper into her. Wrapping her legs around his waist, she gasped, beckoning for more. They made love to each other, and the passion continued throughout the afternoon. Their love for each other was sealed.

It was time for the first wagon train of the season, to come through Fort Kearny. There were twenty wagons, and they circled right outside the gates of the fort. They would rest their stock, replenish their supplies and move on in two days. Mr. and Mrs. Martin and their son were planning to leave with the train when it departed.

They were gathering their supplies at the general store when they met some of the travelers. There was a pot luck supper planned, and the Martins were invited. Mrs. Martin was excited to meet the people that they would spend the next several months with on their journey across America. She made a dish, and they took it out to the circle of wagons and mingled among the passengers.

They met and became instant friends with the Gardner Family. Mr. and Mrs. Gardner were ordinary people from the farmlands of Pennsylvania. Mr. Gardner was chubby and short, and so was his wife. He had bushy curly hair that was over grown and spanned out almost past the brim of his tattered, old straw hat. He was wearing patched overalls and boots with holes worn in the soles that were visible when he sat and crossed his ankles. "Come in! Come in to our camp and eat with us. It is very nice to meet you!" He pointed at Matthew and said, "Help me out here, son! Lets pull up a stump!" Matthew helped him roll three large logs up to the fire and turn them upright, so they could sit on them. "Thank you, son, have a seat!"

Mrs. Gardner was also plump, with rosy red, chubby cheeks and a double chin. She wore an old, but clean dress and a tattered, old apron tied around her large waist. "Come on with me, Mrs. Martin! We'll fix up some supper for these hard workin' men!"

They were jolly, easy-going people with a joyous love for food and life in general. He was quite a joker and shared some whiskey with Mr. Martin and even gave Matthew a sip. "Here you go, son, it'll put some hair on that ther' chest of yours!"

Matthew took a sip and coughed and choked as it burned the back of his throat. He passed it back to Mr. Gardner and said, "I think I'll pass for now, Mr. Gardner."

Mrs. Gardner had a secret flask of whiskey tucked in her apron. She shared it with Mrs. Martin, who was reluctant at first, but soon gave in for a harmless sip. It was the first that she had ever drunk, and she had a terrific time.

The Gardners had a young daughter Katie's age. Her name was Alexandria. Perhaps she was the reason that the Martins became so attached to the family. Alexandria was beautiful and full of life. She was bubbly, and it was so easy to talk to her. She was petite and had long, dark hair and a beautiful oval face with bright, blue eyes and the most beautiful, full, red lips. Matthew was tongue tied around her and struggled just to say hello.

The Martins shared dinner with the Gardners, and they all spent the evening gathered around the fire, getting to know each other. It had been a long time since the Martin family laughed so much. Mr. Gardner kept them in stitches all night with his hilarious sense of humor.

The next day, the Martins hitched their team and gathered their belongings into the wagon. They tied the Jersey cow and the old gelding to the back and took their place behind the Gardners in the wagon train. They would start their journey again, the very next morning, as soon as the sun came up over the horizon.

Jack came to say farewell to the Martins the next morning and watch the train move out. It was a the difficult parting. They were his last link to the young woman that he had such a difficult time putting in his past. The wagon train set off toward the Oregon Territory.

It had been almost a year since Katie was rescued by Sequoya. They had spent many days and nights like their first in the cave under the waterfall. Katie remembered her family often but was happy with Sequoya and the Indians.

Tribal life centered around children, and Katie and Sequoya wanted very much to start a family of their own. Children were especially important to them. Because the Indians did not believe in life after death, continuity came through their children.

Katie went to visit the old woman. Her hut always smelled wonderfully warm and comforting. Winona pulled her in with a smile on her face and sat her down by the fire. "Come in, child. I have missed you since you married," she teased.

Katie did not beat around the bush. "Winona, why am I not able to conceive?"

Winona asked, "Conceive?"

"I haven't been able to have a baby?"

The old woman paused for a few moments, trying to

compose the words that she could use to convey her bad news. Tears formed in her eyes. "You lost the tiny infant you were carrying when we found you, child."

Katie leaned forward and put her hands to her face. She cried. She was devastated.

The old Indian woman told her a story about a legend of the spider. "One day a chief went hunting in the forest. He wanted to find a symbol for his tribe. He saw tracks of a large deer and ran through the woods, following the trail. All of a sudden, he became tangled in an enormous spider web that stretched across the trail. The small spider asked the chief why he ran through the woods with his head down, looking at the ground. The chief explained that he was following the tracks of the deer and was looking for a symbol for his tribe. The spider said that he could be the symbol and the chief laughed. He told the spider that he was to small and weak. The spider told the chief that he was patient, and he watched and waited until things came to him. The spider said that if your people learned to be more like him, they would be strong indeed. So the spider became the symbol for the tribe."

She told Katie, "You need to be strong and patient."

Katie left the woman's hut and told Sequoya about the baby that she had lost. He said that it did not matter to him. As long as he had her for the rest of his life, he would be happy forever.

The wagon train traveled six days, and they were entering somewhat hostile territory. There had been some Indian raids early last summer, but the soldiers had suppressed the Indians, and since then, the situation seemed to be under control. Just the same, the wagon master sent out scouts and all of the passengers were a bit nervous and fidgety. The next day, the wagon train would meet a unit of soldiers heading back to Fort Kearny on their regular rounds. This would put the wagon master and passengers at ease.

It was a long and dusty day, and dusk was closing in on them. The men were driving the wagons across flat land, and the women were walking. It was hot, and everyone was tired. Matthew was riding Mr. Martin's riding horse when the wagon train came upon a river, and the wagon master motioned to circle the wagons for the night. They would cross the river in the morning.

Mr. Martin and the men gathered wood and started fires and Mrs. Martin, Mrs. Gardner and Alexandria prepared supper and made beds. They were tired but still enjoyed visiting and preparing the evening meal together. After dinner, the men worked on the wagons to complete the repairs necessary to cross the river, and the women cleaned up after supper. With the sound of a harmonica playing in the back ground, they all sat by their fires. They visited and passed the whiskey flask around once or twice before everyone retired for the evening.

It was just before dawn, and the women were tearing down the bedding and putting the blankets away in wardrobe trunks that they kept in the wagons. Alexandria heard some screaming and fearfully looked at her mother. Mrs. Gardner quickly covered Alexandria's mouth and listened. The noise was getting closer and louder. There were horrifying screeches coming from Indians, and high pitched shrieks of terror, from unprepared victims, that sent hair-raising goosebumps down Alexandria's back. The sound of gunfire began to fill the air. Mrs. Gardner looked out the rear of the wagon and saw men running to the far side of the circle of wagons. They were using the wagons as blockades and shooting at the Indians on the other side. Some wagons were on fire and some were tipping over.

Mrs. Gardner went back into the wagon and pushed her daughter into the wardrobe trunk. Covering her with a blanket, she closed the lid and told her to stay there no matter what. Mrs. Gardner hid herself under a blanket and watched out the back of the wagon, attempting to protect her daughter. The sun was just coming over the horizon, and the screams from the men, women and children intermingled with gun shots and were deafening.

Mr. Martin grabbed his rifle and ran, taking cover behind a wagon. Matthew ran to join him. Mrs. Martin was climbing into the back of her wagon to hide when an arrow penetrated deep into her back. Matthew heard her scream and ran to her. He held her in his arms with tears streaming from his eyes and said, "Momma, hang on, Momma. It'll be okay!" He looked around with panic in his eyes and screamed, "Help me! Somebody help me!"

She looked into her sons eyes and said, "This isn't how my dream is suppose to end, Matthew." Reaching up to touch his face, with tears coming from her eyes, she pulled his ear close to her mouth and said, "I haven't been very good at telling you this, Matthew, but I love you very much." Her head fell back, and blood trickled from her mouth.

Matthew put his hand behind her neck and lifted her up. He closed her eyes and pulled her body close to him. "Momma! Oh, Momma, please don't leave me, Momma." He held her to his chest and cried, rocking her back and forth.

Mrs. Gardner was terrified and whimpering. An Indian warrior jumped through the canvas opening at the rear of her wagon and heard her gasp in fear. He grabbed her and pulled her from the wagon. Clubbing her several times with the butt of his gun, she screamed with terror.

Alexandria put her hands over her ears and held her

breath, trying not to be heard. Trembling with fear, her heart was pounding in her chest as her mother's screams finally stopped. She was scared, but did as her mother said and stayed in the trunk. Knowing it was a matter of time before the Indians would open the trunk to take its contents, she wondered if she should run, but she stayed as her mother told her.

Mr. Martin looked behind him and saw Matthew, holding Mrs. Martin. He left his cover and ran to them screaming, "No! No!" Arrows were coming down like rain. He was hit. Falling to his knees, he kept crawling toward them. Matthew held his hand out to his father with tears streaming down his face, when his eyes opened widely, and he gasp for air. He had been hit by an arrow in his chest, and he could not breathe. Gasping for air and spitting blood, he slumped over his mother and laid there motionless.

Mr. Martin crawled closer, trying to reach them and save them. He pulled himself, inch by inch, with his fingers digging into the dirt and grass, trying to drag himself to them. Arrows kept coming, and he was hit again and again but was determined to reach them. He crawled slowly, and blood was streaming from his mouth. Closing his eyes, he pulled himself with all of his might. He finally reached them and pulled himself up over them, trying to shelter them from the arrows. Taking several more arrows in his back and legs, he held his family tightly and took his last breath.

Alexandria heard Indians rummaging through her wagon, outside of the trunk. She held her breath, trying to keep quiet, hoping and praying that they did not open the trunk. She stuffed a blanket in her mouth and squeezed her eyes tightly closed. She could hear them opening boxes and throwing out the contents. They were laughing and fighting over her belongings.

She heard the trunk open and froze as the Indian's

pulled the blanket off of her. They screamed with excitement and reached down and pulled her out by her hair. One of the warriors grabbed her, and the other tore at her dress, pulling pieces off of it. She screamed and gasped as they threw her out of the back of the wagon. She landed on the ground and tried to run.

Several more Indians were outside, pillaging through the wagons. They were laughing and screaming. They all ran to her and tugged at her clothing, ripping it off her body. One of them grabbed her and threw her on the ground. The other one jumped on top of her back and held her down, reaching under what was left of her dress and pulling on her undergarments. He pulled them down, exposing her naked body. They were laughing and screaming loudly. Knowing what they were going to do to her, Alexandria started to fight. She bit the Indian on his hand as hard as she could bite, tearing flesh from it. He jumped up off of her and screamed as his hand bled. The others laughed at him, teasing him.

He came back and grasped her hair, holding her head up. He hit her face and made her mouth bleed. She looked at him and spat blood in his face which made him fearsomely angry. She lifted herself up on her hands and knees, and when she started to try to escape, he kicked her in her stomach, making her land on her side and gasp for air. He rolled her over onto her back and sat on her hips. Two other Indians held her down. One held her arms and the other held her feet. The third lifted her dress and tore her undergarments the rest of the way off. They rolled her over onto her stomach, and while the two warriors spread her legs and held her down laughing and screaming, the third raped her. She screamed as he pushed himself deeper inside of her, pounding on her, screaming at her, until he finally stopped.

It was silent for a moment, and Alexandria started to kick and fight. She was able to free herself, but only for a moment. The angry Indian held a knife up to her chest and threatened to cut her heart out. She knew he would kill her, but she would rather be dead, so she struggled to free herself. He hit her again in her face, and she stopped. He tore her dress, at the waist, trying to remove what was left of her clothing.

Suddenly, Alexandria heard trumpets, and her eyes opened wide with hope as she fought desperately to free herself. The Indian pulled her up and turned her back to him, putting the knife to her throat. He looked to see from what direction the sound was coming. He was in a panic, wondering what to do as the other Indians caught their horses and tried to escape. He was using her as a shield while he tried to find a way to flee.

The soldiers entered the circle of wagons shooting and trampled through the dead bodies with their horses.

The Indian pulled Alexandria from side to side, dragging her, trying to find his horse through the smoke and the soldiers. Then suddenly, she felt him jump. His knife fell to the ground, and the weight of his body on her back made her crumble beneath him.

She screamed, and then she froze, realizing that she was hidden under his body. She waited until it was safe to call out to the soldiers. Soon, all the noise stopped, and she could hear voices. She could hear the soldiers working through the rubble. Lifting her head, she looked up and could tell that there were not many survivors. There were dead bodies littering the camp. Some of them had their scalps cut off, and the stench of blood filled the air. She wanted to get out from under the Indian and find her parents, but she was whimpering so badly that she could not call for help.

The soldiers were calling out for survivors.

She faintly screamed, "I am here! Help me! I am here!" She tried to lift the man off her. She finally pushed him off enough to scream louder, "Help me, please! Please help me!"

She kept screaming and finally someone said, "It's alright! I'm here!" A soldier came yelling out, "I found one!"

He pushed the dead body off her. "Are you alright, Ma'am?" He helped her to her feet and wiped the blood off her lip, and she cried. Grabbing what was left of her dress, she tried to hide her naked body. She held herself up by the collar of his uniform and cried loudly.

The soldiers worked all day, gathering the bodies and unhitching the live animals. Alexandria was the sole survivor. Katie's parents and Matthew were dead. Alexandria's mother and father were dead, and she held her mother's bloody body, until the soldiers finally pulled her away and put her on one of their horses.

They brought Alexandria, the dead and a small herd of livestock back to the fort where they had started from six days earlier.

The women at the fort tried to console Alexandria and take care of her. Her experience was horrific, and it would take a long time to heal her heart.

Chapter Fourteen
The Bleeding Heart and The Torn Soul

Katherine woke in tears. She sat up in bed and wept into her pillow. Of course, she always knew there was a lot of war and death throughout history, but it was horrifying to witness it first hand. She realized that she had always chosen to close her eyes to it, never letting the thoughts of war and death enter her mind. Always being shielded from such things, she was over-protected and doted over. How could anyone conceive killing women and children? How could they kill each other?

She finally pulled herself out of bed and showered. She tried to block the dream from her mind as she always did. Instead of death and war, she thought about Katie and Sequoya and how much they loved each other.

She made a pot of coffee in her room and ordered room service. She ate and dressed and wondered how she would be able to find the location of the Osage Indian settlement. She booted her computer and searched for waterfalls in Missouri. She pulled up several photographs and found one called "Mina Sauk Falls" located on Taum

Sauk Mountain in Missouri. After seeing the picture, she knew it was the one. She remembered it from her dream. Locating it on her road atlas, she decided to go there. It was near Arcadia, on the tallest mountain in Missouri. It was a step back to the east, but she had over a week left before her interview, and she could fly out to Los Angeles if needed.

She drove all day and into the night, before she finally reached Springfield, Missouri. After purchasing a room at a hotel, she ate dinner and decided to retire. She would drive to the mountain in the morning.

XXXX

One crisp fall afternoon, after the braves had come home from their hunt, Katie and Sequoya went for a ride. It was a beautiful day. They had gone to one of their favorite private places and made love. Their love making was still always intensely passionate. Sequoya worshiped Katie, and she doted over him.

They returned to camp, and the women were there tending the meat from the hunt. As Katie slipped off the horse to joined them, Sequoya leaned over and whispered in her ear, "I love you!"

"I love you too, Sequoya!" she whispered back to him and kissed him on his cheek.

He rode out past the camp to let his horse loose to graze with the others. As he was about to let his horse go, the rest of the horses became startled and ran off.

Suddenly, a trumpet sounded and soldiers came racing over the hill toward the camp. Katie realized immediately what was happening, but could not believe her eyes. Her first instinct was to run, but she would not leave without Sequoya. The soldiers rode through camp shooting everyone. It was horrifying. Men, women and children

185

were run down and murdered. Cannons blasted. People were running from the camp, screaming and trying to hide.

Sequoya mounted his horse and charged into camp to defend his people.

Katie was trying to help the older women and the children across the river and into the woods. Soldiers were killing them right before her eyes. After all hope had been lost, she ran to her hut, calling for Sequoya. She saw him in the distance, trying to fight the soldiers from his horse. Smoke was filling the camp as the huts were torched and burning. She ran toward Sequoya, screaming for him, and he looked toward her. Then, as he turned to motion for her to run, a soldier shot him. He fell from his horse and on to the ground.

Katie ran to him and held him in her arms. She screamed in horror. A soldier approached her and pulled her away from him. Screaming and kicking at him, she reached for Sequoya. The soldier put her on a horse and took her to a wagon behind the lines. She screamed at them, pleading for them to stop, asking them why and calling them murders. "These people are peaceful! Why are you doing this!"

As she looked behind her, she saw dead, bloody bodies littered throughout the camp. Children's bodies lay crumpled on the ground. The camp was destroyed and, as far as Katie could tell, none of her family were left.

The soldiers took Katie to Fort Kearny which was located along the Oregon Trail west of the Indian Camp. They took her to headquarters and left her in a room.

The room was simple and sparsely decorated with plain furniture. It had a small, iron parlor stove and a small table and chairs on one side and a window in the front, looking out to a wooden walkway covered by a porch. A man came back with a woman and some food. The woman was the General's wife. "My name is Mrs. Smith." She tried to talk to Katie and console her, "Are you alright, Miss? Can you speak English? Do you remember where you came from?"

Katie knew that the woman could do nothing about the undeserved raid on her family. Mrs. Smith brought her food, but she could not eat. She was dazed over what had happened to Sequoya and the rest. Her heart was aching, and her stomach was sick. She was vomiting and could not forget the horror that she had witnessed. She knew that these people believed that they had rescued her, but they had taken the new family that she came to love. There was a time in her life that she would have done anything to be in this room, but now, it disgusted her.

Sequoya woke and lifted his head. The smoke had cleared, and he saw the bloody battlefield and all the mutilated members of his family. The stench of blood and body fluids sicken him, and he laid his head back down and cried. He wanted to lay down and die with them. "Oh, Wakonda, please let me die like the others."

After a few moments, he heard noises. He lifted his head with new determination and hope and saw some movement among the ocean of bodies. He gathered all of his strength and crawled toward the movement, moving some bodies and crawling over others.

He had to stop. He could not go on any further. He rolled a dead soldier over and pulled the belt from his waist. Tying it tight around the cut on his arm, he tore some cloth from the soldiers trousers and tightly bandaged the gunshot wound on his waist. He knew that he had to stop the bleeding. After he had rested a few moments, gathering more strength, he moved closer.

He could see the movement was coming from his young cousin, Muraco. When he finally reached him and wiped the blood from the boys face, he spoke to him, "Muraco, wake up, Muraco!" The young man could not speak, but only moaned. Sequoya found another dead soldier and ripped cloth from his uniform. He bandaged the boys wounds and stopped the blood that was oozing from his body. He rested his head on Muraco's chest, listening to his heart as he gathered more strength.

Katie was moved to another section of the fort and was introduced to Alexandria. Mrs. Smith explained, "You will be staying together here in the quarters. Alexandria has been through some of the same things that you have. You have a lot in common, and she can help you, Katie."

Alexandria was sitting in the chair and looking out the window. She said nothing.

Katie sat in another chair and did not respond.

A while later, Mrs. Smith returned with a dress and some under garments and filled the tub with water that she heated on the stove. She helped Katie bath as she sat motionless in the tub. She dressed her in the clothing and sat her back in the chair.

Katie wanted her Indian clothing. She wanted her husband. She refused to eat or sleep. She would rather die.

Looking around the room, Katie noticed that there were two beds, a wood burning cook stove, a table and chairs and a tub for bathing. She stood and went to the small bed that sat in the corner of the room. It was covered with a comforter, but the room was stuffy and hot, so she laid on top of it and cried. She could not stop.

Sequoya laid on the ground with his head on Muraco's chest, listening to his heart beat, as the sun went down. The stars illuminated like the spirits of the brave young hunters that were taken abruptly and unfairly from this world. He faded in and out of consciousness, so near to death, while his body struggled to repair itself.

The next morning came and Katie watched the sun come up, still trembling, she rolled herself in a ball and rocked back and forth. All her tears were gone. She had hoped all night that Sequoya would come for her. She knew that he would not come, but she hoped, with all her heart and soul, that all that had happened was just a hellish dream.

There was a knock at the door, and she and Alexandria just laid in their beds silently. Soon, there was another knock. Thinking that someone was delivering her morning meal, Katie whispered in a low, weak voice, "Leave it."

The door creaked open slowly, and a soldier entered the room. Katie turned slowly to look. Her face was pale, void of expression, and her eyes had dark circles under them.

She realized it was Jack. He had found her. He had come for her, but it was too late. He looked just as he did before, but this time, she could see pity in his eyes. He did not possess the witty, self-assured attitude that she remembered so well.

The tears returned, and they streamed down Katie's face. She felt relief, knowing that there was someone that might help her. She felt captive in a place where she did not want to be. She sobbed, "Jack, take me back for my husband. Please, Jack!

Jack had a look of devastation in his eyes as he sat down next to her on her bed. She put her arms around him and cried. He sadly lifted his arms and began to put them around her but paused before touching her. His heart went out to her, and it ached with sorrow. He felt such a deep love for her that he wanted to make her pain disappear. As he finally touched her, he pressed her head into his neck and held her tight. Tears began to roll down his face. "Katie, our scout spotted you among the tribe and feared that you had been abducted. They had no idea..."

Just then, Alexandria sat up in her bed, and for the first time since her horrifying rape, she spoke, "How could you live with those dirty, savage murderers?"

Katie looked at her. "They were a friendly, loving tribe. They saved me from a terrible fate and brought me back from near death." She looked back at Jack and again, begged him, "Please take me back."

Alexandria laid back down and turned her back to Katie.

Jack realized the terrible mistake that they had made. "There were no survivors, Katie. I am so sorry."

She pulled herself away from him and pleaded. "Please take me anyway. I want to give them a proper burial. They saved my life, Jack. I want to pray for them."

He pulled her back to him and held her as she cried. "I will see what I can do, Katie." Letting her cry, she finally fell asleep in his arms, and he laid her down on her pillow and kissed her forehead.

Alexandria laid on her bed. She felt angry about her parents and how they died. She was angry at the woman in the bed on the other side of the room. Hating Katie because she wanted to help the savages that were responsible for the death of her family. Hating her for the suffering that she had to endure that terrible morning full of blood and terror. How would she be able to lodge in the same room with her? How was she ever going to get over what had happened to her?

She thought of vengeance. Her Christian background was pushed aside as she thought about overtaking and torturing the Indians for what they had done. She would take the knife and cut them until they begged for her to stop, and then she would do it some more. They would feel the pain that they bestowed on her people. She was glad about the bloody battle that she heard Katie speak of. She was glad that they were murdered. She wished that she could have seen the women and children and men trampled down, shot and smashed into the ground. Bitterness ran thick through her blood. She could not stop it.

Early the next morning, Jack petitioned the General to report the incident and to deploy a unit of soldiers back to the site to care for the dead.

The General denied his request. "Absolutely not, Jack. It would be wasted money. We don't have any extra to spend."

Jack knew that, because the General was the one who gave the order to attack, he was afraid that reporting the incident would tarnish his reputation. He argued, "Listen, General, Miss Martin is not going to give up on this. If the word gets out that we killed innocent people, there will be an outrage among the press. If you were to allow Katie to give the Indians a proper burial, it would put an end to the affair once and for all."

The General finally agreed, "Alright, Jack. You are indeed a silver tongued devil. You may take one unit, but I will not report the incident."

Jack hurried to Katie's room, and they left promptly with the unit toward the battlefield.

Alexandria was setting on the edge of the bed, vomiting in a bucket when Mrs. Smith arrived with her breakfast.

She felt her forehead, "Are you alright, Alexandria?" She thought that her sickness was probably due to the anguish that she was still feeling, but did not want to take any chances, "I am going to get the fort physician."

Alexandria looked up at her, wiping her mouth, "No.

No, I am fine." She leaned over and vomited again.

Mrs. Smith walked to the door. "I will be back directly!"

The physician walked through the door with Mrs. Smith and asked Alexandria, "Tell me how you have been feeling, young lady."

Alexandria looked at him. Her face was pale, and her eyes were pink around the edges and darkened under that. She said nothing.

"Have you been eating?" he asked.

"Yes, I have been very hungry," she said, wiping her mouth again and pushing away the bucket. " I could eat more if they could spare it!"

He looked at her and checked her vitals.

The woman explained, "Her forehead wasn't hot. She has been at the fort for three weeks now, and even though she is still distraught, she is beginning to eat exceedingly well."

He poked, prodded and pressed on her abdomen and then put his tools back into his bag and walked toward the door.

Alexandria watched as Mrs. Smith followed him out the door. She was upset that he did not tell her anything before he walked out of the room. "What is wrong with me, Doc? Why aren't you telling me...."

After closing the door, the Doctor looked at Mrs. Smith, shaking his head with a disparaging look upon his face, "The poor girl is pregnant."

The woman took a deep breath and put her fingers on her mouth, "Are you certain?"

"No, I can't be certain, but there is nothing else wrong with her. We know that she was brutally raped by those savage animals."

Looking toward the sky, Mrs. Smith said, "Oh, my

Lord! How could it get any worse for her!"

The sun was high in the sky when Sequoya woke. He coughed and held his chest while the pain in his side slowly passed. He knew that if Muraco were to survive, he would need food, water, herbs and bark to dress his wounds. Using his legs as a travois, he pulled Muraco up on them and slowly with his arms, scooted and pulled him toward the river. He pushed dead bodies aside, making a trail. He cried as he passed the mangled bodies of his people. Finally reaching the river, he cupped his hands and filled them with water. He sipped from them and then lifted Muraco's head to put some water in his mouth. Muraco choked and coughed and then opened his eyes. He held Sequoya's hand, and tears came to his eyes, "Thank you, Sequoya, for saving my life."

"Thank you for living, cousin," Sequoya smiled, trying to be light-hearted. He rested Muraco against a tree and then lifted his own body, slowly, as he braced himself against the same tree. He stood there for a moment, catching his breath and resting. He slowly walked to the river and leaned over a log, managing to catch some fish from the river. He did not have the strength to build a fire, so the men ate them raw and rested again.

They gathered their strength and searched for more survivors. They were able to save five men, two women and a small child. They gathered medicine herbs and bark and dressed and bandaged their wounds. Then, they built a fire and caught more fish to feed them. While the survivors recuperated, the two men carried the dead to the burial ground and built elevated beds where they could place them. They decorated the graves with any belongings they could find in the rubble under the burnt huts.

The ten survivors prayed for the dead and fled into the

woods.

As Sequoya and Muraco slowly helped the survivors up the hill, well hidden in the woods, he saw the cavalry men coming. He tucked the wounded safely behind some bushes, and he and Muraco gathered their weapons and hid behind a rock to watched.

When the woman came back into the room, Alexandria asked, "Is it as bad as that? Am I dying?"

"No, child. You are not dying." Mrs. Smith did not know how she was going to tell Alexandria. In fact, she thought about waiting until she felt better.

Alexandria felt relieved and picked up the breakfast tray. She took a bite of the food which was cold by now and chewed it. Then she took another and another as if she had not eaten in days. With her mouth half full, she asked, "Than what is wrong with me. Why do I keep vomiting?"

The woman took the fork from Alexandria and put it on the tray. She took the tray and set it on the table.

Alexandria sat with her empty hand still held up over her lap, watching the tray as Mrs. Smith sat it down on the table. "What are you doing? I am still hungry!"

"I need to tell you something, Alexandria. It's not easy for me to say this." She turned around and paused, looking out the window. She searched for the words to say.

"What is it?" Alexandria was confused and getting angry.

The woman turned toward her and took a deep breath. She started to speak, "You are...."

Alexandria looked at her anxiously, "What? I am what?"

Mrs. Smith closed her eyes tightly and covered her face with her hands, pausing. Then she forced the words out of her mouth, "You are with child."

194

Alexandria sat with her mouth open, completely still, not even breathing. Then, she started to cry.

Mrs. Smith went to her side and sat next to her on her bed. She held her tight as she cried.

When Jack, Katie and the soldiers reached the Indian camp, the area reeked with the stench of death, making Katie sick to her stomach. She leaned over the edge of the wagon and vomited. As she got closer, she realized that all of the Indians were gone. They searched the area for them, and finally, Katie saw that they were all placed on elevated graves in the burial ground. Each grave was decorated, honoring the dead.

Katie searched among them and found the old woman. It was the middle of summer, and the bodies were deteriorating, but Katie touched her face and said a prayer. Her tears dropped down on the woman. "I am so sorry, Winona. None of this had to happen. You should have let me die! It is all my fault, all my fault." Katie could not help but feel responsible for their deaths.

Sequoya watched and, with tears in his eyes, his heart ached as Katie prayed over the dead. His first instinct was to go to her and bring her back. He started back down the hill, passing the other survivors. Muraco ran and reached out, grabbing his arm. Sequoya pulled away and continued. Muraco ran after him and knocked him down. He pleaded with Sequoya in a low whisper, "Please Sequoya. Please don't go. The future of our tribe is at stake, and I don't have the strength to handle the burden that you would leave me with if you were killed."

"I have to let her know that I am alive, Muraco!"

Muraco told Sequoya, "You were trained as a 'Little Old Man,' and you have to care for the last remaining members of this tribe.

"I can't just leave her!" Sequoya said.

"Katie will be safe with her people, more safe than with us, but the last survivors of our clan will not make it without you. I am young. I am not a leader and do not know how to save them."

Sequoya knew he was right and, after pausing briefly, he reluctantly turned back toward his people. With tears streaming down his face, he slowly walked. His plan was to lead his tribe southward toward the Comanche tribes. The Osage traded with them from time to time, and they were allies. They did not speak the same language, but in the past, had communicated with them using the Plains sign language.

Katie searched all the other graves and prayed for all of them, but she did not find Sequoya and several of the other young men. "They have to be alive!" She was so relieved that Sequoya was not among the dead. She suddenly became sad and looked at Jack, "Where could they have gone? How will I find them!" She called out for Sequoya with tears streaming from her face.

Sequoya heard her cry out for him and stopped in his tracks. He stood dead still as Muraco looked at him with panic in his eyes. He knew how hard it was for Sequoya to turn his back on her. He loved her so. Sequoya fell to his knees and cried as he listened to her tearfully scream his name.

Jack reached out and held her arm, pulling her back toward the wagon. She pulled away from him and fell to her knees. She wept as she cried for Sequoya.

Sequoya turned and watched with tears streaming from his face, and his own heart felt as it was tearing away from his chest.

Chapter Fifteen
New Friends and Old Friends

Katherine could not take any more. It was too painful. She wanted the dreams to stop? She wanted to put this all behind her and go on with her life. She packed her bag quickly and deliberately. She wanted to run. She wanted to get out of town and drive to Los Angeles and forget all of her dreams. Throwing her bag into the trunk of her car, she jumped into the seat.

The Rand McNally Road Atlas was on the passenger seat, opened to the Missouri map. She looked at the area that was circled with a red marker. She stopped for a moment and thought about what she was about to do. She had always run from the pain. She thought, "If everyone faced the painful things and did something about them instead of ignoring them, the world would surely be a better place to live. Maybe this is what would make a difference in my life."

The Indians attacked the wagon train and tortured Alexandria. They were wrong. The soldiers attacked Katie's tribe and nearly wiped them out. They were wrong.

Alexandria felt hatred for Katie. She was wrong. Why does this happen? Our history is filled with wrongs. How do we make them right?

She started her car, pulled out of the parking lot and drove east toward the mountain. After a couple of hours of driving up the most beautiful mountain she had ever seen, Katherine's attitude mellowed. She thought about Katie and Sequoya and how beautiful it must have been for them. When she finally arrived at the waterfall, she walked to it and slipped under it. She drenched herself under the falling water and cooled herself, just as they did. As she went further under the cave, the sun made strobes of light bounce off the cave walls. She laid down on the rock ledge and watched the water and the light, thinking of the romantic wedding night that Katie and Sequoya spent there. She fell asleep.

XXXX

Katie rode back to the fort with Jack in silence.

He looked over at her, and he felt her pain. He loved her so much. It tore his heart apart to see her suffer as she was. He knew it probably was not an opportune time, but he told her anyway. He wanted her to know that she was loved, and she had someone that she could trust. "Katie, I have been searching for you since the day I heard that you vanished. I stayed on at Fort Kearny because it was the closest to where you disappeared."

She was distracted with another thought and did not hear a thing that he had told her, "Do you know where my parents are, Jack?"

Jack hesitated, "I didn't want to tell you this because you have gone through so much already..."

Katie looked at him with tears welling in her eyes,

"Oh no, Jack. Not my family!"

"I'm sorry, Katie." He explained, "Your parents and Matthew decided to move on after we searched for you all winter. We couldn't find any clue as to what happened to you and thought that you had drown in the river."

"Indians attacked and killed all but Alexandria and some stock. That's why she is so bitter. They raped her, and they were about to kill her when we saved her. She hasn't healed from it yet."

Katie put her head on his shoulder and sobbed, "Is that why the soldiers attacked my tribe, Jack?"

"It is what fueled the fire and made the soldiers more hostile and uneasy about the Indians. It set the stage for the attack on your friends, especially when it was revealed that you were among them. They thought that the Indians were holding you against your will."

Jack knew that she had been through so much but wanted her to know that he was there for her. "I still love you, Katie, and I will always be here for you."

Katie was in tears when she told him, "Sequoya may still be alive, and he is my husband, Jack. He will come for me."

Jack loved her more than anything else in his life. He would be patient and would wait as long as it took to get her back.

When Katie returned to her quarters, she over heard Mrs. Smith trying to console Alexandria. Katie felt remorseful for Alexandria and wanted to help her. She walked over to the bed and sat on the other side of her. Alexandria jerked away from her screaming, "Don't touch me!"

Knowing exactly what Alexandria had gone through, Katie said, "I know what you have been through. I was raped. It wasn't by an Indian. It was a white man. Not all

Indians are savages, just as not all white men are good. I can help you. Please let me be your friend."

Alexandria burst into tears. "Do you have a savage growing in your stomach?" She screamed loudly, "Do you know how that feels?"

"No, but I lost my child because I was raped, and I don't know if I will ever be able to have another," Katie sobbed.

Katie looked at Mrs. Smith. The women laid Alexandria down on the bed and walked outside with Katie. She explained, "Yes, she is with child. I don't know what to do for her. She is very angry, and I am afraid she will not accept the child!"

Katie wiped her eyes and sighed, "I will try and befriend her. She has been through a horrid time, and I know how she feels. It will take time, lots of time."

Katie walked back into the room. Sitting beside Alexandria on the bed, she told her, "I am here, and I will be here for you when you decide you need someone. I know you will, because I did. I found a dear, dear, friend in my time of need, and someday, I will be yours."

Sequoya and his small tribe traveled a long distance, and finally found a Comanche tribe about fifty miles south of their home. The tribal doctor cared for the sick, fed them and nursed them back to health. The Comanche were more aggressive than the Osage and were notorious for winning wars. When Sequoya met with the Comanche chief, Chief Wichita, he was eager to help Sequoya plot revenge for the terrible attack on his people.

Katie agreed to stay on at the fort through the winter. She spent her time with Alexandria, the children and attending services in the Grand Hall that her father helped to build. She went for long rides with Jack, secretly hoping she would find Sequoya, or he would find her.

She wondered where his home was or if he were truly alive. She often thought of looking for him but did not know where to look. She would not be able to survive alone in the wilderness.

Katie spent a lot of time with Jack but always made it exceedingly clear to him that she would wait for her husband. Jack knew that if Sequoya had not come yet, he most likely would not. Katie knew it too, but she was not ready to give up hope.

One Morning, Jack came to get Katie, "I have a surprise for you, Katie!"

"What, Jack? What is it?" She loved surprises and the suspense cheered her up.

He put his handkerchief around her eyes and led her outside. She had no idea where he was taking her. He stopped and aligned her with something, then he untied the handkerchief.

"Oh! Oh, Jack, he's beautiful!" Katie opened the corral where a palomino gelding was standing. "Is he for me?"

"Of coarse he is!" Jack said smiling.

"I love him!" She turned, and something caught her eye. "Oh, my God, Jack! It couldn't be! It just couldn't be!"

Jack stood and looked at her curiously, "What, Katie?"

She walked to the next paddock and opened the gate. As she fell to her knees, the Jersey cow came walking up to her and licked her right across her face with her abrasive tongue. Katie exploded with tears of joy. "Maggie! My dear friend, Maggie!"

Alexandria eventually opened up to Katie, and they

made incredible friends. They spoke of their experiences, and Katie discovered that Alexandria knew her parents and Matthew. They talked for hours about their lives and the things that they had so much in common. They had been taken from their families and left alone with no one.

Alexandria took Katie to the cemetery, and they prayed for their parents and Matthew. Katie looked to the heavens and spoke to them, "I am so very sorry that I left that night."

Alexandria and Katie spent a lot of time together and came to be very close friends.

Sequoya and Chief Wichita worked hard to condition their tribes for the raid that they had planned for the soldiers. The Osage trained themselves as warriors and learned how to use the guns that the Comanche tribe had traded for. They traveled far to scout the movements of the soldiers and learn their vulnerable tendencies.

Chief Wichita had long, black hair and a rounded face with high cheek bones. He was feared by everyone, including Sequoya and the other Osage survivors. He was easily angered, and if crossed, he would not hesitate to kill. Sequoya was decidedly cautious around him and made sure to follow directions carefully and exactly.

Chief Wichita explained his plan to Sequoya. "We will hunt them in the same manner that we hunt animals. We will quietly sneak up on them, so they will have no warning. We will kill as many as we can, quietly with our knifes, one at a time. There is a boxed canyon at the end of their trail where the soldiers camp for the night. We will be able to surprise them in their sleep and trap them there."

February was coming, and the women all made clothing for the baby that Alexandria was about to bring into this world. Alexandria had gotten over the bitterness that she felt for the infant. As it grew in her womb, her instincts took over, and she grew to love it more every day.

When the time came, Katie sent Jack to get the doctor, and she helped him bring the baby boy into the world. From that day forward, she would always feel a distinct bond with Alexandria and her son.

It was approaching Easter, and the General was hosting the first community party at the new hall. Jack asked Katie, "Would you do me the honor of being my guest at the Easter Ball, Katie?"

"Yes!" she said excitedly. "I would love to, Jack."

He surprised her with a new gown that he had asked the General to pick up for him when he went to Washington D.C. the month before.

"Oh, Jack, it's beautiful. I love it!" She held it up and twirled around.

He handed her another package that he had been trying to hide behind him.

Because she could see it all along, and she knew he had it, she laughed at him playfully. She unwrapped the package and unfolded a petticoat, matching hat with feathers and shoes with buckles. "She threw her arms around Jack and kissed his cheek." She put the hat on and said, "Do you like it, Jack?"

He smiled. "I like it very much." He loved to make her happy, and she could see it by the glow on his face. She was excited about the occasion.

On her way back to her quarters, Katie stopped to tell Maggie all about her excitement. She had Maggie back, and along with the palomino gelding whom she shared a stall, Katie had confidants once again.

When she returned to her quarters, Alexandria had another surprise for her, "I have been asked to the Easter

Ball, Katie!"

"That is perfect, Alexandria, we can sit together at a table and visit and dance!" Katie got them some tea. "Tell me about this new, young man of yours!"

"Actually, he is a friend of Jack's! They are in the same unit. His name is Michael, and he is very handsome."

"I am so happy for you, Alexandria. I am happy that you found someone to help fill your days!" Katie was happy for her and anxious to get to know him. It will be nice for her and Jack to spend time with another couple.

The Easter Ball was held in the Grand Hall on the Saturday night before Easter. Several married couples were present and many men of high stature. The room was round, had an extraordinarily high ceiling and columns to support it. The floors were wood inlay and had beautiful designs. The building was full of men in clean, starched uniforms and beautiful women in gowns of the latest fashions. Katie was especially beautiful and certainly the belle of the ball. Her dress was pale blue, just like her eyes, and it came off her shoulders. With her hair up, it complemented her long neck and petite shoulders. All the men wanted introductions, but Jack stayed extremely close to her and doted over her constantly.

Alexandria and Michael sat at their table, and they all visited and laughed and forgot all that had happened to them in the past. Alexandria was terribly bubbly and vivacious, but she was also a bit spoiled and was used to being pampered by her parents. Like Michael, she was exceptionally well educated. Michael seemed to love the fact that she required so much attention. They were a perfect couple and Michael adored Alexandria's son, Jacob.

They danced and danced, over and over again. Katie had a fabulous time, and the nightmare at the Indian camp never entered her mind.

Jack escorted Katie to the beverage table, poured her some punch, and then he walked her out to the terrace. It was a beautiful, spring night. The breeze was cool and smelled fresh and fragrant. Ivy spread its limbs wide among the terrace railings and climbed just over the edges. The stars were bright and lit the sky, and the moon was full with a ring radiating off it. The breeze blew across them and made Katie's hair blow back from her face. "You are beautiful," Jack told her. He held her hand, and staring into her eyes, he pulled her close to him.

His eyes were still as captivating as Katie remembered, and at that moment, she felt the same love for him that she had felt so long ago. It is possible to love two men. It must be, for there was a time that she loved Jack and fell in love with Sequoya. Now, she still loved Sequoya, and she is falling back in love with Jack.

Jack placed his finger on her jaw bone and raised her lips up to his and kissed her softly. "I love you, Katie. Please tell me that you still love me too."

Katie looked into his eyes, and hers became heavy with tears. "Yes, Jack. Yes, I do love you."

Jack reached into his coat pocket and knelt on the floor with Katie's hand in his. "Katie Martin, will you make me the happiest man in the world and marry me."

Tears of joy flowed from Katie's eyes, "Yes, Jack, yes! I will marry you!" She pulled him up and threw her arms around him.

He kissed her again, and he was indeed a happy man.

After Katie had told Jack about her terrible experience with the renegade and rescue by the Indians, he was determined to keep her safe. He never left her alone, always leaving someone to keep watch over her. He took care of her, and they planned to marry at Christmas. Jack and Katie loved each other very much and spent all their spare time together.

She planned the wedding, and Jack made sure that she had everything she needed to make it the best. It would be even more grand than the Easter Ball. Katie commissioned the seamstress to make her wedding dress of white satin and lace. She would wear a corset and her dress would spread graciously over a wide hoop. Jack would marry in his uniform. She arranged for a beautiful cake from the baker, and Jack even talked the men into helping him cut and haul the tallest tree to put up in the middle of the hall. The children will decorate the tree with lace and candles. Katie could not wait to be Jack's wife.

The anticipation of the wedding made the summer drag by, but fall was just around the corner. The leaves eventually turned golden and the air crispy. Excitement filled the fort as children prepared for Halloween. Jack came to Katie's quarters to help her hand out the cookies and caramel apples that she had made the day before. They giggled as the children knocked on the door. They both pretended that they did not recognize them as they came, "Katie, who is that?"

"Hmmm, I don't know, Jack. I have never seen this little goblin before?"

"It's me, Johnny!" the child replied.

"No, this is not the Johnny I know," Jack teased.

The children had so much fun. Katie loved them and, thinking of Winona and the story of patience, she wondered if she would ever have any of her own.

As the last child came, and the last caramel apple was given out, Jack and Katie were exhausted. They both plopped down on the sofa and put their feet up on the ottoman.

"You would think that I have worked in the field all day. I am so exhausted," Katie said.

Jack was stoking the fire. "It was worth it though, wasn't it? Those kids were so cute!"

"Yes, I can't believe little Johnny. I really didn't recognize him." She sipped her tea.

They talked and laughed about the children and their costumes. Jack put the fire prod down by the fireplace and sat down beside Katie. "Maybe someday, we will be walking our children down the streets on Halloween."

Katie sat up and looked at Jack. Tears started to roll down her eyes.

Jack took her hand, "What's wrong, Katie. Did I say something to upset you?"

"No, Jack, there is something that I have to tell you." Katie wiped her eyes. "I should have told you a long time ago."

Jack smiled at her, "Katie, don't cry. There is nothing you could tell me that would make me love you less."

"When I was recovering from the renegade...." she paused to compose herself.

"It's okay, Katie. I promise," he urged her to continue.

"I lost our baby, Jack." Katie sobbed and could not stop. "I don't know if I can ever have children."

"Oh, Katie. I am so sorry. I am so, so sorry," he said. "It will be okay, even if we never have children, I will still be the happiest man in the world." Jack picked up Katie's chin, and smiling, he looked into her eyes.

She has still never gotten over how handsome he was. She smiled back, wiping the tears from her face, and he kissed her. He placed his hand on the back of her neck and moved her closer, gently pressing her body up against his. She wanted him, and he wanted her. She wanted him to make love to her. Jack kissed her, and he leaned over, pushing her down on the sofa and laying her down with his body over hers. They kissed, and her body tingled as Jack pressed against her, making her moan.

There was a knock on the door and the two lovers jumped to their feet, straightening their hair and clothing. Jack answered the door, "Trick or Treat"!

Thanksgiving came and went, and Christmas was just around the corner. The wedding was growing into a huge event, combining a small-town wedding and a holiday party, all into one celebration. The women spent every Saturday evening in November and December decorating the Hall.

The men helped them with any of the building, lifting or heavy work, but they were mainly just looking forward to the celebration itself. Of course, Jack looked forward to the wedding night and getting on with a normal life. All the hoopla was starting to wear on him.

A week before Christmas the men went on their tree cutting outing. They were gone the whole day and returned silly drunk, dragging a gigantic tree behind them. Stumbling through the main corridor of the fort, they were singing Christmas carols mixed with "Here comes the Bride." The women could not help laughing at them but acted entirely out of sorts like dutiful, Christian women were suppose to, dragging their men home by the ears. They let them get away with it because it was their version of a bachelor party.

The women threw a lovely wedding shower for Katie, and she had almost enough household items to stock her and Jacks new quarters. She was exhausted, also ready to get on with her life with Jack. Katie had matured so much since she left her hometown on that wagon train. She started out as a young girl, full of romantic dreams for her life, and so much had happened to her since then. She was blossoming into a mature woman and had all the comforts that she could ever ask for. She had so much to be thankful for, including life itself.

Jack and Katie LeShea were married December 25,

1851 in the Grand Hall at Fort Kearny, Nebraska. The reception was also held at the Hall, and everyone at the fort was invited. There were also several people from Washington D.C.

It was a wonderful party. Champagne was served, and toasts were given, and the cake was beautiful. The huge tree in the middle of the Hall was a conversation piece among the men who had such a jolly time cutting it down and dragging it back to the fort. The music and laughter filled the Hall and Jack and Katie danced through the late hours of the night.

When the clock struck twelve, Jack picked his wife up and carried her out the door. The crowd threw rice at them, as he carried her across the road and into their new quarters. They were finally alone.

Jack let Katie down gently on the bed and pulled her up close to his body. He kissed her, "Mrs. LeShea...."

Katie giggled, "Mr. LeShea...." She was reminded of her parents and how they called each Mr. and Mrs. Martin. They looked into each others eyes which were full of sparkles and joy.

Jack kissed Katie's forehead and then her lips. Kissing her neck, he loosened her corset. He undressed her slowly as if he wanted her to remember this moment forever. Then he stood and slowly undressed himself. Katie saw his naked body again. It had not changed. He was still as fit as he was when she first met him. His muscles bulged at his neck and shoulders and rippled down his waist. Sloping perfectly from the curve of his back, his butt was full and firm. His legs were strong, and she wanted to touch them. She wanted to touch every muscle in his body and get to know every inch of him.

Jack reached across and touched Katie's ankle. He kissed it and followed her long, lean leg upward with his lips. As he kissed her, the intensity of her passion began to build and her breath became labored. She savored every second, as he made his way up her thigh and the anticipation made her excited. He kissed her stomach and continued up until he reached her neck. He kissed her neck and then her lips. It was a beautiful moment. Katie felt so close to Jack that it felt as they were one. Their emotions heightened as Jack and Katie's lovemaking peaked and they exploded with love.

Jack held Katie close, "I love you, Katie LeShea."

"I love you, too, Jack LeShea."

They kissed and held each other tight and fell asleep exhausted.

Only a few days later, Jack had to leave with the cavalry to patrol the trail. That morning, Jack prepared breakfast for her. He cooked oatmeal and honey with a ham steak.

Katie woke to the smell of ham cooking and stumbled out to the stove with a smile on her face, "Good morning, Mr. LeShea," she said, putting her arms around his neck and squeezing him.

"Good morning, Mrs. LeShea, did you sleep well?" He got oatmeal on her neck when he kissed her, so he playfully kissed her neck until it was gone.

Katie giggled, "Like a baby, Mr. LeShea." Her giggles turned to moans as he loosened her robe and let if fall to the floor. He admired her body in the sunlight that was rising in the window. Jack pulled Katie close to him and made love to her against the kitchen cupboard. He sighed and kissed her. "It is the best morning that I have ever had Mrs. LeShea."

Chapter Sixteen
Marital Bliss and Sorrowful Good-Byes

Katherine felt warm and content about Katie's happiness. It was beautiful, what Katie shared with Sequoya, and she could not help but feel regretful that Katie was not able to share her whole life with him. He was her husband, and she loved him. She was able to feel Katie's pain and knew it was not easy for her to get over him. Because she had been through so much, it was a wonder that she was still sane. Katherine was thankful that Katie was able to find happiness again with Jack.

She sat under the fall for a while longer. She would never forget this place because it was so beautiful. She stepped outside and made her way back to her car. She drove back to Springfield where she would spend the night before going back to Kearney and then on to Los Angeles.

When she reached Springfield, she stopped for dinner and purchased a room at the same hotel that she had stayed the night before. She slipped into her night gown and then into bed. She turned the television on and soon fell asleep.

Jack kissed his new bride, "Good bye, Mrs. LeShea. I will miss you, while I am gone."

"I don't know what I will do while your gone, Jack." Katie hugged him, "I wish you didn't have to go so soon."

He held her face and told her, "Two weeks and we will be together again, sweetheart." He mounted his horse, and bending down, he gave her one more kiss before he rode off with Michael and thirty-eight other soldiers.

Katie truly did not know what she was going to do with herself for two weeks without him. The women were going to paint the new church that had just been completed at the fort, so at least that would keep her and Alexandria busy during the daylight hours.

The next day, Katie arrived at the church right before lunch. "Good morning, Alexandria," she hurried into the church with her pot luck dish.

Alexandria put her paint brush down and wiped the moisture from her forehead. "I was beginning to worry about you, Katie." She had paint on her face and in her hair.

Jacob waddled over to her, "Katty!"

She laughed at him. "I couldn't sleep last night. I don't think I fell asleep until daylight. I miss Jack. I just don't feel good about this trip."

"I miss Michael too, Katie." They both dished up their lunch and ate with the other ladies.

The General's wife, who Katie admired, knew that Jack's absence was difficult for Katie, so she tried to lighten her spirits. "Just wait until you are married for ten years, honey. You will be glad to have the peace and quiet." Her husband did not patrol anymore, but they were both very busy and involved both in Washington D. C. and the fort.

The rest of the women talked about their husbands

and how impossible they were. Katie did not have anything to say about Jack, but thought someday when they were old and gray, she might find something impossible about him. For now, he was perfect. At night, she thought about how they made love and that made her miss him more. She could not wait for him to return.

The men traveled westward, twenty miles a day to keep the peace on the Oregon Trail. Since it was winter, there were few travelers on the trail and no reason for raids. There had not been a raid on the settlers for months now, and the soldiers did not expect any trouble. None the less, the men were restless, also anxious to get home to their wives.

Their meals were cooked by the camp cook, and there was not much variety. Jack did not mind the cook's chow. Katie was not a particularly talented cook. She tried but did not have much experience in the kitchen. That is why Jack cooked most of the time. From time to time, the soldiers came upon wild game which gave them a break from the beans and biscuits. Because of the size of the unit, the game often saw them coming and were far from shooting range. It did not happen often, but when there was meat on the fire, there was a reason for a celebration. This was one of those nights. Michael shot an antelope while he and Jack were returning from a scouting trip. The men ate well after setting up camp and went to bed with full stomachs.

The Indians were lurking, waiting to take their revenge on the soldiers. Their plan fell into place perfectly. As the soldiers slept in the canyon, the Indians closed in on them. They were deadly quiet, creeping up behind them in the dark through the trees, like a cat stalking its prey. They were perfectly camouflaged and out numbered the soldiers by two to one. As they slipped into their camp, they separated two or three men per tent. They were quiet, like a deadly mist, creeping into their tents and surprising them, one by one. They killed most of them with their knifes quietly in their tents while they were totally unprepared. Some never even woke. There were very few left when the soldiers finally realized that the Indians were there. Then, the fight broke out into a loud battle. Gunshots were ringing through the air, and the soldiers were trapped.

Sequoya was with the Comanche Chief and watched as he was shot down beside him. He never welcomed death, but he felt a sense of relief because Chief Wichita was an evil man. He was known for kidnapping whites and torturing them, sometimes slowly until they died, and sometimes, he traded their mangled bodies back to the whites.

When the fight was finally over, Sequoya wrapped the Chief's body in a blanket and tied him up on his horse. The Indians lost only five men. Sequoya mourned over them and the soldiers. Even though he wanted revenge for his people, he was sad that they killed them. He knew that there would be mourning families that would miss them. He knew it would cause a lot of aching hearts, just as his heart had ached when his people had been murdered. He and his tribe dragged them into their tents and secured them so that the wild animals would not get to them.

It took the women two weeks to paint and set up the church for Sunday service. The men would be returning soon to share it's beauty. The Pastor was proud as he gave the first service in the new church. Katie thought about what it would be like when Jack could attend the service with her. She remembered the day she first saw Jack. It was in the beautiful, little, whitewashed church back home. Much has happened since then. Everyone that remained at the fort was in the church for Sunday service, and it still seemed empty.

They were singing from the hymn book when the door slammed open. A tattered, bloody soldier fell down to his knees and screamed "Indian raid!" He gasped for air and blood oozed from the corner of his mouth. The Pastor and the doctor ran to him and carried him off as he continued rambling. The women gathered and followed, holding each other in horror. They knew that what ever happened was awful.

When the Doctor finally came out of his office, the look on his face was disbelief. He explained to the others that the Indians had taken the soldiers at a canyon one hundred miles west of the fort. The soldiers were on their way back, and the Indians trapped them in the canyon. It was a massacre. Mac said that as far as he could tell, he was the only survivor.

Katie and the other women were silent with disbelief. The General deployed his second unit to find them, and he went to his office to send a wire for more troops. There was nothing to be done until the unit returned with the dead.

Katie felt as if she had a hole in her heart as she fell to her knees in tears. She had so much pain in her life. She felt dead inside. Her mind was numb, and her heart was empty. Alexandria helped Katie to her feet, and the women went to the church to pray and hope, against all odds, that their husbands somehow survived.

Two weeks later, the soldiers returned with wagons full of dead and grossly decomposed bodies. The General and the women identified their husbands. Katie held Jack in her arms and could not let go. She did not have the chance to mourn for Sequoya, and now she could not let go of Jack. She wanted to hold him forever. She wanted to join him in heaven. She vowed that she would never marry, and she would meet him in heaven as soon as the Lord would take her. The General had to force Katie off Jack's dead body, and he and his wife helped her to her quarters. "Katie, is there anything we can do for you?"

"No thank you," she whispered.

The new troops arrived and all of the soldiers began digging graves. The coroner built caskets, and the funeral was scheduled for Sunday. Katie stayed with Alexandria because she could not bare to be alone. The fort was somber and silent with morning women.

The Pastor performed a long funeral, addressing each man and his family. They all prayed. Dreams were shattered, and tears were shed, not only for Katie, but for all the women, including Alexandria. Katie placed a red rose on Jack's casket and kissed it with her lips. She told him good-bye for now and left with the precession of mourners.

There was nothing left here for Katie, and she decided to sell her goods and take a stagecoach west with Alexandria who was joining her sister in Virginia City.

Alexandria found Katie in the barn that evening. She was on her knees holding Maggie's neck. She silently watched as Katie cried. Katie knew that she would not be able to take her beloved Jersey or the gelding. She sold them to the General's wife and knew they would have a good life with them. She still would miss her terribly. Understanding Katie's sorrow, she waited until Katie finished saying good-bye, and then she walked her back to their quarters.

Because Sequoya knew the soldiers would soon look for them, he led his people deeper into to the wilderness. They had previously scouted a new camp, well hidden and protected. They packed their homes and moved them further southwest. Their numbers were many, but they moved swiftly. Every member of the tribe was fit, and they worked hard to carry their plan out perfectly.

Their new home was situated on a hilltop that provided cover and lookout points. They would be able to see anyone coming for miles and could protect themselves easily. There was ample water, and plenty of wild game to hunt.

Sequoya knew he would not be able to find Katie and bring her back. If he did, her life would be in danger, just as their lives were. He spent a lot of time alone and thought of her often. Although his life would never be the same without her, he finally took a Comanche bride. He was now the clan's Chief, and it was essential to his tribe that he take a woman. He must have children to carry on for him when he was gone. Her name was Kahuu, and although he did not love her, she was a dutiful wife. She was a beautiful, young woman and loved him immensely.

The soldiers never found them, and the tribe lived in peace and happiness, until the white man eventually pushed their way into their lives. The white people they met were friendly, and they traded among them. They brought white Priests that taught of their God. The white God was strange to Sequoya because he was so different from Wakonda and the spirits. He struggled with the possibility that the white man's God must be much more powerful than Wakonda to allow the white man to win this battle and push them from their homeland.

Chapter Seventeen
The Bandits and The Opera

"How could one persons' life hold so much sorrow?" Katherine sobbed as she pulled herself out of her bed. She reflected on her trip across the trail and pondered where the battle might have taken place.

If Sequoya knew who he was killing, he would never have done it. She felt the sorrow and regret that he felt, and it was killing her. She felt the pain that Katie felt, and it was also killing her. She did not know if she could watch Katie go through anymore anguish. Katie had changed. She was dead and empty inside. She did not care if she lived or died. Katherine hoped that one day Katie would reunite with Sequoya and that she would never know what he did.

Because she had to go west to Los Angeles, Katherine decided she would continue her journey with Katie to Virginia City. She hoped that the move would bring happiness to Katie.

She drove across the country, thinking of Katie's journey and how awful it must have been in her mental state. She drove all day and stopped in Salt Lake City for the night. She updated her journal and went to sleep early.

XXXX

Katie spent the morning at Jack's grave. "It is so hard for me to leave you here, Jack, but I can't stay. I have nothing left. Everything has been taken from me. I'm going to Virginia City with Alexandria. I know you wouldn't approve, but I'm not afraid of the danger. If I die, I'll be with you, my dear husband." She paused trying to fight off the tears. "I can't wait until I can be with you again. I know I'll be able to talk to you anywhere, so I won't say farewell."

She walked back to town and attempted to eat breakfast with Alexandria. Both of the women were melancholy and silent.

The stage left at nine in the morning, and Katie and Alexandria were on it. Katie gazed out the window and thought about Jack. She thought about how they spent their time together, and how she missed his touch. She felt dead inside. All was lost to her. She thought she would welcome death, so she could be reunited with Jack again in heaven.

The women did not talk about their sorrow. They were both feeling the same feelings and did not feel the need to share them. When they were alone, Alexandria cried a lot, and Katie just held her with silent acknowledgment and understanding. They stared out the windows empty minded and numb.

The stage stopped each night at small settlements along the Oregon Trail where they roomed together to save money. Each morning they ate breakfast before boarding the stage. They were joined by many passengers for short distances, but all had gotten off at different destinations. Many passengers told them stories, and they politely listened but could not wait to be alone again. They had seen the landscape change across the country from wooded hills, to endless prairies and then to vast salt flats. They would be turning south soon to take the California Trail to Virginia City.

When the stage driver announced that they were entering Utah Territory, the women watched for a change of scenery. They climbed a long pass and were going down the other side. The view was fantastic. The rocky hills were dotted with junipers and sagebrush that filled the air with the most sensational aroma as they drove through it. Katie thought again about Jack and how she missed him and Sequoya. She wondered if they watched down on her and could see this strange land. She wished that she was with them where ever they were.

As they descended down the canyon, they heard gun shots. They looked out the window of the stage to see some bandits chasing them with guns blazing. The drivers brought the stage to a halt, and the girls held each other in the seat of the stage braced for what was to happen next. Katie's heart was beating fast and hard in her chest, and Alexandria began to cry. "Katie, what will happen to us next! Will it never end?"

"It's alright, Alexandria. It's alright," Katie whispered, putting her arms around her.

Two men pointed their six guns on the drivers, and the third pointed his gun at Katie and Alexandria. The man that seemed to be the gang boss told the drivers, "Get down off the stage, boys."

The men were wearing hats and black cloth handkerchiefs covering their faces. Katie could only see their eyes.

The same man shouted at the second man, "Get the bags down." Then he told the third, "Get those women out of there!" He grabbed Katie by her arm and then Alexandra, pulling them from the stage. He slammed them up against the stage and touched Katie's chin with his gun. He pushed the gun into her cheek and put his hand on her breast. He started to kiss her face when the boss scorned him, "There is no time for that." Katie looked at Alexandria with relief. Tears were streaming down Alexandria's face as she tried to be silent and hold them back.

The second man scavenged through the baggage, throwing the contents through the air and out onto the desert. Loading the saddle bags that were strapped onto their horses, they took anything of value. The third man pushed his gun into Katie's cheek and kissed her on the lips, pushing her up against the stage. He pointed his gun at her head, and she closed her eyes.

Finally, the boss shouted, "Lets go!"

The second man backed up slowly with his gun still pointing at the women and mounted his horse. They ran up into the canyon.

Katie and Alexandria cried and held each other as the drivers picked up all the pieces and loaded them and the women into the stage. They headed on to Virginia City with nothing left but their clothes.

The white men met with Sequoya and his tribe and spoke of a treaty. They promised a safe and fruitful place for the tribe to live and safe passage to it. Sequoya wanted his tribe and his new bride to be safe. He knew that a war would never be won with the white soldiers and their white God. So he agreed to the treaty.

It was late when Katie and Alexandria arrived in Virginia City. They were surprised at the size of the city and the activity that was still going on there so late at night. "Maybe we should stay at a hotel for the night and find my sister in the morning," Alexandria said. She was staring with amazement at the lights and noise in the streets.

"I think that would probably be a good idea. Your sister is probably sleeping by now and since she is not expecting us, it would probably be best."

The driver got their bags and took them into the hotel. He took the liberty of explaining the robbery to the Hotel owner and said that he would pay for the Katie and Alexandria's room personally after he spoke to the stage office in the morning. The women went up to their room and fell asleep, exhausted.

The next morning they cleaned up in the bath house and ate breakfast before asking the hotel clerk if he knew Alexandria's sister, Annabelle.

"Why yes, Miss Gardner, but I don't think you will find her awake at this hour!" he looked puzzled.

Alexandria looked at Katie confused. "What do you mean?"

"She didn't tell you?" he said.

"I haven't seen my sister in over four years, Sir." Alexandria was loosing her patients. "What is it?"

"Ma'am," he paused. "I don't know how to tell you this, but Annabelle owns the saloon next door."

Alexandria's mouth fell open as she turned and looked at Katie. "What shall I do?"

Katie immediately replied, "We go and see her, of course!"

The two women went next door, and the saloon doors were locked. A sign in door read, "Closed - Open at 11:00 am."

Alexandria looked at Katie with determination and rapped loudly on the door.

Katie smiled for the first time in weeks. She was amused by Alexandria's reaction to the news of her sisters profession.

Finally, a man came to the door and pulled the curtains aside to look out. He was in his night clothes, and Alexandria turned around quickly and looked the other way.

Katie giggled at her.

The man unlocked the door and said, "I am sorry, Miss, but you must have the wrong place!"

Katie spoke for Alexandria, "No Sir, we have the right place. This is Alexandria Gardner, and she is looking for her sister, Annabelle.

"Well, I'll be!" the man said with a surprised expression. "Well, come right in and I'll fetch her!"

Katie grabbed Alexandria's arm and turned her around and pushed her through the door. The man locked the door behind them and said, "I'll be right back!"

The saloon had an overpowering scent of blooming roses. Katie assumed it was meant to cover up the smell of whiskey and tobacco. Neither of the women had ever been in a saloon, but then, not many women had. There was a long bar lined with stools on the right side, and against the wall behind it, was a large cabinet with whiskey bottles, glasses and two of the most beautiful cash registers that she had ever seen. Three large mirrors and candle chandeliers lit the area. On the other side of the room, was several small tables and chairs and, in the back corner, was a gambling table. Two glass doors went into a back room. Above the glass doors, overlooking the saloon was one glass door. She wondered what it was for. There was no way to get down from it. She glanced over at Alexandria, who was still in shock with her mouth open. She looked as if she were lost and looking for a way out. Again, Katie laughed and said, "Look, Alexandria, this is nothing compared to what we have been through! Toughen up!"

"Katie!" She gave her a shocked look.

Annabelle finally came through the glass doors. She was coming toward Alexandria at a full run with her arms out. Her hair was down, it was shiny, with curls that bounced as she ran. She was as beautiful as Alexandria but a little older.

Annabelle was extremely excited to see Alexandria. Tears filled her eyes as she held her sister in her arm. "Alexandria, I thought I would never see you again." Katie could see the shame in Annabelle's eyes when she explained her heart breaking story. "I didn't ever want you to see me like this and certainly didn't want you to know what I do." She held her sister back and took a long look at her. "You are so beautiful! Come! Come up to the kitchen and sit." She started to drag her along beside her. Katie followed with Alexandria's son, Jacob.

"Oh wait, this is my friend, Katie," Alexandria introduced them.

"Oh, welcome. Please come along." She took them through the glass doors, up a spiral staircase, down to the end of a hall and into a kitchen.

Katie guessed that all of the doors down the hallway were rooms and that the upstairs was a hotel. She asked, "You also board out rooms? It looks very nice."

"Sit down here. I will make some coffee and explain it all to you both." Annabelle pulled out two chairs at the table and put a pot of water to boil on the cook stove. She sat with them, "My husband, Tom, and I moved here four years ago. Two years ago, he was killed in a mining accident. The mine caved in and killed twelve men, including Tom."

Alexandria was starting to feel as though the whole world was falling apart. It seemed as if everyone that she knew were coming on hard times. "I am sorry, Annabelle."

Annabelle continued, "My husband was good friends

with Bill who tends bar here at the saloon." Annabelle lifted her chin and continued, "I was lucky that we had been able to save enough to purchase it. I know it isn't what you were expecting, but it isn't the sort of thing that you write home about." Katie could tell that she had been hardened by her circumstances, just as her and Alexandria had become. "Where are Ma and Pa?"

"Our wagons were attacked by Indians, Annabelle..." Alexandria explained.

"Oh, my God, Alexandria! You poor thing!" She held her sister while they both cried.

Katie excused herself and went back down stairs and sat at the bar to give them time to mourn. Katie was quiet, so the bartender set a bottle of whiskey and a tumbler in front of her.

She held the glass in her hand and looked at him, "I have never tasted it."

He picked up the bottle and poured a bit in the bottom of the glass. "It's better if ya drink it right down. All at once. Real fast like."

She lifted the glass and drank it down, all in one swift gulp. Her face turned red, and she made a funny face.

The bartender giggled when she slid the glass back toward him, "Another, please."

"Well, at least ya have manners!" He poured her another, and she drank it.

"What is your name?" she asked.

"Just call me Rick," he said offering his hand to her.

She shook it and turned, "What's the door up there for?"

"You don't know?" he paused for a moment and thought before sighing deeply. "Well, I guess ya wouldn't. Well, this is a saloon and it's a brothel." He looked at her and noticed the blank stare on her face. "Do you know what a brothel is, Miss Katie?"

She looked into his eyes and cocked her brows, "I guess I don't."

He put his elbows on the bar and leaned in toward her. He lowered his voice. "Do you know what a prostitute is?"

Katie felt a bit sassy from the whiskey and slurred her words a bit. "No, I guess I don't know that either."

"They sell sexual favors to men that come into the saloon," he whispered.

She leaned in closer toward him and whisper back, "Oh My! She paused for a moment trying to grasp the idea. "What's that got to do with the door?"

He could not help himself any longer, and he laughed loudly. Katie was drunk, and she was truly comical. "The women aren't allowed down here, so they show themselves up there in that doorway. If a man wants 'em, he picks 'em."

Katie sat back on the bar stool and thought for a moment before asking, "Do they make a lot of money?"

"I reckon they do," he replied.

Just then Alexandria came through the glass doors and sat down beside Katie.

Rick put another glass down beside her and pushed the whiskey bottle toward her.

Alexandria looked at Katie scornfully and lifted her brow, "You've been drinking?"

"I thank yer gonna need a couple of those, before I go and tell ya what that there door's for," she slurred and grinned at Alexandria trying to look serious.

Alexandria looked at Rick, and he tilted his head and shrugged his shoulders in agreement. She looked back at Katie defiantly and grabbed the glass.

Rick filled the bottom of her glass, and she sipped it, spitting it out on the floor in front of her. "That's terrible!"

"No, Alexandria, ya gotta drink it real fast, like this,"

she took the glass from Alexandria's hand and drank the rest of it.

Looking at Katie with her mouth gaping open, Alexandria finally smiled at her and said with much determination, "If you can do it, I can do it."

Rick filled the bottom of the glass again, "I guarantee ya, your much more fun than the stuffy, old businessmen that come in here!" Rick was nice to them.

Somehow, with the assistance of the whiskey and Ricks' sense of humor, the girls began to loosen up and their moods lightened.

Rick's hair was slicked back, and he had a long, well groomed mustache. He wore a white shirt with a garter on his sleeve and a vest, pants and boots. He was a middle aged man but carried himself well, and his stature demanded respect.

Alexandria drank one and then another. She looked at Katie with a serious expression and leaned over to whisper in her ear. "My sister told me what the door is for and asked me if I wanted to stay!"

"I'm stayin', if they'll have me," Katie said.

Just then, Annabelle approached them, "That sounds great! I am glad to have you!"

"If your stayin', I'm stayin'," Alexandria said.

They sat and drank all morning, as Annabelle explained the rules to them. "You need not use your real names. I use Belle, and I never tell anyone my last name. Alexandria, you can go by Alex. Katie..."

"Kit," Katie interrupted, "I'll go by Kit!"

"You aren't allowed downstairs. The men around here are highfalutin, and they don't want their wives thinkin' that their messin' around," she said. "You'll use the window, and they'll come up if they want ya.

Rick doesn't allow any misconduct in his bar. He has

a way with people and is usually able to talk them out of drunken foolishness. He is able to prod a conversation out of anyone and will let me know about any unsavory characters." Belle showed them around and gave them their own rooms. The rooms were meticulous; meals were provided and prepared by a cook, and the pay was excellent.

They all sat and ate lunch, and soon each of their individual stories were revealed. Katie was reluctant but told her story to Belle, and Alexandria told hers. Belle was highly sympathetic to them both and was excited about her new nephew. She was devastated about her parents. She wished that she could have seen them or at least seen their graves. She had not been able to say good-bye. Belle excused herself and went to her room quietly.

Katie and Alexandria finished their lunch and went up to their rooms to unpack and take a nap before the evening crowd arrived. They were both intensely nervous, but Belle told them that after the first time, it would all be "old hat." By this time, they both seemed to face whatever life dealt to them. They did not have a choice.

Many men came into the saloon. Some were wealthy, and some were hard working miners. They were all there to have fun. Alexandria was terribly nervous, and Katie was anxious to be done with it, so she went first. She followed another woman that had been there for a while. She stood in front of the glass doorway, just as Belle had shown her. She was dressed in a camisole, net stockings with a garter and shoes with heals. Her hair was up with a few tight curls falling down her back and she wore some feathers in it. She could not hear the men below, but she noticed they all looked at her and some were pointing and cheering. She was embarrassed but hoped that it did not show. The men starting raising their hands. They were bidding. Her emotions were mixed. She was ashamed but flattered. She decided to concentrate on the flattered feeling, because she knew that it would not do her any good to feel ashamed. The cheering and bidding stopped, and a young, handsome and strong looking man stood and walked to the double glass doors. She went down the hall way and greeted him on the spiral stair case. He walked up the staircase with a bottle of whiskey and two glasses in his hand. He put his arm around her, and she took him to her room.

It was not long before the effect of the alcohol relaxed Katie. She laughed and found herself wanting to be held. She needed the affection that the man wanted to give her. He asked her name, and she told him, "My name is Kit."

"It is very nice to meet you, Kit." He introduced himself, "My name is Jim. I come to town quite often. I do some engineering for a mining company here in Virginia City."

The night grew old, and Jim laughed and joked with Kit. Soon, one thing led to another. Jim sat in a chair and pulled Kit down, straddling his lap. He pulled her closer and kissed her. The lanterns were low, and it was almost dark. The whiskey and the low lights made Kit's imagination soar. As Jim touched her softly, she closed her eyes and, deep in her mind, she dreamed that he was Jack. It was so much easier than she had imagined. The mood was set by the lighting and the alcohol. She knew that he was not Jack, but she was desperately clinging to his memory.

He was kissing her and began to untie her corset. He was freshly bathed and shaved and was wearing an inviting cologne. He smelled masculine, and she let him undress her. Piece by piece, her clothing fell to the floor until she found herself naked. She helped Jim remove his clothing, and they moved to the bed. As he pressed against her body, she began to move with his movements. She thought of Jack and she let it happen, not once looking back to regret it. The room felt steamy with sexual excitement. When the hour passed, they fell to the bed and slept naked tell daylight.

Kit woke up about noon. She found money on her pillow, and Jim was gone. Katie went down to the kitchen. Alex turned and looked at her, with curious eyes. They both began to giggle and held their heads. They had hangovers from the whiskey they drank the night before. Both in their night clothes, they went down the hall into the bath house. There was a copper tub they filled with hot water that they had warmed on the wood stove. Kit dropped her clothes on the floor. Her body was still as beautiful as ever, since she never bore children. Alex and Kit bathed together, washing the soreness away from the night before.

"Tell me what happened, Katie!" Alexandria could hardly stand the suspense.

"It was easy, Alexandria. I don't know how to explain this, but I just pretended it was Jack, and it was easy! Tell me about your night?"

"It wasn't as easy. I will have to remember that. Maybe, if I think of Michael, it won't be so bad. He was very handsome, and he let me drink some more whiskey and, after a while, it wasn't so bad."

Katie felt sorry for Alexandria. She had never had a sexual experience with someone she loved, but maybe it was better for her, not to know what she is missing.

After their bath, the girls dressed and went down the hall for coffee and a late breakfast. Belle was up, and the girls all ate together with Jacob. They went from the kitchen to the bar. It was quiet, and the girls sat and talked to Rick. Jacob played on the floor with some toys that Cookie had bought for him. Rick said that the day had been slow, but he expected it to be busy tonight. Kit drank a couple shots of whiskey and went up to her room and laid down on her bed. She thought about Jack and Sequoya and drifted into a deep slumber.

Kahuu was at the river bathing with the other women and children. When Sequoya and the men returned from their hunt, they brought their kill to the women as usual. As his horse stepped into the river, he heard Kahuu scream. He looked and saw a moving mass of water moccasins coiling up around her, biting her. He jumped from his horse and ran to her, beating the snakes away with his long bow. He grabbed a hold of her and picked her up out of the water. He stood holding her in a panic. He looked her over and saw where she had been bitten several times on her arms, neck and chest. She looked into her husbands eyes and choked and wheezed, and blood started to come from her mouth. She had a look of panic and disbelief in her eyes. She knew, as did he, that there was nothing that could be done. She looked into his eyes and said, "I am scared, Sequoya."

He kissed her cheek and her forehead and held her face close to his. He did not know what to do. He did not know what to say. If he could only save her from her fate, he would gladly take her place.

She whispered in his ear, as he held her close to him, "Good bye, Sequoya," and faded away in his arms.

Sequoya held her close, rocking back and forth with her body in his arms and cried loudly. He could not save her like he saved Katie that day, such a long time ago.

Virginia City was a bustling city. The amount of gold there was more than anywhere else in the world, and people were coming from everywhere. The bar was busy every night and so was Kit. She met a lot of men and made a great deal of money. Rick was a shrewd businessman and took her to the bank to open an account. She saved all of her money in it. She told him, "One day, I will go to California and retire in comfort," but for now, she was busy and enjoyed her business. Not all the men were as nice to her as her first, and not all were as young and strong and clean. Sometimes, she did not enjoy it as much as others, but for the most part, it was a decent job.

Jim came to see Kit often. He came in and bid until he won and one night he asked her to attend the Opera with him. They had just finished the construction of the Piper Opera House and the grand opening would be a monumental affair. Only the best entertainers were invited to perform there. She agreed to go, and Jim bought her a new dress. He paid handsomely for two seats in one of the boxes in the front that they would share with some of the most influential people of Virginia City.

It was a enormous building made of stone. The entry way was large and had a small window where one could present or buy tickets. There was a window next to it where the men were required to check their guns. A large doorway opened up into a great hall with rounded ceilings lined with linen. Chairs were crowded on the floor with a narrow aisle in between them. They were among the first to enter and were escorted directly to their seats and served champagne. Katie was amazed. It was two or three times as large as the grand hall at the fort. "It's beautiful, Jim!"

Jim liked Katie a great deal, and she thought that he would marry her if she would agree. He knew about her life, and she had told him that she would never again marry. "Nothing is as beautiful as you are, Kit!" He took her hand and kissed it.

The box where they sat had red velvet and gold wall covering and was trimmed in heavy, red-velvet curtains. It was funny in a way, the view of the stage from the box was not particularly good, but everyone else in Pipers Opera House was sure to see the wealthy and influential people who sat in them. It was more for status than for comfort and visibility.

None the less, Katie cried as the Opera was presented and the beautiful woman sang. Her voice was astonishing. None of the women knew who Katie was, and she felt like a princess.

For the amount of money that was being circulated in Virginia City, it was surprisingly calm most of the time. There was gambling and drinking and laughter and fights, but the girls were not allowed downstairs, so it was relatively safe. A time or two, there was even gunshots but that only happened when someone was cheating at Faro. Rick and Belle did not let questionable men upstairs and sometimes they sent for the sheriff to haul the rough men out of the saloon. The sheriff was a genial man. He even frequented the saloon, a time or two, but usually on off hours.

Sequoya and a few of his men were invited and escorted to Washington D.C. They were to sign the treaty that was to protect their tribe. The white man's world was so different from theirs. They had so many material things, but they did not worship the land like the Indians did. White people believed that they owned the land, while the Indians just used it carefully and left it as they found it. It seemed strange for the Indians that the white man was giving them land that did not belong to them to give. They met with the whites, and Sequoya trusted them and did as they said. He believed that it was the best thing for his people.

Sequoya watched in amazement while a man stood behind a little box that sat on a stool. The man covered himself with a black cloth, and Sequoya jumped when it popped loudly and a flash of light came from it. It startled Sequoya and his people. The box made a photograph that was given to them when they left to return home.

After returning home, the tribe packed their homes and moved a long distance to a reservation in the unorganized territory to the west. The trip was long, and most of the promises made to them were not kept. Ample food was not provided, and the trip was hard. The Indians were able to hunt and provide food for their people.

When they reached their destination, their supplies were not enough. Again, they possessed the skills and were able to provide for their tribe.

Chapter Eighteen
The Desire and The Disappointment

When Katherine woke, she giggled. "What would mother say?" She wondered if this were the reason her mother did not speak of her ancestors. She always wanted everyone to think that her past was free of blemishes. Katherine was a bit bitter when it came to her mother and father. They both gave her what ever she wanted except for love. Love is all Katherine ever wanted.

She knew how Katie felt. She longed to be loved. Until now, Katherine was not sure that real love existed. She never took it seriously because her mother and father seemed so miserable. Never seeing them touch or kiss or even speak nicely to each other, she always thought that she could easily get through life without love. She did not need the money. Even if she did not have the family fortune, she was smart enough to take care of herself.

"Poor Katie." She was smart enough, but she had such rotten luck.

As soon as Katherine ate and gassed her car up, she headed west. She crossed the vast expanse of salt flats. She

thought it would never end. Then she came upon a summit.
The countryside looked just like it did in her dream where
the bandits stopped the stage. She stopped and looked at the
juniper covered hills. She took deep breaths. The sweet
smell of sage was incredible. She had a long drive ahead
and only stopped for coffee and drive-through meals.
Passing through Reno, she climbed the long mountain to the
top where Virginia City was located. In a rugged sort of
way, it was breathtakingly beautiful. She knew it would be
late when she arrived, so she had called ahead and reserved
a room at a historic hotel. She went straight up and got into
bed.

XXXX

One morning, Kit sat reading a newspaper at breakfast
and noticed a familiar picture on the front page. A chill ran
down her spine, "Oh, my dear Lord, it's Sequoya." She
could not believe her eyes. He was in Washington D.C.
meeting with the President to sign a peace treaty. Her heart
filled with joy and her blood seemed to pump new hope into
her body. He was alive. What would she do? Could she
find him? Did she want to find him? So much had
happened in her life since they were together. She did not
know if she could go back to the Indian way of life. She
knew that he could not live in the white man's world. She
looked at the photo again. He was wearing white man's
clothes, but it was him. He looked healthy. The article said
that Indians were being moved to a reservation in the
unorganized territory just to the west of Missouri.

She wondered if he remarried, or if he could still be
looking for her. She felt at peace, knowing that he did not
die on that terrible day so many years ago.

Kit was drinking with a man that had come upstairs

for her. She had never seen him before. He was young and handsome, but she was distracted by the news that she had discovered in the paper that very morning. They drank some whiskey, but her mind was wandering.

He put his glass down and pulled her up close to him. He slammed her up against the door passionately and pressed himself into her and kissed her.

Kit closed her eyes, and in her mind, the tall, dark, handsome man turned into Sequoya. She was numb to her surroundings. Her mind was somewhere else, far away in Sequoya's arms under the waterfall where they used to go to make love. It was as if he were beckoning her to come to him. She held him tight and made passionate love to him. Kissing his body, she told him that she loved him. Katie was deep into the emotional daydream that she was having about Sequoya. With a smile on her face, she opened her eyes, that were now sparkling with love.

Coming to her senses, she apologized to the tall, dark haired man as the smile left her face and the sparkle left her eyes. He accepted her apology, paid her and left the room. Katie laid on the bed thinking of Sequoya and fell asleep.

When she woke, she still could not get Sequoya off her mind. Missing him so, she wanted to see him again. She had been happy in Virginia City only because she was dead to everything else. Realizing that she wanted more than anything, to be loved by Sequoya again, she decided that she was going to find him.

The next morning at breakfast Katie told Rick, Alex and Belle about his picture in the paper. "I have to find him. I need to let him know that I am alive, and I still love him. I am going to travel to the reservation to find him."

They understood. "We will miss you, Katie," Alexandria sobbed. "You are like a sister to me, and I don't know what I'll do without you!"

"You are always welcome back here, Kit, if you ever want to return," Belle told her as she held her tight.

Rick just hugged her with sadness in his eyes, "We will never forget you, Kit. Don't forget us!"

She assured them that she would remember them always. They held a portion of her heart forever.

Katie boarded the stage the next morning after the last breakfast that she would ever spend with her friends. They saw her off, and she waved to them with excitement.

The journey to her destination was a long one. She had no trouble with bandits. She had sewn her bank draft in her corset, just in case. She traveled with just enough money to get there. When she arrived, it was mid summer. The air was dry and brisk at night.

The stagecoach stopped at the town nearest to the reservation, and she purchased a meal and a room for the night. She spoke to the desk clerk, "I need to hire transportation to the Osage Reservation tomorrow."

He advised against it, "Ma'am, that is no place for a lady. Ya never know what those savages are gonna do."

"I know the people there. I am not afraid," she told him, trying to shame him with her tone.

He looked at her curiously, "Maybe, I can get George to take ya on out there."

The next morning, Katie ate her breakfast and her driver, George, picked her up on time in front of the hotel. He was annoyingly talkative, "I know the Indians well, Ma'am. I come out here every week to bring 'em their supplies. I'll be goin' back out there tomorrow."

The drive took half of a day, and when she arrived, the men were on a hunt just like the days when she was with the tribe. She knew no one. George asked for an interpreter, and they brought a woman about Katie's age. Katie was surprised and laughed with excitement when she recognized her. "Tanis! You are alive!" She was a survivor from the attack and recognized Katie instantly.

Tanis took her into their village. The women of the tribe welcomed her, and she sat with them while they made moccasins. They had beads made of turquoise and laces made of leather. Katie spent the afternoon with the women and children and felt so much at home. She was excited to see Sequoya, but Tanis told her that he would not return until the next day. "Their hunting trips take days now that we are on the reservation.

Sequoya is our chief now." She told her about how they survived, "Sequoya was there when you called out to him from the burial grounds. He felt so much pain when he could not come to you. Because he knew that you would be safer with your people, he let you go. He had to take care of us, but he wanted to go to you. There were only a few of us left, and we were all hurt. So was he."

She saw the tears in Katie's eyes when she told her, "He still rides in the hills. I know he is thinking about you. He married, but his Comanche wife was killed by water moccasins.

She began to tell Katie about the revenge that the Indians took on the white soldiers.

Realizing what Tanis was saying, Katie jumped to her feet and ran to the wagon, as Tanis called to her wondering what was the matter.

George was at the wagon napping while he waited for Katie. "Take me back to town, George."

He scurried to his feet. "But, Ma'am..."

"Now, George, take me now!" she screamed.

Tears were in her eyes, and she cried while George sat speechless. All of the things that Tanis had told her ran through her mind over and over. She loved Sequoya with all her heart, but she could not come to terms with the fact that he could have been the one that killed her husband.   She had nowhere to turn. Then she remembered Abby.

She asked George, "Is there a stage to Independence, Missouri?"

"Yes, Ma'am," He said. There is one that leaves first thing in the morning. What happened."

I don't want to talk about it," she snapped at him. "I have an old friend there."

I lived in Independence for a spell. Who is it?" He looked at her, waiting for an answer.

"Abby Sternwall," she said.

"I know her. She works at one of the nicest hotels in Independence. Poor thing, her husband left her and never came back to get her," he spit over his side of the wagon and wiped his mouth with his sleeve.

Katie purchased her stage tickets and went back to her hotel room. She packed her bags and sat in the chair by the window that overlooked the street. She sat there all night, thinking of Sequoya. She knew it was not his fault. She had told him about Jack, and how she fell in love with him in Pennsylvania, but Sequoya did not know he was with the soldiers the day of the battle. She still could not forgive him.

In the morning, Katie boarded the stage to Independence, Missouri. She felt as if her dreams had been snatched away from her again. She was alone on the stage, and she laid across the bench. Using her bag as a pillow, she fell asleep.

Chapter Nineteen
The Mad Man and The Rescue

"Oh no! Katie, don't do it. He loves you, and you love him. It is not his fault. Don't leave him!" Katherine could not believe she left without seeing him. "Katie should have spoken to him."

She sat on the edge of her bed and held her head. She wished that she could go back and change it for her. She would tell her to go back and live happily.

Katherine remembered the death certificate. Mrs. Mary Kate Martin Standing Bear. "She must go back. She has too!"

She knew it was time. She had to go to Los Angeles, but she wanted to walk up and down the streets of Virginia City first. Some of the buildings that still stand today were present in the 1850's, and she wanted to see them. After she showered, packed her bag, ate her breakfast, she bought her coffee and walked down the street. She stopped anywhere that looked familiar. Opening a door to a bar, she recognized it immediately. It was almost the same! The door was still hovering up on the second floor with no steps to get down. She went through the glass doors and touched the old, spiral staircase. The upstairs was blockaded, no longer safe due to its age. She had a Bloody Mary at the bar and talked to the barmaid about the history of the building. It was amazing. Story has it, there is a ghost in the building. The ghost is supposedly a "woman in blue," who was a madame in the 1850's. She died there. Katherine looked around and wondered if it might be Belle.

She crossed the Sierra Nevada Mountain range and into California. She stopped in Sacramento for lunch, San Francisco for Dinner and then into Los Angeles. She arrived late, purchased a room and slipped into bed.

XXXX

Katie arrived at the Hotel where she and her family had left Abby. She went inside and asked the clerk about Abby. The young man did not know Abby, but said he would go and ask the manager. The stage driver brought Katie's bag and the man returned and told Katie that the Sternwall's lived a mile south of town, just past the bridge on the left. He asked Katie if she would like a room. She said yes, and decided to eat, bathe and sleep before searching for Abby.

Later that night, Katie stood and looked out the window. She noticed the construction of a hangman's platform. She thought about how awful it would be for the man to watch the platform construction from his jail cell. It gave her the chills, and she closed the window and went to bed.

The next morning, Katie woke to cheering in the streets. The sun was trying to push its rays through the drapes that covered the window in her room. She went to the window and opened the drapes. She saw a crowd gathering around the hangman's platform and remembered what she had seen the night before. She watched as they led the man out of the sheriff's office. The crowd hovered closer and closer, and she could not see him. Katie thought about how morbid the hanging would be and was about to close the window when she caught a glimpse of him. She stepped closer to the window to take a closer look. Her heart began to pound in her chest when she realized it was the renegade. She watched closely as they walked him up the twelve steps and onto the platform. They stood him over the trap door in the floor and placed the rope around his neck that hung from the heavy beam above. Just then, as she looked at his face, she saw that he was looking at her. He glared at her and spit. She raised her brow and glared back at him with a slight squint in her eyes. She had never hated anyone more than she hated that man and she asked God to forgive her for wanting to see him hang. The trap door opened, and he dropped. She could see him kick his feet and wiggle on the rope for what seemed to take an eternaty. She let a long breath of relief escape from deep in her chest, and she closed the curtains.

It was a sunny day and after the crowd had dispersed, she took her bag and went to the livery stable. She did not feel like talking to anyone, so she decided to drive herself. She rented a horse and buggy and set off toward Abby's house.

While she drove, Katie thought about how Sequoya saved her from that dreadful man. She drove a mile south and crossed the bridge. She turned a corner and on the left, was a prodigious entrance to a beautiful ranch. The pastures were filled with cattle as far as she could see. She looked up at the iron entry and "Sternwall" was written over the driveway. She drove her buggy down the long drive and came to a cluster of buildings and barns. The house was the furthest building down the lane, and she continued until she reached it. It was a grand, two story mansion with beautiful grounds surrounding it. Katie hesitated a moment, not knowing if she had the right Sternwall house. As she positioned her brake and wrapped her reins around the hook on her buggy, two men rode up on horses. One man spoke in an unfriendly manner, asking what she was doing there. She looked up starting to apologize and recognized the man. It was Billy Sternwall. He had matured into a handsome man but seemed very unkind when he excused the man beside him. She thought to herself, "He must have had a bad day."

Billy recognized her immediately and the rude and irritated facial expression vanished from his face. "Katie? Katie Martin?" He dismounted and ran to her side of the carriage. He stretched out his arm and offered her his hand.

She put her hand in his, "Yes, it is me, Billy. How are you?"

"I am wonderful now, Katie!" He put her hand on the inside of his elbow and led her to the house. " Please, Katie, stay and dine with me, won't you?"

"I would love to, Billy," she said.

Katie sat with him in the parlor. The room was decorated in the best furnishing from Europe, but the heavy drapes that covered the windows made it dark and cold in the room. The room gave Katie an eerie feeling.

An Asian women entered the room with some tea. The woman set the tea tray down on the table. She seemed terribly timid and nervous and asked Katie, "Would you like some sugar?"

Her nervousness puzzled Katie, "Oh, yes, please. Thank you!"

The women put some sugar in Katie's tea and left the room.

Katie asked Billy, "How is your mother, Billy? Is she home?"

His face grew serious, and his mood was bitter and cold, "They killed her."

"What do you mean, Billy?" Katie was sad and shocked.

"They worked her to death." He looked crazed with anger. "She worked so hard at that hotel when I was away working. When I returned she was sick, Katie. She was dying, and I couldn't save her." He fought the tears from his eyes.

Then Katie noticed that Billy's mood changed back to friendly almost as fast as it had gone sour. It was like there were two people in his body. His thoughts turned to supper, and he became excited.

He called the Asian woman into the room and told her, "Set the table for two. Miss Martin will be joining me for supper."

Katie felt uneasy, and she interrupted, "I really need to get back to town and take the buggy back before dark."

Billy insisted, "I won't hear of it. I will have my man take it back, and I will drive you back to town in the morning. You can stay in the guest room tonight."

Billy poured a glass of whiskey, "Would you like a drink, Katie?"

"No thank you, Billy," she replied.

"You know, after you left us here, all I had was my fathers riding horse, so I got on with a man, herding cattle from Texas. I helped to organized the first cattle drive to Independence. In no time, I was able to build an empire from scratch."

Katie quickly realized that Billy had changed. He had become consumed with conceit, greed and power. He took her hand and led her to the dining room. A huge, long table filled the room and was lined with eight bulky, tall-backed, wooden chairs. A crystal chandelier hung over the table filled with several candles.

The Asian woman served dinner from the sideboard situated along the wall next to the table. Katie sat at the table, picking at her food and listening to Billy. She wondered what she was going to do. Abby was gone, and she regretted that she did not stay at the reservation. She knew that she loved Sequoya and, even though he led the raid that killed her husband, nothing would stop the love that she felt for him.

The Asia woman was serving some wine to Billy when she lost her grip, and the crystal long-stem glass slid from her hand. It broke when it hit the floor right by Billy's feet. Katie jumped up to help her pick up the pieces. The woman began to cry, and Katie tried to console her. "It's alright, Ma'am! Are you alright?"

Billy turned his chair and kicked her, pushing her up against the wall. "You are a clumsy tramp!"

"Billy," Katie gasped. "What are you doing?" She helped the woman to her feet. "Are you alright?" She looked back at Billy, "I can't believe you just did that, Billy!"

He snapped at her, "My name is William!"

Katie pulled the woman by her arm and started for the door.

When Billy realized what she was doing, he ran in front of her. Grabbing her by both her arms, he held her there and said, "Katie, Katie, please, don't go!" He begged her. By this time, he was calm and collected. He apologized, "I am so sorry, I don't know what has come over me. It has been so hard for me since Ma died. I promise. I don't usually act this way!"

"I have to go, Billy. I need to get back to the hotel."

He squeezed her arms and pulled her up the stairs. "I won't hear of it. You will stay here with me. He marched her up the stairs, dragging her by her arm. He told the Asian woman, "Bring Katie's bags."

The woman paused. Her eyes were still full of tears and fear.

"Now, woman! Get the bag!" he screamed at her.

Billy opened the door to a room with a beautiful, Victorian, four-post bed, a wardrobe and a fireplace that had already been lit to warm the room. He pushed Katie in the room and closed the door behind them.

"Billy, you are frightening me!" she said.

His face became red with anger, "I am used to getting what I want, Katie, and I want you to stay."

"You can't make me stay, Billy," she said.

"You will learn to love it here! I have worked hard to make sure that my home has everything anyone could ever want. You will love me too, Katie. I have always loved you!"

He opened the door and took the bag out of the Asian woman's hands, tossing it into the room. He shut the door, and Katie could hear the key turn that locked her in.

Katie went to the window and looked out. She tried to open it, but it was locked. She quickly scanned the room for a chair, or something to throw through the window, so she could climb out and run. Looking down, she realized that it was a long way to the ground, and she had no way to climb down. She was trapped. She tried to open the door, but as she suspected, it was locked. She sat on the edge of the bed in frustration. "There must be a way out. Why do I always do such irrational things and make such poor decisions?" She was always getting herself into trouble and wished that she would have waited at the reservation for Sequoya.

The next morning, Katie woke to a knock on her door.

She was still fully clothed, and she sat up startled as Billy opened the door. He held a tray with breakfast on it. He sat it on the table by the door and turned around and locked the door. "Good morning, Katie. How do you feel today?" He put the key in his pocket. "I brought you some breakfast. You need to eat. I don't want you to get sick." He acted as if nothing had happened. "I am going to take your carriage back to town and tell them that you will be staying on here with me."

Katie pleaded, "Billy, please, let me go. I don't want to stay here with you. I don't love you, Billy."

He looked at her with glazed, empty eyes, "I will bring some suitable clothing back from town for you. You will be dining with me downstairs, and you will need to dress appropriately." He turned and left, locking the door behind him.

It had become obvious to Katie that Billy had gone mad. His money and power had disillusioned him, and his mother's death had pushed him over the edge. She looked at the food on the tray and pushed it onto the floor in a fit of rage and frustration. She fell onto the bed and cried.

It was late afternoon, and Katie could hear the key turning in the door. She grabbed the heavy vase that sat on the table and lifted it high above her head. The door slowly crept open and, just as Katie was going to slam the vase down, the Asian woman entered the room. Katie dropped the vase and held her hand to her chest, letting out a deep breath. She pulled the woman in and closed the door.

The woman told her, "You must hurry! Go! You must hurry!"

Katie asked, "Are you a prisoner here?"

"William brought me here as his concubine," she said.

"You must come with me then!" Katie demanded.

"I can not go. My family works for William. I have

to stay! You go now! Hurry!" she said. "He will come back soon."

Katie took the money from her bag and put it in her corset. She left her bag behind so that she could run. She ran down the staircase and looked out the window by the front entry. It was being guarded. She went to the kitchen and looked out the window there. It was also being guarded. Katie's heart was pounding, and she did not know what to do. The Asian woman came into the kitchen, "Come!" and took Katie's hand. She pulled Katie into a doorway that led down a stairway and into a cellar. Their was a small opening in the foundation that vented the cellar. The woman reached up and unlatched it. Katie peered through the hole as the woman boosted her up. No one was there. Katie could see the barn. She looked both directions and saw nothing. She slipped through the vent hole and ran as fast as she could run without looking back. She ran up and down the barn, looking in the stalls for a horse to saddle. There were none. The sun was beginning to set. She heard a buggy coming down the road. She heard a man shout, "He is here! Get the buggy."

She heard them talking and searched for a place to hide. She found a pile of hay. She grabbed a pitch fork and ran and hid behind it trying to quiet her breathing. Her heart was racing and pounding hard in her chest, as she heard Billy tell another man to put his horse and buggy up and bring the packages into the house. She was frightened and wondered what Billy would do to the Asian woman when he discovered that she was gone. Katie crouched down behind some hay and looked around her to see if there was a way to escape. She would have to escape on foot. The man drove the buggy through the barn door and set the brake. He got out of the buggy and started to unhitch the horse.

Katie could hear screams come from the house and

then she heard Billy shout. The man in the barn dropped what he was doing and ran out the door. Katie listened. She heard voices and stood in a panic. She did not know how to get out of the barn without being seen. She ran to the door and hid beside the opening. She tried to peek out so that they could not see her. Billy saw her and pointed. She ran to the back of the barn as the two men came through the doorway. She pointed the pitch fork at them and told them, "Stay back, Billy! I am warning you! Stay back!"

Just then, someone jumped down from the hay loft onto the hired hand. It was Sequoya. He knocked him down and hit him, easily knocking him out. Sequoya stood and faced Billy. He had his club in his hand and was crouched slightly, waiting to pounce on him. Billy reached into his coat. Katie screamed, "He has a gun!"

Sequoya threw his club at Billy's shins knocking him down. He jumped onto Billy while he was unprepared, and put his hands around his neck, trying to strangle him. Billy broke loose and hit Sequoya with his fist on his jaw. Sequoya hit him back, and Billy grabbed a hammer. He hit Sequoya over the head with it, and Sequoya fell to the ground.

As Billy slowly tried to stand, gathering his wits, Katie hit him across the back of his head with the blunt side of the pitch fork. He fell to the ground, and Katie ran to Sequoya. Sequoya stood and took the long leather reins from the carriage. He tied each man and unhitched the horse. He put Katie up on it and jumped up behind her. They fled through the field as fast as the horse could run.

Katie looked behind her and could see lanterns moving back and forth across the grounds and loud voices shouting. They came to the bridge and slipped under it where Muroco was waiting with Sequoya's horse. Sequoya put Katie on his horse and jumped back up on Billy's horse.

They fled down the river to safety.   When Sequoya finally thought they had reached safety, he stopped and dismounted his horse. He helped Katie down and held her tight and kissed her neck and cheek, thankful that she was safe. She vowed that she would never leave him again.

Chapter 20
The Child and The Force

The suspense-filled dream made Katherine wake exhilarated. Her heart was beating fast, and her palms were wet. The relief that she felt for Katie was indescribable. She loved happy endings and hoped their love would be everlasting, because Katie had suffered terribly throughout her life.

As for Billy, Katherine now knew where William Sternwall's oriental lineage came from.

Katherine unpacked the notes that she had taken. According to her research, a daughter was born to Katie and Sequoya Standing Bear in 1863. As her mother said, "Patience is a wonderful virtue." Winona had told her in the legend of the spider that she need only be patient.

Her thoughts went back to the long list of women that had just one child, all at the age of 30 and all female offspring. It made her wonder, "Is it just a coincidence or is there a reason? If so, what was the reason?"

Because it would be much easier than driving in Los

Angeles, Katherine dressed and took a cab to the Mayo clinic. She arrived a few minutes early and decided to walk around and look at the facility. It was an excellent opportunity for her, and the hospital offered her the most up-to-date equipment and an exceptionally high pay scale. Money was not essential to her. She wanted to do something with her skill that would make a difference in the world. Being skeptical, she felt that there was something about this position that would not fulfill her hopes.

When she reached the administrative offices, she checked in and sat in the waiting room, collecting her composure and trying not to show her nervousness. A few minutes later, Dr. Gates came through the door and extended his hand to Katherine. "Hello, Miss Hampton, can I call you Katherine?"

"Please do, Dr. Gates." She shook his hand, stood and followed him back through the door.

They meandered through a long hall way. The furnishings in the offices were impressive. "Please sit down, Katherine." He pointed to a very nice, burgundy, leather chair in front of his desk. His office was beautifully decorated. He was obviously generously compensated.

"Thank you, Sir." Katherine sat square and confident with her ankles crossed and waited for his first question.

"Katherine, I have reviewed your transcripts, and I will not beat around the bush. Your grades and attendance records tell me all that I need to know. So I am just going to get to the point. I want to offer you an internship in our surgical department. You will have an open option to specialize in any field that you wish." He went over the compensation and benefit package and then waited for Katherine's response.

"At the risk of sounding ungrateful, Sir, I would like to think about it." She wanted to give herself time. "I will need at least a month to wrap up the details at home."

"I understand Katherine, why don't you give me a call when you get home after you have figured out a time line," he said.

"Yes, Sir, I will." She stood and extended her hand.

When she stepped into the cab, her thoughts went back to Katie. Not yet wanting to let go of her journey, she decided to stop in Oklahoma on her way home.

After packing her bags, she opened her atlas and plotted her trip. Her route would take her through California, Nevada, New Mexico, Arizona, the top of Texas and into Oklahoma. It would take a couple of days if she drove as much as possible. She spent the day clearing her mind, listening to the radio and driving. Flagstaff was a beautiful place, so she decided it would be the perfect place to stop for the night. The scent of pine seeped into the cab of her car as the trees thickened and finally, engulfed the hillsides in front of her. A refreshing breeze cooled the summer air, and she even saw a small group of elk stop at the road before crossing it. The balcony from her hotel room had a splendid view, and she decided to eat her dinner there. When room service arrived, she ate and sipped a couple glasses of wine. After reading over her journal, she fell asleep.

XXXX

Katie and Sequoya arrived at the reservation at dawn. He slid down off his horse, and helped Katie down, hugging her. She felt so safe and so complete.

They made love in his hut, just like they had made love so long ago. Katie did not care about anything in the past and was only looking forward to her future with her husband. Peace and love was the main focus in her life. To her, every day was a new day, and she would never take her happiness for granted. She made a conscious effort to live and love as if it were the last day of her life. It was just the way it should be.

XXXX

Katherine woke and looked at the digital clock that was attached to the table in her room. It was only 2:00 am. She stretched and smiled. She loved happy endings. She drank a glass of water and went back to sleep.

XXXX

It was summer, and Katie and Sequoya had a blissful and peaceful life on the reservation. It was her 30th birthday, and after a day of celebration, they slipped into their bed, covering with a light, cloth cover. Rolling over on to her side, she held his face in her hands, looked into Sequoya's eyes and told him, "I am with child."

Sequoya smiled and held her tight. Except for the day that he found her again, he had never been so happy. From that day forward, Sequoya was careful that Katie did not do anything that might jeopardize her or her unborn child's safety. Being completely capable of small tasks, she laughed when he insisted on doing them for her, but she enjoyed it, just the same.

One night several months later, Katie gave birth to a beautiful daughter. They named her Margaret after Katie's mother, and they loved her more than anything else in their lives.

XXXX

Katherine woke happy and slowly enjoyed her breakfast before showering and packing to leave for Oklahoma. After purchasing a large Latte at Starbucks, she pulled onto the freeway and headed east toward Pawhuska, Oklahoma.

The land was flat and green. Pretty in a way, but nothing like the land that the Osage once inhabited. She knew that it must have been a disappointment for the tribe when they arrived. When she entered the reservation, she sensed the hurt that the people must have felt being forced into a strange land and losing their freedom. The reservation was filled with moderate homes and seemed to be neat and well kept.

She found the Osage Indian Museum and parked the car. She opened the doors, and she could see the pride that the Indians had for their heritage. She moved slowly from one display to the next. It was particularly intriguing now that she had re-lived the life of Katie Martin Running Bear. While she admired a beautifully beaded, buckskin dress in a display case, something caught her attention. A man was quietly watching her. When she turned to look at him, he smiled. He was very handsome, and she was instantly smitten. He looked so much like Sequoya when he smiled. He curiously watched her. "Can I help you find anything?"

"I was just looking." She blushed and fidgeted nervously. "I recently found out that a distant relative of mine was a member of the Osage tribe, and I was curious about our heritage."

"Really? Which relative, a Grandfather?" he asked.

"My Great, Great, Great Grandfather," she smiled.

"What was his name?" he asked. "Maybe, I could look him up for you."

She followed him to the front counter where the computer was located. "Thank you, his name was Sequoya

Standing Bear."

He stopped in his tracks and immediately turned looking surprised, "Your kidding, right?"

"No, my Great, Great, Great Grandmother was Mary Kate Martin Standing Bear." She was confused by his comment. "Why?"

"He was a legend, that's all!" He looked at her as if she should have known that. "When our tribe was brought to this reservation, he was our Chief and kept our tribe alive."

"Really!" Katherine was excited and anxious. "Please, tell me more!"

"Come with me." He led her to a wall of photographs. "Look, this is when he went to Washington D.C. He went there to sign the treaty that moved us here."

"I have seen that photo!" It was the one Katherine saw in her dream when Katie was in Virginia City and realized that Sequoya was alive.

He looked at her and paused. They both smiled. "Would you like to join me for dinner tonight?"

"I would love to, but I don't even know your name!" She wanted to get to know him, so she waited for him to introduce himself.

"Oh, I am so sorry. My name is Justin Long Spear." he said as he extended his hand.

"My name is Katherine Hampton." She gave him her hand, and as he kissed it, she said, "Nice to meet you, Justin."

"I am thinking you probably know better than to get into a strangers automobile so, would you like to meet me at the cafe down town?" He asked while still holding tightly to her hand.

"I would!" she pulled her hand back slightly trying not to be rude, but he had forgotten to let go.

"Oh, sorry! He smiled and let her take her hand. "Six o'clock?"

She looked at her watch. "That would be perfect," she said. That gave her time to purchase a room and clean up.

She met Justin Long Spear for dinner and had a fantastic time. They had a glass of wine, a superb steak dinner and a great conversation. She was extremely attracted to him and did not want the evening to end.

"How long are you going to be in town," he asked. "Can I see you again?"

"I would love to, but I can't stay long. I am on my way home and then I have a new job in Los Angeles." She could have stayed longer, but she honestly did like him a lot and was afraid that she would become attached to him. "I have to be there as soon as I can get my affairs in order."

"You are a wonderful person, and I am so disappointed. It is my loss, not to be able to spend more time with you." He smiled at her. "Not to mention that you are the most beautiful woman that I have ever seen! What kind of job are you taking? Maybe you could visit again when you get a vacation?" He was teasing her.

"I will be completing my internship at the Mayo Hospital." She sipped her wine.

"Very impressive! I am the Family Physician here at the reservation." He blotted his lips with his napkin. "I have dedicated my career to my people."

"Now, I'm impressed." She looked at her watch. "It is getting very late. I should be going."

"Of course!" He stood and pulled her chair out for her. "I am very glad that I met you, and I really hope there will be a day that we meet again!"

"Thank you. I hope so, too," she said.

He paid the check and walked Katherine to her car.

"Thank you so much for dinner. I had a wonderful

258

time, Justin Long Spear," she said with a smile.

"I did too, Katherine Hampton." He closed her door and waved as she pulled out of the parking lot.

Katherine went up to her room and laid down on the bed. She smiled and thought about the incredible journey she had. She thought that her dinner was a perfect end to it. She fell asleep.

XXXX

Like the first time she had her dream, the air was filled with smoke, blocking her vision. The sound of a hawk screeched loudly, and she could hear a rattle in the back ground. First the noise was distant and then it got louder and louder until she could hardly stand it. Then, all at once, the noise stopped, and a bright light nearly blinded her vision. The smoke cleared, and Katherine could see Winona. There was still some smoke and the aroma of sage filled the room. It was wonderfully tranquil. Winona was chanting and waving her idles over the fire. She spoke, "Itsike, Itsike, Itsike."

Katherine could see a vision appear in front of Winona and speak to her. The vision was not human. It was a shape shifting mist, and it moved like a cloud of smoke. It spoke in a strange language that Katherine could not understand.

Winona gasped and screamed as if she were in pain, "Itsike, Itsike, Itsike." She wept as the vision spoke. "No, Itsike, no, no, no!

XXXX

Katherine woke slowly trying to lift herself, but felt as if she had a weight holding her down. When she finally pulled herself from the dream and sat up in bed, her heart was pounding, and sweat had drenched her night gown. She was terrified. She took several deep breaths as she stumbled to the bathroom and wet her face with a cold cloth. After showering and dressing, she took Justin's business card out of her wallet and searched the address for the clinic on the GPS in her phone.

When she arrived at the clinic, Justin was just parking his car. After opening his door and stepping out, he saw her standing by her car. "Good morning! What a wonderful surprise!"

"Good morning," she smiled as he walked toward her with some file folders in his hands. "Do you have a full schedule today?"

"Nothing I couldn't put off until tomorrow!" he laughed. "What's up?"

She looked down at the ground. "What do you know about Itsike?"

He bent down slightly to see her face, "Itsike is an old Indian legend. Itsike is a negative force. It is a trickster."

"Do you believe it could be real?" she said in a whisper.

He lifted her face with his hand, so that he could see her face, "I believe that anything is possible. We can't pretend to know everything. There is too much left unknown. Would you like to have breakfast and talk about it? I have to be somewhere. I would love it, if you would join me."

"Sure, I can join you." She followed him into his office while he dropped the files off with his nurse and they left.

Katherine looked out the window as they pulled down a dirt road. There were rows and rows of horse trailers and pick up trucks. "What is going on here?"

"It's our annual Indian ranch-hand rodeo. You will love it!" He stepped out and opened her door for her.

She stood on the dusty roadway and looked at him. "I am not really dressed for a rodeo."

Justin laughed and said, "Don't worry, we have front-row seats!" He took her hand and walked her to the ambulance that was situated behind the bucking chutes. "It will be a while before they get started. Would you like to talk about Itsike?"

She paused and turned her head to him, "You might very well think that I am going mad if I tell you my story."

"I try not to pass judgments." He held her hand and helped her into the passenger side of the ambulance. "Trust me! Give it a whirl, what do you have to lose?"

Katherine told him about the dreams she had, the research she has done and about her last dream.

"So you couldn't understand what Itsike said?" he asked. "Do you remember any of the words that he spoke? I know the language."

"No." Katherine shook her head. "So, professionally speaking, do you think I am going mad?"

"Not at all! I have heard about many of my people having visions. Some even have had special powers like yours." He continued. "I recommend you learn the language. Itsike is known for making curses. If you solve the mystery, you might be able to stop the curse."

"Really! You believe in this, because I am struggling with it." She pulled her purse up off the floor boards.

Justin looked at her seriously. "It seems that you have plenty of proof that your dreams actually happened. The photographs, newspaper articles and locations. To many for coincidence."

"I suppose you are right." Katherine shuffled through her purse to find her wallet. "Do you think anyone might have any coffee brewed?"

"I'd bet they do. He took her hand and walked her to the concession stand.

It was an awesome rodeo and Katherine enjoyed herself immensely. She enjoyed Justin's company and the members of the community were extraordinarily friendly. The day passed quickly and safely for everyone.

When the rodeo ended, Justin took Katherine to the museum and gave her a copy of Osage Language book. He asked her to join him for dinner, and she did. They laughed and joked, and she had a terrific time. Her evening with Justin lightened her mood, and for the first time, Katherine did not think about her dreams.

When the evening was over, Justin walked her to her car and opened her door for her. He placed his hand behind her neck and kissed her softly, then looked into her eyes. "You know, I do have an opening for a surgeon at the hospital here. I know it wouldn't be near the opportunity that you have in Los Angeles, but you would undoubtedly make a difference here in this community.

Katherine could not believe he said that. How did he know that making a difference was what was important to her. "Thank you. I will keep that in mind."

When she walked back into her room, she looked at the bed and realized that she did not want to fall back to sleep. She was afraid of Itsike. Looking at the cover of the Osage Language book, she packed her suit case and put the book on top of her clothes. Taking one last look at the bed, she closed the door and checked out of her room.

It was dark when she drove out of town, and she thought about Justin. She wondered if she had made a mistake by leaving him. He was the only man in which she ever thought seriously about having a relationship. She was at ease with him and there was something wonderful about him.

The road that led out of town was slightly curved, and some fog had thickened around it. Suddenly a white buffalo appeared in front of Katherine's car, and she jerked the wheel and slammed on her brakes sliding, off the road and hitting a tree. Before her sight went black, Katherine saw Itsike in her mind.

The car behind her stopped. The driver opened his door and told the passenger, "Call an ambulance!" He ran to her car and opened her door, checking her pulse, he shouted, "She's alive! Tell them to hurry!"

CPSIA information can be obtained at www.ICGtesting.com
Printed in the USA
BVOW012241180313

315870BV00011B/309/P